IF YOU FIGHT

(CORRUPTED LOVE #2)

K.M. SCOTT

Books by K.M. Scott

If I Dream (Corrupted Love #1)
If You Fight (Corrupted Love #2)

Crash Into Me (Heart of Stone #1)
Fall Into Me (Heart of Stone #2)
Give In To Me (Heart of Stone #3)
Heart of Stone Volume One Box Set
Ever After (Heart of Stone #4)
A Heart of Stone Christmas (Heart of Stone #5)
Unforgettable (Heart of Stone #6)
Unbreakable (Heart of Stone #7)
Heart of Stone Volume Two Box Set

Temptation (Club X #1)
Surrender (Club X #2)
Possession (Club X #3)
Satisfaction (Club X #4)
Acceptance (Club X #5)

SILK Volume One
SILK Volume Two
SILK Volume Three
SILK Volume Four
The SILK Box Set

Books by K.M. Scott writing as Gabrielle Bisset

Blood Avenged (Sons of Navarus #1)

Blood Betrayed (Sons of Navarus #2)

Longing (A Sons of Navarus Short Story)

Blood Spirit (Sons of Navarus #3)

The Deepest Cut (A Sons of Navarus Short Story)

Blood Prophecy (Sons of Navarus #4)

Blood Craving (Sons of Navarus #5)

Blood Eclipse (Sons of Navarus #6)

The Sons of Navarus Box Set #1

The Sons of Navarus Box Set #2

Stolen Destiny (Destined Ones Duology #1)

Destiny Redeemed (Destined Ones Duology #2)

Love's Master

Masquerade

The Victorian Erotic Romance Trilogy

If You Fight

If you fight, will we last?

Serena
All my life, everyone around me made sure I was weak. My father. My sister. And now the man my father forced me to marry. But Oliver doesn't know what I know. Strength can come even in the hardest times, and if you're willing to fight for love, nothing can stand in your way.

For the first time in my life, I'm fighting back, and with Ryder by my side, I'm never letting myself be weak again.

Ryder
They want us to be their pawns, but I won't let them use her like that. I promised I'd protect Serena, and if it costs me everything in this world, I will.

Even if it means returning to the one place I swore I'd never go back to again.

PART ONE

Chapter One

Serena

ALL AROUND ME I heard silence. Where was I? What happened? I slowly opened my eyes and saw through the haze stark white walls and a window with pale orange draperies pulled closed. Instantly, all that happened flooded into my brain. Fighting with Oliver. Hands pushing me down the stairs. Lying on the floor. Him standing over me kicking my stomach with the point of his shoe.

Emotions swirled inside me as I remembered it all. I looked beneath the white sheet covering me to see a bloody maxi-pad in my underwear, and my heart clenched, aching for what I'd lost.

For what Ryder and I had lost.

I remembered every hateful word that spewed from Oliver's mouth. Every terrible word he said to me before pushing me down those stairs and taking my child from me.

Before he tried to kill me.

Rolling over, I curled up into a ball and closed my eyes as the tears came and wouldn't stop. Not when the nurse asked me if I needed anything for pain. Not when she told me I'd be okay and I could have more children. Not when she placed her hand gently on my shoulder and said God knew about my pain.

What God? God hadn't kept his eye on me not a day of my entire life. If he had, my mother wouldn't have been sent away from me in the dark of night. If God had cared, my father wouldn't have auctioned me off to the highest bidder, a man who not a day earlier had threatened to kill me and then pushed me down a flight of stairs.

If God even knew I existed, I wouldn't have been shown happiness with Ryder only to have it yanked away from me at every turn.

No, God knew nothing of my pain, or if he did, he didn't give one damn. God wasn't going to save me from the world I was in. Only I could do that.

I will not die at the hands of my husband. I will not die because I'm merely a female. I won't let Oliver or my father do this to me.

Over and over, the words repeated in my mind until my lips began to move and the words met the air around me, each one feeling like it clawed its way out of my injured throat, still raw from Oliver's attempt to strangle me.

"I will not die at the hands of my husband. I will not die because I'm merely female. I won't let Oliver or my father do this to me."

I said those words until nothing else came to my mind. I wanted those words to be truth. Never before had I believed in myself enough to take that stand and refuse to be discarded for who I was.

But could I be that strong? I wanted nothing more than to be that woman who could face the monsters all around her and make them fear me like I feared them.

Ryder could. He scared them. He had enchanted my father in ways my sister and I never could, and from that first day, my father respected him. Needed him. Wanted him around.

Watching him do it so effortlessly thrilled me nearly as much as being with him did. Strength exuded from him even as he stood silently staring straight ahead there in my father's office day after day.

And my husband knew it. He knew Ryder possessed a strength he never would, and it terrified him. I may not have, but Ryder did.

I stared at those ugly orange draperies and repeated my mantra, but slightly different now. I would not let them kill me. I would be strong. Or die trying to be that person.

And from that moment on I would do everything in my power to escape from that world that had trapped me for so long I wasn't sure I'd recognize life without the manipulation and heartache my father and husband force fed me. But deep down inside where only Ryder had seen, I craved that life away from all I'd ever known.

Drying my eyes, I set my mind to a singular thought. I would survive, and I'd get out. And I'd do whatever I had to.

Trapped in that bed as a captive audience, I watched as my husband entered my hospital room and noted the look of surprise in his beady eyes. *Thought you got rid of me, did you? Not so quickly, Oliver. I'm tougher than I look.*

Behind him, my father followed, along with Ryder. Overjoyed to see him, I didn't even attempt to hide how happy I was he'd come to be with me. I'd pretended long enough for a man who tried to kill me.

Oliver spun around to see who had made my eyes light up and brought a smile to my face. Pointing his finger at Ryder, he barked, "Get him out of here! He doesn't belong here!"

Ryder leveled his gaze on him and didn't waver, but my father spoke up to defend his presence there. "You should be thankful for him. He's the reason your wife is still alive. If he hadn't found Serena in time, we'd be meeting to discuss her funeral instead of seeing her lying there in that hospital bed."

Rage simmered beneath Oliver's façade of worry

for me, but he said nothing in response to my father's dictate, even though I knew how much he chafed under his orders. He turned back to look at me and as if on cue, he played the loving husband act like a pro.

Taking my hand in his own far-too-soft hand, he held it just tightly enough that I couldn't pull away without causing a scene. "How do you feel, honey? Your father told me the horrible news, but don't worry. We'll have other children."

So that's how he planned to play it. Would he say it was an accident that caused me to fall down a flight of stairs in my own home while he was there? Or would he claim complete ignorance and continue with the desperately concerned husband act?

Out of the corner of my eye, I saw Ryder react to Oliver's words, his eyes opening wide and filling with anger. My father watched Oliver carefully, hanging on every word he said like he wasn't sure if his son-in-law had been involved in hurting me.

I opened my mouth to speak but only got a few words out before the pain in my throat from being choked made talking almost unbearable. Clutching my neck, I mouthed, "It hurts to speak."

Like the dutiful husband, Oliver gently patted my leg and said, "You don't have to say anything, Serena. There's time for that later. Now you just need to rest."

I saw in his eyes the terrible fear that I would start talking and tell anyone who'd listen exactly who'd done this to me. But I had other plans for my dear husband.

Forcing the words out, I whispered, "No, I want to speak. It's important to me that I tell my father what happened before I forget the details."

Oliver protested my attempts to speak. "You need to rest. We can do this later. Rest now."

But my father wasn't interested in his idea of my resting. Eager to know who had done this to me, he stepped toward the bed and asked, "Do you remember what happened, Serena?"

In that moment, it felt like time stopped as I looked from my father to Oliver and then to Ryder. Only I knew what had happened and who had attacked me, and each man waited to hear my answer. I held Oliver's entire future in my hands, and for the first time in my life, the feeling of real power rushed through me.

It would be nothing to tell the truth about what he'd done. He wouldn't make it out of my hospital room before Ryder jumped him, and I sensed that my father already had his suspicions and likely wouldn't have stopped his employee from exacting his revenge.

Oliver would be arrested and out of my life as he sat in prison for attempted murder. I'd get what I wanted and have my freedom. My father probably wouldn't even give me a hard time about divorcing the son of a bitch.

But as that scenario played out in my head, I knew that would be too easy for him. He might get himself a good lawyer and never spend a day in jail. He might contest the divorce and keep me tied to him for years, and if my father wanted me to stay married to the bastard, then where would I be?

No freedom. Same trapped existence.

No, that wouldn't do. I couldn't let that happen.

Reaching out for my father's hand, I took a deep breath and made the decision to use the power I finally had. "It was an intruder, Daddy. He broke into the house and attacked me. He wanted to kill me."

With those words, I set into motion my plan for freedom.

A look of true concern settled into my father's features, drawing his mouth into a deep frown. "You're lucky you're alive then. But why would an intruder attack you?"

Knowing my father had doubts why anyone would want to hurt me, especially some unknown assailant, I croaked out, "I think he was looking for Oliver but I happened to be in the wrong place at the wrong time."

And with that, the lie made sense. While I, a

simple woman who rarely even left the estate, would be an unlikely target for an attacker, Oliver certainly could be. A businessman, he made enemies every day.

Or at least my father would think that since he made enemies all the time through the course of his wheeling and dealing. I may never have had much of a head for business, but I paid attention whenever I could to what my father said about running his companies.

Turning toward Oliver, my father said, "Who would want you dead? We need to figure that out to find out who was behind this."

In a flash, the dutiful, concerned husband morphed into the outraged husband. Flailing his hands, he said, "It's outrageous! I demand the security be improved at the estate. My wife and I have lost something precious today. This can't be allowed!"

From behind my father, Ryder said in a flat voice devoid of emotion, "The security cameras will show us exactly who the attacker was, Robert."

Oliver immediately grew flustered at the thought that he'd been caught by none other than the man he'd ordered out of my hospital room. "Is he saying you have security cameras in our apartment? Why wasn't I told about this? Why have you been watching us?"

"No, no, there are no cameras in any of the apartments, Oliver," my father answered as he tried to ease his troubled mind about being spied on in his own home. "The security cameras are on the outside around the estate. But Ryder's right. We'll be able to see anyone who left the area near your apartment in the past twenty-four hours, so rest assured, we'll know who did this. Don't worry about that."

My father's reassurances did nothing to calm Oliver's fears, though, naturally since he knew what they'd see on the security footage. The only person other than Ryder to leave our apartment in that time was the very person who'd done this to me.

"Did the man say anything to you?" my father asked, thoroughly convinced some intruder had found a way onto the estate.

I shook my head and took a sip of water to ease the pain in my throat. "No. One moment I was alone in the kitchen, and then the next moment he was coming at me. I threw a glass to stop him, but it was no use. His hands were around my neck in seconds choking me."

Completely ignoring my father's interest in my attacker, Oliver asked, "Do you need anything from home? I can go get you whatever you need, honey."

So now I was honey. He hadn't called me that once in all the time we were married, and now he'd called me honey twice in the span of a few minutes.

Oliver may not have been much of a husband, but he was a hell of an actor.

I smiled like a thankful wife would and answered sweetly, "Just a change of clothes for when I go home tomorrow, please."

Like he couldn't get out of that room fast enough, he nodded and announced he'd return with exactly what I asked for. Kissing me goodbye, he said in his kindest voice, "I love you, Serena. I'm so happy you're going to be okay."

He had no idea how not okay I was going to be until I made him pay for what he'd done. But I smiled and pretended to be thankful for such a wonderfully thoughtful husband.

"I'm going to go too. You need your rest, sweetheart," my father said as he gave my hand a gentle squeeze. Another manipulator pretending to care.

"Thank you. I am feeling a little tired, I guess."

"Well, we'll get out of here, but you have Ryder to thank once again for the fact that you're alive. If he hadn't been there to save you, God only knows what may have happened."

If God was paying attention, he knew exactly what would have happened.

I smiled at Ryder, and he took a step toward the bed. The troubled look on his face told me he didn't understand what he'd just witnessed. Confused by my insistence that I'd been attacked by an intruder when he knew full well who had done this to me, he remained silent but tried to smile.

"Thank you again for saving my life. One of these days I'm going to have to repay the favor."

"I just wish I got there in time to stop him. I'm sorry I didn't."

The pain in his voice told me he was sorry for more than that. We'd lost something beautiful we'd created. It was taken away by a hateful man I swore would pay back someday soon.

I reached out for his hand and took it in mine, soothed by him being there with me. "You saved me. I can't tell you what that means to me, Ryder."

"Well, we're going to leave you to get some rest. If you need anything that Oliver doesn't bring you, just call me, sweetheart," my father said as he kissed my cheek and turned to leave.

"I want to talk to Ryder. Give us a few minutes, okay?"

"Okay. Ryder, I'll be down at the car."

Happy to get a few moments alone with him, I clung to Ryder's hand as I waited for the door to close behind my father. When we were finally alone, I didn't hold back my tears any longer. I didn't have to.

As they rolled down my cheeks, he pulled me close and held me to him as I sobbed over what we'd lost. I felt the sadness in him and wished I could do more than simply fall apart.

He pressed his lips to the top of my head and whispered, "Why did you lie? You could have outed him right here and been done with him, Serena. Why let him off so easy?"

I leaned back and looked up into those green eyes so full of confusion, hoping he'd understand what I'd had to do. "That would have been too easy for him, Ryder. I couldn't risk him somehow getting out of paying for what he'd done to me, to our baby, because of some slick lawyer. No way."

My mention of the baby made Ryder wince, and he turned away from me. "I hate him, Serena. I hate the very sight of him," he said quietly, his voice cracking.

"I know. I do too."

"I swear, if I could, I would—" He stopped speaking and sighed as his shoulders sagged. "I hate him for what he did to you. To our baby."

Tugging on his arm, I pleaded for him to look at me. I needed him to know I wasn't going to just return to Oliver and that hateful life I had with him.

"Ryder, I want you to look at me. Please."

He slowly turned his head, and his gaze zeroed in on my bruised neck. "He could have killed you, Serena."

I placed my palm on his cheek and directed his

eyes to mine. "I swear to you he won't get away with this. I just need you to trust me. Please, I know what I'm doing."

"What are you doing? Why not just show him to be the fuck he is and let the cops take care of him?" he asked, exasperation filling each word.

"Because I won't risk not getting my revenge like that. He took something from me today, from us. I won't let him get away with that."

Ryder stared down at me sadly. "You sound like your father. You know that?"

He wasn't wrong. I did sound like my father now. I'd heard my father threaten to exact his revenge on people nearly every day of my life, and I'd sworn I would never become that person. Now that Oliver had taken something so precious from me, I couldn't help myself. I needed revenge for that.

"Is it so bad to want revenge on someone who hurt you?" I asked, desperate to hear him say he didn't hate the person I'd become as I lay in that hospital bed.

"No, but revenge is a tricky thing. It starts out feeling good, but in the end, you get consumed by it."

Turning away from him, I looked out the window and tried to explain what I felt. "All my life, I've been at the mercy of my father and what he wanted. And when he decided it was time, he gave me away to a husband who doesn't care about me. Somehow, they both thought I'd be okay with that."

"I'm not saying you ever deserved that, Serena. I just don't want to see you become like them."

I looked back at him and saw the concern in his eyes. "Maybe I've been wrong all this time. Maybe if I'd been more like my father this would have never happened."

Ryder shook his head as his frown deepened. "Don't. Don't take the blame for what that bastard did."

I wasn't. The days of me taking the blame for what the monsters in my life did to me were over.

Chapter Two

Ryder

S ERENA'S EYES FILLED with tears. "I need you to understand what I'm feeling now. This wasn't just a fight that got out of hand, Ryder. He pushed me down those stairs after I told him I was pregnant. He wanted me and our baby dead. I don't want to be a victim this time. Can you still love me if I'm not going to be just a victim for once?"

I smoothed her soft brown hair back off her face and looked into those sad, dark eyes so full of emotion. "I never loved you because you were a victim of what your father did or what Oliver did, Serena. I love you because of who you are. Because you're gentle and kind in a world full of people like them."

Squeezing my hand, she said, "I'm still that person, if only with you, but he took our baby from me and I can't forgive that and I can't let it go."

"I just don't want to lose you to this."

She wiped away the tears from her cheeks and took a deep breath. "You're not going to, Ryder, but

I'm tired of living my life in fear."

I stepped away from the bed, hating what I was hearing. The beautiful soul I'd fallen in love with was hardening over before my eyes. Her father and Oliver had succeeded in forcing her to be like them.

Callous and vengeful.

But what would happen to us when she became that person?

"Why did you walk away?" she asked as I stood at the window looking out toward the nearby mountains still dotted with the reds and golds of the fall season.

How much I wanted to take her in my arms and run away into those hills until we reached a place no one would find us. We could leave our pasts behind and start again. Now as I looked toward the horizon, I worried when we finally did get the chance to do that, we wouldn't be the two people who'd first dreamed about running away together as we lay in each other's arms in that bed in the guest room all that time ago.

"Why aren't you angry like I am, Ryder? He killed our baby. I thought you'd be furious."

Inside, rage bubbled up, touching every part of me. I spun around to face her, letting her see for the first time how what he'd done made me feel.

"I hate him, Serena. I hate him like I've never hated anyone before in my life. It wasn't bad enough that he had you there in his bed, but then he took our baby away."

"You want to kill him, don't you?"

I wanted to kill Oliver with my bare hands and knew exactly how I'd do it. No pushing him under the water in a hot tub or a gunshot to the back of his head. No, I wanted to do to him what I'd done in The Pit because what he took from me made me feel like I used to when I fought.

Like an animal fighting for its very survival.

After what he'd done to Serena and the baby she carried, only one of us could remain in this world. Either he disappeared or I did, but I wouldn't be able to continue living with him walking around like he'd gotten away with his crime.

Quietly, I admitted to her for the first time what we never talked about before. "I've killed other men for your father. He'll be no different."

I watched for horror to fill her eyes as she finally understood what kind of man I truly was, but it never came. Instead, she simply shook her head.

"I don't want you to be the one who does this, Ryder."

Walking back to the side of the bed, I searched her face for the answer to why. Why couldn't I avenge the death of our child?

"What does it matter if it's me who does it? You'll be free and I would have protected you, finally."

"Is that what this is about to you? You being some big protector for sad, pathetic Serena?"

My emotions spun out of control after everything that had happened that day. "I promised to protect you and I failed! How do you think that makes me feel?"

Exhausted from my failure once again to protect her from being hurt, I sank down in the chair next to the bed and hung my head. I understood that she didn't want to be a victim anymore, but that didn't mean I didn't want to protect her because she was the woman I loved.

She gently stroked her hand across my back as I sat there hating what was happening to us. "Ryder, I don't need you to protect me. All I need from you is your love."

Looking back toward her, I asked, "What if I want to protect you? What if that means something important to me?"

Her hand trailed down my arm and she weaved her fingers through mine, squeezing our hands together. "There was a time that all I thought I needed was someone to protect me, first from my father and then from Oliver. In fact, if you had asked me this afternoon if I needed you to protect me, I would have said yes. But something happened when he pushed me down those stairs and I lost the baby. I woke up in this bed and all I knew for sure was I never wanted to feel that weak again. I never wanted to feel like I had no power ever again in my life. I won't."

I looked down at where our hands met and brought her fingertips to my lips in a kiss. "What does that mean for us? What am I if I'm not the one person you trust to protect you?"

She smiled for one of the first times since I'd entered her hospital room. "Equals, like a man and woman should be."

I didn't mind the idea of Serena being my equal. From the first moment she appeared at my room right after I arrived at the house, I'd thought she was far superior to me, and not only because she came from money and I came from The Pit. Something inside her made her sweeter and kinder than anyone I'd ever met. I wanted to have someone with those qualities in my life.

"You've always been better than me," I said quietly, slipping my hand from hers as I stood to walk to the window again.

"That's not true, and you know it. I'm just some poor little rich girl with a powerful father. At least that's all I've been, but now I want to be more. I want to be someone who has control over her life instead of being sold to the highest bidder and forced to live with other people's decisions."

As I gazed out at that place I imagined in the mountains where we could finally be free, I said, "You want to be like your father."

From behind me, she said, "Maybe I want to be like you."

Her answer made me chuckle. Turning back to face her, I asked, "Like a junkyard dog? You're not the biting type."

"Not the biting type but the type of person who has the power to say no."

Her newfound strength didn't frighten me, but I worried what she might want to say no to. Or who.

"I would never say no to you, Ryder, if that's what the look on your face means. You're the only person I know cares for me."

"So this is about having the power to get your revenge on Oliver? Because I meant what I said about revenge. I've seen what it does to people like you. It'll eat you up from the inside, Serena."

She placed her hands over her belly and nodded. "I want the chance to make him pay. I need to do this. I hope you can understand why."

Part of me did. Although I'd come around to wanting a child after she told me, Serena had lived with the baby inside her, something I could never truly feel. Whatever Oliver had taken away from me, he'd taken more from her when he decided to kill her and our baby.

But another part of me didn't want to think about how different things were for her and simply wanted to exact revenge on the man who had hurt the woman I loved and killed my child. That part didn't want to stand aside and let her do just that. That part wanted to look him dead in the eyes as the life drained out of his body so he'd know who he'd crossed before he left this world.

Accepting for the moment that Serena needed me to support her in this, I asked, "So what do you plan to do? I can't stand the idea that you're going to have to go back to that apartment and live in the same house as him. I don't trust that he won't try to kill you again."

"He won't. He pushed me down the stairs because of the baby," she answered as she fought back tears.

And for that one horrible act I'd someday get my revenge, even if it didn't mean killing him.

"My father will be watching. I saw how suspicious he was when he was here listening to me tell my story. I want him to be suspicious so Oliver knows he's being watched. One word from me and he'll be under arrest, but I'd rather him live in terror that I'm going to finally tell the truth one day."

"Why? Why not tell the truth and be done with him?"

I knew the answer before she said it. It would

never be that easy.

"Because he might get some sleazy lawyer who finds a way for him to wriggle out of any charges the police bring. No, I'm not leaving my revenge to more men in expensive suits. I want him to leave me because he can't take the threat of me telling the truth one of these days. Then my father won't have anything to say about it and I'll finally be free."

"And then what, Serena?"

My question confused her. "What do you mean? Then I'm free to be with you."

I shook my head at how simple that sounded and how impossible it would be. "Don't fool yourself. He's never going to let that happen. You know that. He married you to Oliver because it helped his bottom line, and if Oliver leaves you, he'll make sure the divorce is quick and your second marriage happens even quicker."

Serena seemed to think about what we both knew was the truth and then nodded her agreement. "Then knowing my father, I'm going to have to make sure that doesn't happen."

As I began to ask how she'd do that, she reached for my hand and kissed it. "I'm tired now, Ryder. I think I need to rest. Promise me you won't take this into your own hands and steal my revenge from me."

Leaning down, I pressed a soft kiss onto her lips.

"I promise. Now I want you to promise me something."

She looked up at me and smiled. "Anything."

"Promise me if your plan doesn't work that you'll accept the fact that I will kill him for what he's done to you."

Cradling my face, she pressed her forehead to mine. "To us."

I LEFT SERENA lying there in that bed with her dreams of revenge and worried she was underestimating her father and Oliver. He'd tried to kill her once already. What would stop him from trying again?

By the time I reached Robert still standing outside the car, his look of fatherly concern had disappeared, replaced by a far flintier look. I braced myself for his interrogation since I'd been up there with Serena for a while, but the first words out of his mouth weren't questions about me or what we'd talked about at all.

"I want to see those security tapes tonight. I already called Johnson about them while I was waiting for you. If an intruder could get onto the estate and into Serena's home, I damn well want to know how."

Knowing what he'd find on them, I nodded in agreement, as I had to. "Sounds like a good idea."

We rode back to the estate in silence as I eagerly waited for him to see the proof of who had come and go from Serena's apartment that day. The question was what would Robert do when he found out that the only person who could have done that to Serena was her husband.

He waved at me to follow him to where Johnson and the other real security guys spent their days on the first floor directly beneath the bedroom wing of the main house. He sat in a room full of monitors that showed the outside areas around Serena's apartment, Robert's townhouse at the far end of the estate, the front door to the main house, the side and front doors of the garage, and the main door leading to the apartments where I and the rest of his on-site employees stayed.

Johnson, a tall lanky guy with closely cropped jet black hair that looked startling compared to his silver beard, swiveled around to face us and began talking as soon as Robert entered the room. Pointing at his monitors like we knew what had gotten him so excited, he said quickly, "I've looked through every bit of footage you asked me to and there's a problem."

Those were exactly the words Robert hated to hear. His body tensed up until he looked as stiff as an ironing board next to me, and I took a step back toward the door, knowing what would likely happen next.

Too bad. Johnson was a decent guy, even if he tended to ramble on about fishing when he got you alone.

"You know what I think of when I hear someone say that, don't you, Johnson? I think someone's not taking care of business, which in my mind is the worst thing a person can do, especially when he's been ordered not an hour before to take care of exactly that fucking business!"

Robert's voice echoed off the walls and shook the equipment. Johnson's eyes bugged open like being yelled at startled him, and he began explaining himself. "It's nothing I or any of us did. I swear, sir. It's just that whoever went into that apartment must have known exactly where the cameras were located because it's like some kind of fog or something affected the view of the camera outside her apartment, and the front gate camera has been on the fritz for the past week, as Snyder told you when it first happened. Look for yourself."

"Fog? What are you talking about? Fog doesn't just drop itself in front of a goddamned camera while the rest of them work," Robert bellowed, just slightly quieter this time.

Johnson nodded his head up and down so fast he looked like a bobble head doll. "I know. That's just what I thought too, sir. But that's exactly what happened. Take a look. You can see it as clear as day right there on the tape."

Robert glared at him, and I winced at his poor choice of words. He spun around in his chair to point at the monitor that showed what the camera outside of Serena's apartment recorded that evening. A few minutes before she said she was attacked, the camera shot became cloudy, obscuring the view for an hour's time. Then he pointed to the monitor next to it and we saw the front gate camera going black for long periods of time as it had for the past week.

I stared over Robert's shoulder knowing it had been Oliver who did it. Probably with something sprayed directly onto the lens. It wouldn't have been difficult.

But did Robert suspect him?

I had no idea, and as he stood hunched over Johnson staring at the monitor, he said nothing. Finally, when he stood up, he simply shook his head.

But there were other ways to make sure he suspected Oliver. Quickly, I suggested he look at the tapes from the other cameras around the estate. "Whoever did this didn't just disappear into thin air. What about looking at the footage from the side door of the garage? That should show if anyone drove past anytime during the night."

As if my idea made him happy, he nodded and patted me on the shoulder. "Good idea." Then he turned to Johnson, who was already loading up the garage door footage. "Why didn't you think of this? Does Ryder have to do everything here? He saved Serena, for God's sake. I'd think someone else who works for me could pick up the ball here."

Johnson didn't have an answer for Robert's questions, so he wisely kept his mouth shut until the footage was available. "Here it is, sir."

The three of us watched, and I waited with my heart in my throat to see Oliver's car pass by on his way out of the estate after attacking Serena. The angle wasn't perfect, so there was no way the driver of any car going by could be seen, but at least if Robert could see proof that a car like Oliver's had driven by during that time he might put the pieces together.

Minute after minute passed with no sign that anyone had gone near the garage door, but then a single car sped by, barely visible on the security tape. My heart sank. It wouldn't be enough to point the finger at that fucker, even though I knew it was his car.

Robert and Johnson saw it too, and Robert yelled, "Wait! Back it up! I saw something pass by. Ryder, did you see that? There's a car there."

Johnson did as ordered and slowed the tape down to show that a car had gone by during the window of time Serena's attacker would have fled the scene. The problem was between the angle and the darkness of the camera shot, the car may have been black or even a dark green or blue. It wasn't definitive.

"What color is that car?" Robert asked the two of us. "We need to know the color of that car."

Johnson guessed it was probably black, and knowing Oliver drove a dark blue BMW, I said, "Black or blue. Either one."

I hoped Robert took the hint.

He looked off in the distance like he was running through every car that he knew could be on the estate, and then he narrowed his eyes.

"Hmmm."

I wanted to ask if he'd remembered something, but I didn't have the chance. Spinning on his heels, he pushed past me as he barked, "Johnson, keep looking at those tapes! Ryder, be ready when I call you."

All I could hope for was he had finally come to the realization that the only person who could have hurt Serena was her husband. When the time came and he gave me the order to take care of Oliver for what he'd done, she'd have to understand.

Even if I had a choice, he'd be dead. Thankfully, I wouldn't have a choice.

Chapter Three

Serena

OLIVER'S FOOTSTEPS COMING toward the kitchen made my stomach tense up, and a second later he appeared in the doorway sneering at me like he always did since I'd returned home from the hospital.

"Are you planning to just sit there moping all day like usual?" he asked as his disgusted sneer morphed into an angry glare.

"I'm not moping. I'm just sitting here having a cup of tea. Aren't you late for work?"

His face twisted into an ugly grimace. "Even if it wasn't, I wouldn't be staying here another minute anyway."

The sun streamed in through the kitchen window, warming my back and making me feel safe, for the moment. I wanted to tell him he hadn't succeeded in hurting me. He'd taken my baby, but I was still here, and I was getting stronger every day.

The time would come for those words to be spoken and many others, but not today. For the time being, I'd take his insults and nastiness and file it all away in my mind so when the moment came that I could get my revenge, all of it would be right there for me to draw on so my hatred for him couldn't wane.

"Will you be home at the same time as always?" I asked.

His eyes narrowed to spiteful slits as he shook his head. "I'm going to find out whose fucking bastard that was, and when I do, Serena, the two of you are going to pay."

I didn't reply to his threat. There was no point. If he ever did find out Ryder had been the father before I had a chance to exact my revenge on him, he'd be the one who'd pay. I knew Ryder well enough to be sure of that.

But that's not what I wanted. What I still prayed for every night was revenge. Sweet revenge that would show Oliver I wasn't some unwanted thing he could just discard by throwing it down the stairs.

The kind of revenge that would show him that I was as strong as I wanted to believe I could be.

The door slammed behind him, leaving me sitting alone in the warm sun. Closing my eyes, I tried to push away the ugliness he made me feel and focused on how much I wished Ryder was there with me.

✧　✧　✧

THE DOCTORS TOLD me I had to be on bed rest for a few days after getting home, but all I could think about was finding some way to see Ryder. Oliver didn't bother to pretend he cared one bit about me when we were alone in our apartment together, and each night I knew I could rely on him staying at the appraisal office until at least eight o'clock.

The problem was my father. Every evening, he seemed to have something or other for Ryder to do that kept him busy until after I knew it would be safe for us to meet. I began to wonder if he knew about the two of us, but every time I messaged Ryder about it, he tried to ease my mind and told me there was no chance he knew.

I didn't care if he found out, to be honest. What could he do to us worse than what Oliver had done already? I knew my father depended on Ryder too much to send him away. I'd probably get the worst of it from him anyway, but it would be worth it if we could finally be together.

Finally, nearly a week after coming home from the hospital, I walked down to my father's office pretending to want to see him. Maybe if I made it seem like I had something I wanted to say, he'd let Ryder go for the night so I could sneak up to his place right after finishing with my father.

For ten minutes, I lurked outside his door as he sat at his desk reading emails. Ryder saw me and gave me a tiny smile, forced to pretend that my presence meant nothing to him because two other men who worked for my father were also there.

Being so close to him yet not being able to touch him since that night in the hospital made my heart ache. I knew he was going through the same thing I was and if only we could be alone we'd finally be able to talk about what we'd lost. Neither of us had been able to do that in the hospital, but since I came home, the reality of how much I needed to speak to him about it pressed down on me every moment of the day.

"Serena, is something wrong? Why are you hovering around my office door?" my father finally yelled out to me.

I peeked my head in and smiled, putting on my happiest face. "Nothing's wrong. I just hoped to see you because I haven't since I got home."

My father's face grew stern. "You're supposed to be on bed rest, aren't you? The doctors stressed that you needed to rest to recuperate."

Left unsaid were the words *after your attack*, or the real truth, *after your miscarriage*. My father had never been the kind of man to want to talk about things like that with me, though.

"It's been almost a week, Daddy. They said I should be okay to move around now," I explained as I took a single step into the room to stand next to

Ryder who stood at his post beside the door.

Sneaking a brief look at him, I saw his expression and my heart skipped a beat. Never before had he appeared so serious. It was like his face had been turned to stone, even when he looked at me.

My father closed his laptop and gave me the most genuine smile I'd ever received from him. "Sit down. I don't want you hurting yourself because you're bored in that apartment of yours. That is why you're here, isn't it?"

I wasn't sure if he knew how little time Oliver spent at home, but by the sharpness of his tone, I sensed he might and how he disapproved. He had no idea how happy it made me that my dear husband didn't care to be around me at all now.

"It does get a little boring sitting around all day," I admitted as I sat down in one of the red leather chairs in front of his desk.

He studied me for a moment and smiled again before waving away the two men standing on the opposite side of the room near the bookcases. "Perhaps if we got you a kitten you'd be happy."

"I don't need a kitten. I miss human contact with other people, Daddy. That's why I came down to see you tonight."

"Human contact? Perhaps it's time I had your sister come to stay for a few days. It could be nice for the two of you to spend some time together. I think she told me that husband of hers was out of town on business this week when I spoke to her the other day, so it could be good for both of you."

Having my sister under foot was exactly what I didn't want. She had only called me once after my father told her what happened, and that phone call had consisted entirely of her bragging about how she and her husband would be taking a vacation to Jamaica once he returned from his business trip and not even once asking if I needed anything or how I felt. I'd lived with her narcissism growing up. I didn't want to deal with any more of it now.

"Oh no, I don't know if I'm up to that. Janelle has a very busy life of her own too, so I doubt she'd want to sit around with me for a few days. She has to get ready for that vacation Charles is taking her on when he gets back."

My father nodded. Apparently, he'd heard chapter and verse about her oh so wonderful vacation too.

"That's right. They're spending two weeks in Jamaica at the end of the month. Well, there has to be something we can get you to keep you occupied until you're one hundred percent again."

He tapped his fingertips off his desktop as he thought about what possible entertainment he could find for me, but all I wanted to do was spend some time alone with the person who still stood silently near the door. I didn't dare look over at Ryder, but I felt his stare on me whenever my father wasn't looking.

"What about if I helped you around your office here? I could file things away for you and little jobs like that," I suggested, knowing he would dismiss the very idea out of hand.

Quickly, he shook his head. "No, I don't want you working for me like a secretary. I do my own filing. Plus, this is where I conduct business, and you don't want to be involved in that."

No, I didn't, but if it meant I'd get to at least spend time near Ryder and possibly have the chance to speak a few words to him each day, then I'd do menial jobs around my father's office. Anything to be close to him.

"I just want to not be alone, Daddy," I said, admitting what was brutally true on more levels than he understood.

A flash of sadness passed over his face for a moment, and he looked over toward his office door. "Ryder, leave us. I'll call you when I need you."

My heart sank, and I turned to see the only soul I wanted to truly speak to silently walk out, leaving me with a man who'd married me to the monster who'd tried to kill me a week before.

When we were alone, my father leaned forward

toward me and frowned like I'd done something that displeased him. "Serena, I know what's going on here. I just don't know what to do about it."

As he spoke, my stomach turned at the thought that he knew about Ryder and me and even knew about the baby. "What's going on? What do you mean?"

"I mean you've lost a baby and now you're feeling lost yourself. I don't know how to make that go away."

My father had so rarely said anything genuinely kind to me that I suddenly broke down and began crying. He didn't know how close to the truth his assessment of my problem was. He thought I felt lost because my husband was rarely home with me since I'd been released from the hospital. If he only knew the truth that the person I needed to be with lived only a few yards away from me and suffered in silence just as I had.

I buried my face in my hands and sobbed at how much I needed Ryder, wishing I could tell my father the truth, even if it made a mess of things worse than they already were.

"Serena, I'm sorry this happened to you. I don't know what to do to fix it, though. Perhaps if you returned to volunteering like you used to when you were in high school that might make you feel better. You'd get out of the house a few times a week, and you'd be able to see other people."

Drying my eyes, I thought about his suggestion and saw at least the possibility of a light at the end of the tunnel. Maybe if he had Ryder drive me to the soup kitchen I used to volunteer at, we'd have the chance to speak to each other for a few minutes, at least.

"I hadn't thought of that. Maybe it would do me good to help others now. I don't know if I can drive yet, though. Can you have Ryder drive me? I'd like to go as soon as possible."

My enthusiasm for his idea pleased him, and he picked up his office phone without saying another word to me. "Ryder, I have a job for you. Come to my office."

As he hung up, I stood to leave. "Thank you, Daddy. I knew coming down here was a good idea."

On my way out, he stopped me. "Serena, I want you to know lately you've shown a strength I didn't know you had. I'm not sure your sister would have been able to deal with all of this like you have."

Surprised to hear my father compliment me on the one thing he'd always said I lacked, I smiled. He had no idea how strong I could be.

Or how strong I planned to be.

"Thank you. Maybe I'm more like you than you always thought."

His eyebrows slowly raised up into his forehead.

"Maybe you are. Let Ryder know your volunteer schedule and if Oliver can't take you, I'll make sure he will. And you know what else I think we should do? I think this house needs something to celebrate."

"Celebrate? Like what?" I asked, unsure what he could mean.

Taking me by the shoulders, he smiled and nodded as he explained what he wanted to do. "Since you're feeling better now, I think a party would be just what the doctor ordered. I'll get your sister and Charles to come for the night since I think he's returning tomorrow, and I'll invite some people. You'll see. You and Oliver will have a good time."

I thought about my father's parties, most of which did little to bring out any happiness in me, and remembered the last one. "Will there be dancing? I'd like that."

"Of course there will be dancing!" he said with a big smile. "I'll make sure Ryder is there since I know he loves that too."

Stifling a chuckle, I tried not to look too surprised by his claim that Ryder loved to dance. "Okay, Dad. That sounds nice. Black tie or more casual?"

"Let's do more casual this time since it's going to be an impromptu get-together. We'll make it for this weekend."

My father opened his arms and hugged me for

the first time in longer than I could remember. It felt utterly foreign but some part of me felt comforted by his attempt to be more than the tyrant he'd always been.

Looking up at him, I smiled. I didn't expect him to become father of the year, but I liked this small effort. "Thank you, Daddy."

He kissed the top of my head and whispered, "And don't you worry. We'll have a wonderful time and you'll forget all about your troubles. But never doubt that the person who did this to you will pay. Never doubt that. Never."

"I don't doubt it. Not in the least."

I SAT IN the backseat of the black town car as Ryder slowly drove through the estate gates and could barely wait to finally get a chance to speak to him without anyone else around. My father insisted on having me come to his office so we could leave from there, and with so many eyes on us, we hadn't said two words to each other by the time we reached the car out front.

"Stop the car, please," I said as I grabbed the handle to open the door.

Ryder looked around as if to check to see if the coast was clear and pulled off the side of the road. Hurriedly, I jumped out and got into the front seat, finally able to look into his eyes and say what I'd wanted to for days.

"Tell me you're okay, Ryder. I need to know."

His face remained as stony as it had been the day before in my father's office. In a low voice, he said, "I'm fine."

He moved his hand to shift the car into drive, but I caught it and weaved my fingers through his, and he stopped dead. Slowly, he turned his head and let out a heavy sigh. He wasn't fine just like I wasn't.

I brought our entwined hands to my lips and kissed his rough knuckles, loving the feel of them scraping against the soft skin of my lips. "Talk to me. Please. Tell me what you're feeling."

Quietly, like the words were being torn from his throat, he said, "I can't do this with you, Serena. I can't. This is torture."

"Why? Look at me. Why is this torture?"

He refused to face me. "We're never going to be together. I know that now. All we're ever going to have are moments like this, and I can't do that. It's not enough."

I turned his head so I could see his expression. I needed to see the truth in his eyes. What I saw was the purest sadness I'd ever seen in my life. "I know you miss me. I miss you. I miss our baby. I know you need someone to talk to about what we lost like I do. Please talk to me, Ryder."

Closing his eyes, he lowered his head. "I can't do this. I spent the last week wishing I could just hold you just to feel you next to me so I knew you were safe. Worried what was happening with you and Oliver. I was scared to death he'd hurt you again, or maybe this time he'd get his wish and you'd end up dead. We're never going to be together. Your plan isn't going to work."

"Why? Won't you wait until it does? You just have to be patient."

He turned his head to look at me and I saw tears in his eyes. "Your father knows it was Oliver. When he has me take care of him, he's just going to find someone else for you. We're never going to be together, Serena. We have to accept that. It might hurt to be apart now, but it's going to hurt a lot more if we continue this."

I felt like my entire world was crumbling away around me. In the week since I returned home, Ryder had come to the decision that there was no hope for us. He'd given up on me.

On us.

Clutching his hand, I begged, "Don't do this. Don't give up so easily. My father just told me yesterday that he thought I was strong. Maybe he won't try to force me to marry another man after Oliver. Please, Ryder! Don't give up on our dream now. It's all I have to hang onto."

"That's all it's ever going to be. A dream. We're trapped in this world of your father's, this nightmare where I do his dirty work and you're traded away to further his business interests. How can we ever be together in that world?"

I pulled him close and began to cry. "It doesn't matter what we are right now. We're going to be together. Please don't give up on us. I can't go on if all I have is a life without you."

A car drove up behind us and Ryder pulled away until it passed us. Shaking his head, he pointed to it. "Do you see what I have to do? I can't even hold you in my arms because I'm afraid that someone will see us."

Laying my head on his shoulder, I tried to find the words that would convince him not to give up. "I know it's hard now. It's always been hard for us. We made it through my father sending me away. We made it through me trying to kill myself. We've made it through him forcing me to marry someone else. We can make it through this too."

Ryder turned his head to look out the window and in a voice full of pain said, "Between your father and Oliver, they've taken everything away from us. What do we have left but stolen moments like this as I drive you places? How can this be enough?"

"Because it has to be. I love you. If this is all I can have of you right now, then I'll take it. It's not perfect, but it's never been for us."

He remained silent for a long time before he turned to look at me. Pressing a soft kiss onto my lips, he whispered against them, "I'm sorry that I couldn't be there this week."

I kissed him as the tears rolled down my cheeks. "I know you needed me too. It won't always be like this. Please, don't give up yet."

Ryder cradled my face in his hands, and as I reveled in the feel of his strength, he pressed his forehead to mine. "What are we going to do?"

I may not have known the answer to many of his questions, but I knew the answer to that one. It was the only answer available to us.

"We're not going to give up. No matter what they do to us, we can't give up. That dream can come true. We just have to fight for it."

As he took me in his arms and held me, he whispered, "God, I hope so. It's all that keeps me going some days."

I knew just how he felt.

Chapter Four

Ryder

THE HOUSE BUZZED with staff hurrying to and from the front door preparing for the party Robert insisted would bring happiness and celebration back to the house. Trays of food, cases of alcohol, and more flowers than a coronation called for came in deliveries all day so the hallway outside his office looked like a busy city street with people marching back and forth with arms full of everything needed to make his plans come to life.

I had little interest in attending his party, but it didn't matter if I wanted to or not. I'd be expected to be there and play my part, just like at all his get-togethers. I'd had to pretend Serena's accident and the miscarriage hadn't torn me up inside from the moment I heard that doctor say she lost our baby, remaining stoic and cold while all the while I wanted to take out my rage on that fuck Oliver for what he'd done to her and our child. The last thing I wanted to do was perform my show horse act at another of Robert's parties and have to watch Oliver mope around like some grieving husband trying his best to get over the loss.

"Ryder, you're practically sullen today. I'm certainly hoping I can expect you to be livelier tonight at the party," Robert said, rousing me from my daydreaming about the night's festivities and how much I wanted to pull Oliver into a side hallway and slit his fucking throat.

I forced a smile and nodded. "I'll be there with bells on. You know me."

He stared at me for a moment like he was studying me. "I do, son. I know you well, so I can say without a doubt that something's wrong lately. What is it?"

The last thing I wanted to do was tell Robert what was bothering me. If I mentioned anything about Serena or her injuries, I ran the risk of him suspecting we were far closer than we pretended to be. And anything else that might have been wrong with me he wouldn't understand or care about anyway, so what was the point of mentioning any of it?

Shaking my head, I answered, "Nothing at all. I'm the same as always."

He studied me again for a few more seconds and frowned. "Well, whatever it is, the answer to whatever problem you're dealing with is tonight's party. Did I tell you Janelle and her husband will be there too, so we'll have the whole family back together, at least for one night?"

Whenever he included me in his idea of family, I wanted to believe that I could tell him what I knew about Oliver and what he'd done to Serena. Families protected one another, so maybe he'd take care of that son of a bitch once and for all and Serena would be free.

But then the reality I knew to be the truth always rushed into my brain, pushing out whatever fantasies of family loyalty I wished existed. If I told him Oliver pushed Serena down the stairs, he'd know she and I were far more than just two people who lived in the same house and who he pretended were actually family.

"Janelle and Charles too? That's great," I answered with as much enthusiasm as I could muster for the thought of seeing those two. I disliked and distrusted her, and I didn't give a damn about him.

"Yes, and I think having all her family around her will do wonders for Serena, don't you?"

Nodding, I silently catalogued how much I knew Serena wouldn't care about her sister and brother-in-law being at the party. Janelle's presence never failed to make her wish she was anywhere else but near her, and Charles was practically a stranger to her.

"And I'm hoping that this little get-together will help her husband to feel better about things too. He lost a child just like she did, so they both need our support."

I clenched my jaw and nodded once again as Robert's kind words for Oliver made my stomach churn. That fuck had lost nothing and deserved no support. What he deserved was what I'd someday give him when I finally got the chance to exact my revenge.

If he was lucky, I'd do it quickly. If he wasn't, I'd torture the motherfucker for taking something so precious away from me.

"You might as well go get ready. I want you there front and center at seven sharp."

Always happy to have a reprieve from Robert, I smiled and meant it for the first time in our conversation. "I'll be there like usual. You know me."

He winked and smiled back at me. "That I do, son. That I do."

AT EXACTLY SEVEN o'clock, I took my place next to Robert, just like he instructed, and did my show horse act for each person who approached him. With every one, he said the same thing.

"You remember my adopted son, Ryder, don't you?"

And every important looking man who heard it

looked me up and down and confidently replied, "Of course. It's good to see you again."

None of them meant a word they said, and those words were no exception. I suspected a few of them may have remembered me, but I served no purpose in their world, so their claims that it was good to see me again rang hollow.

They said what they knew Robert wanted to hear because they wanted to be on his good side. Nothing more. It didn't bother me how meaningless I was in the world he shared with them, though. I didn't care. All I cared about stood on the opposite side of the room next to her husband and pretended to want to be there just as I did.

"And there's his sister and her husband," Robert announced when he noticed Serena had arrived. "Now to find my other daughter and her husband and we can begin."

Eager to escape, even for just a few moments, I turned to him and said, "I can go look for her, if you'd like."

The thin woman standing with one of Robert's favorite congressmen smiled at hearing my offer. "Isn't he wonderful? Robert, you're very lucky to have a son like him."

Nodding, he beamed like she'd just told him he'd won a billion dollars. "I am very lucky."

I excused myself and headed out toward the

main hallway, glancing over at Serena as I made my way to the door. The frightened look in her eyes told me she worried I wouldn't be coming back, so I mouthed I'd be right back, and she smiled.

Janelle came through the front door a few seconds later dressed in a tiny red dress far too formal for the occasion, but her husband wasn't behind her. She walked quickly toward me, her high heels clicking off the marble floor, and before I could say a word, she said, "Don't bother looking for him. He's not coming tonight."

"Your father will be disappointed. He wanted the entire family around him tonight."

My statement made her laugh, and then she twisted her face into an expression that showed how little she believed it. "He'll be fine as long as Serena and I are here. And you too, of course, his adopted son."

The snide way she said that indicated she disliked how Robert referred to me as much as Serena and I did. I had a feeling she was jealous, like my presence meant she'd be cheated out of something she thought was rightfully hers someday because he liked to call me his son.

She had nothing to worry about. I wanted nothing he could give me.

"He's already in there," I said as she breezed by me toward the dining room.

Before she walked in, she turned around and asked, "Has he moved the chairs already? I'm assuming there will be dancing like always?"

"You know him. I'd bet money on it."

"Well, then tonight's your lucky night. My husband's absent, so you get to be my partner since Serena will be with Oliver, I'm sure."

Forcing a smile, I tried not to look as disgusted as I felt at the thought of Oliver touching Serena. In addition, I'd hoped to have as little contact as possible with Janelle tonight, so having to dance with her or do anything at all with her made me hate this party even more.

Robert announced Janelle's arrival while I faded into the background, thankful for at least a few minutes of not having to be his favorite show horse. Taking a spot against the wall at the opposite side of the room, I watched Serena stand stiffly next to Oliver, who looked more bored than anything else. Every ounce of my being wanted to walk over to her to close to her. I thought of how I could tell her how beautiful she looked in her deep green velvet dress, but I knew that fuck of a husband of hers would just make a scene, so I simply stared at her, wishing we were anywhere else in the world but there.

As long as we were together, it didn't matter where we were.

For nearly a half hour, I had my reprieve from

Robert and socializing with people I barely knew. From my vantage point, I watched as he flattered his guests, likely in an effort to take their money in an upcoming business deal, and Janelle slipped easily back into her drunken party girl routine she'd practiced before her marriage. Oliver joined them and seemed to be happier without his wife than with her, while Serena stood alone at the party that was supposed to be for her.

While they enjoyed themselves, I made my way over near her and whispered, "You look beautiful tonight. Are you okay?"

She didn't turn her head but moved her eyes to look toward me. "My wonderful husband told me as we were leaving the apartment that if he saw me talking to you I would regret it, Ryder. I don't want to start anything here tonight. Not with all these people around."

"Does he know?" I asked as I watched him glad-hand some man and his wife.

"I don't think so. He just has a problem with you. He always has."

From across the room, Robert said loudly, "Where are my daughter and Ryder? Come over here. I want to make sure everyone has met you two."

Suddenly, every head turned and looked at us as we walked over to join Robert and the rest of the family. Out of habit, I put my hand on Serena's lower back to guide her and saw Oliver's face twist into a look of hate as he saw me touch her.

"Everyone, I think you know my daughter Serena and my adopted son Ryder," Robert said as he wrapped his arms around us. "Tonight I have almost my entire family here. We're missing my daughter Janelle's husband Charles, but we do have Serena's husband Oliver. One big happy family, right?"

As he said this, he looked around at the four of us like he wanted to see our reaction to his ridiculous claim. Janelle lifted her wine glass in salute to his words while Oliver merely smiled through gritted teeth as he glared at me. Serena and I exchanged glances and played our parts, like we knew we must.

We'd done this enough times to know how we had to act.

"Music! We need music and dancing. Ryder, since Janelle is without her husband tonight, you're going to have to take his place. Serena, your husband promises me he'll do his best, even though he says he's not much of a dancer."

"Daddy, it's not fair to put that kind of pressure on Oliver. Not everyone can be as good as Ryder," she said, hate for her husband dripping off each word.

I stood in shock as Serena spoke. Robert's eyes

opened wide like he understood she hadn't been trying to be complimentary.

"Ryder does seem to have dancing in his blood, but Oliver, all you have to do is give it your best shot," Robert said with a wry grin, almost as if he enjoyed tweaking his son-in-law's ego.

As I paid attention to the tension-filled look Serena and her husband shared, Janelle grabbed my arm and twirled in a circle next to me. "Time to dance, brother."

Thankfully, other couples began to move toward the empty space at the end of the room so it wouldn't just be the four of us on display. I'd be able to watch out for Serena easier with others around me to distract Robert.

Janelle took my hand in hers and waited for me to slide my arm around her waist before she began moving her feet. Already too drunk to do much of anything close to dancing, she smiled up at me and asked, "Do you remember that night after Serena went away and Daddy made us dance together at that party he had outside? It was right after she went to Italy."

The memory of that night raced through my mind, leaving little to mention. Janelle had been drunk and just like that first party, she spent as much time falling into me as she did dancing. She also let her hands wander, grabbing my dick like she had the first time too.

Looking away to get a glance at Serena, I answered, "Yeah."

I saw Serena and Oliver dancing nearby, the two of them barely touching one another and both of them looking miserable. I wanted to grab that husband of hers and dump Janelle on him so I could dance with Serena and bring a smile back to her face.

"You were still nursing a broken heart over my sister leaving, so nothing happened between us. But it could have if you weren't so lost without her."

I turned back to look at Janelle and saw her watching me carefully. "I didn't realize you ever wanted something to happen between us. You are my sister, after all."

She laughed at my attempt to use her father's words against her. "That's ridiculous, and you know it. You're no more my brother than Oliver is. By the way, he hates you. Did you know that?"

I nodded, not wanting to act like that fact wasn't well-known to even me. "I've heard."

"He's sure she's in love with you. That's why their marriage is in shambles. Have you heard that?"

Glancing over at Serena, I saw her walk away from Oliver, even though the music hadn't stopped. Worried about her, I forgot what Janelle had asked me, but she grabbed my jaw and turned my head to face her again as I mindlessly moved my feet and pretended to dance.

"I think he's got it all wrong, though. I think you're the one in love with her. You can't keep your eyes off her, Ryder. I wonder if she knows, though. Does she?"

"There's nothing to know. I care about Serena like I care about you. That's what family does," I answered, staring straight down into her brown eyes as they watched carefully for any sign she was right about how I felt for her sister.

As the music began to fade away, she smiled and said, "I wonder how my father would feel if he knew how you felt about her. He's very invested in that marriage working, Ryder, so I assume he'd be unhappy if anything upset that."

I stopped dancing and shrugged. "Then maybe he should talk to his son-in-law and tell him how to treat his wife. Thanks for the dance, Janelle. It was a pleasure as always, even without you palming my cock."

The mention of her copping a feel on my crotch made her smile, but I had nothing more to say to her. All I could think about was Serena and making sure she was okay.

Oliver stood at the bar downing a drink, so I hurried out to look for her. Passing a few guests who stood talking about some deal they wanted to make with Robert, I walked down the hallway and as I glanced into the kitchen, I saw her standing at the counter looking out the window into the courtyard.

"Not in a dancing mood?" I asked quietly so the people in the hall couldn't hear me.

She turned around and wiped under her eyes. "Not with him."

Stepping toward her, I took her hand in mine and instinctively looked around to see if anyone was nearby. "Did something happen? Are you okay?"

A look of pain settled into her beautiful face. "In front of my father, he pretends to be the comforting and loving husband, but when we're alone, I can't stand to be near him he's so vicious."

"What did he say? You look like you've been crying."

Serena swiveled her head to look around for anyone who might see us and then tugged me toward the back of the house. "Nothing more than usual. He hates me as much as I hate him. Let's go somewhere we can be alone."

We hurried to the utility room at the end of the hallway leading out to the apartments, and I closed the door behind us, happy to finally be alone with her. She quickly wrapped her arms around me and lay her head on my chest, making me wish we never had to return to the party, Robert, Janelle, or Oliver ever again.

I held her to me and whispered against the top of

her head, "Are you still sure you want to go through with this whole revenge plan of yours, Serena? Is it really worth it? You're miserable, and every minute you have to spend with him..."

She looked up at me and frowned. "I know it's hard on you. I know and I'm sorry. Just give me the chance to do this."

"It's killing me knowing you're over there with him every night," I said, barely able to hold back the rage inside me at how much I hated him for what he'd done. "That he thinks he got away with hurting you and killing..."

I couldn't finish my sentence and looked away. I imagined he walked around their apartment like some fucking king who felt he had the right to do whatever the fuck he wanted and he'd never have to pay the price. I wanted to make him pay and pay dearly.

Serena kissed me softly on the lips and cradled my face. "I know. I promise it won't be for long. I just need to do this, Ryder. I need to prove to myself that I'm strong enough. You can understand that, right?"

That I understood her need for revenge didn't make it any easier to deal with him still walking around with that smug look on his face whenever I saw him. But I didn't want to make her think I doubted her, so as much as I wanted to put an end to all of it with Oliver, I said nothing and pulled her to me.

"It won't be for long. He'll get what he deserves and that will be that. My father might even figure out it was him and do it for us," she said against my chest.

Every day, I secretly prayed Robert would give me the order to take care of that fuck, but every day came and went and he never said a thing about whether he knew who had attacked Serena or not. And every day, Oliver continued to exist in the same world our child didn't.

Tilting her head, Serena looked up at me and smiled that gentle smile I loved. "I love you. Please don't forget that, okay?"

I pressed my lips to her forehead and whispered against her soft skin, "I could never forget. It's the only thing that gets me through most days. That and the dream of us getting away from here."

"We're going to be okay. I believe that, Ryder."

Closing my eyes, I tried to believe that too. I wanted to. I did. But sometimes when I sat alone thinking about her just a few doors away in that apartment with him, I wondered if we'd ever find that happiness we'd promised one another.

Serena backed away from me even as she held my hand. "I better get back in there. I'm sure my father is wondering where we are."

"I'm sure Janelle is keeping him busy. She's in rare form tonight. When we were dancing, she told me we could have gotten together one night right after you left for Italy, but she said I was too busy being lost without you."

"I'm surprised," Serena said with a chuckle. "I thought she didn't like you. It never occurred to me that she might make a move on you while I was gone."

"Me neither. She's convinced she knows that I'm in love with you, but she isn't sure if you feel the same."

Serena brought my hand to her lips and kissed it. "As long as you know how I feel, that's all that matters. I'll come to your place if I can tonight. If not, I promise I'll come as soon as I can, okay? I better get back now."

As much as I wanted to wrap her in my arms and make her stay, I knew she had to leave or risk us being found out. I watched her walk away from me like always and hated it, even though I knew it had to be this way.

At least for a little while longer.

Chapter Five

Ryder

THE DARKNESS OF my apartment swallowed me up, just as I'd hoped it would when I began drinking an hour earlier after it became obvious tonight would be another night without Serena. After spending an entire week driving her to and from the soup kitchen on Federal Street and enjoying those hours more than any others in my days, I craved her touch so much I was afraid I might do something stupid like go to her apartment.

So I drank. And when thoughts of her popped into my mind, I drank more. I didn't know how much it would take to forget her, at least for one night, but I had to try.

If I didn't, I'd go out of my mind wishing she was in my arms.

I wanted to believe what she said in the car that first day we were together after she came home from the hospital. I wanted to be strong for her after all she'd gone through. I did, but every day the chances of us ever being together felt like they shrank smaller and smaller while my need to have her at my side grew until she was all I could think about.

Lifting the whisky bottle to my lips, I let the alcohol sit in my mouth for a moment before it slid down my throat. It had been too long since Serena was in my arms. My body ached for her.

I needed to drink more. Whatever it took to stop thinking. I closed my eyes and tried to remember a time before I came to this place, but all I was then was a fighter who lived day to day to inflict pain on others.

Some would have said my life at the estate amounted to the same thing. I couldn't count how many people I'd punished for Robert in the time since he made me one of his guards. Some weeks it was the only thing I did, and then sometimes I didn't lay a hand on anyone for a month at a time.

But no matter if he called us guards, and no matter if my job only occasionally required me to rough someone up, I was who I'd always been. I knew that should make me feel something, but it didn't.

I only felt for Serena.

When I wasn't with her, I became more machine than anything else. Robert dictated what I did and to whom, and I did his bidding. No more, no less. None of it required feelings one way or the other.

I'd always been that way. When my uncle forced

me into fighting, I didn't cry or complain. What would have been the point? Then instead of me beating others he would have beaten me. I may not have been good in school, but I could figure out that equation pretty quickly.

So I did what he made me do, and when I got old enough and could make my own decisions, I continued fighting. And when I made some bad mistakes with money and got into Floyd for more than I could afford, I accepted he'd basically own me until I could pay him off.

I was the king of accepting the shit the world handed me and smiling as I said thank you for it. It's all I'd ever been since I was old enough to know what life was about.

Then I met Serena and for the first time in my life, I let myself dare to dream. To really dream, not just look forward to a day when things would be better but to think that life had something better in store for me than the constant helpings of shit it dumped on me.

I didn't understand how she had the strength to dream after everything her life had been. She'd had the best of everything money could buy, but when it came to things money couldn't buy, she was piss poor.

A mother gone in the middle of the night and no hope ever given that she'd be back. A father who saw her in terms of what use she could be to him. A sister who'd stab her in the back for a kind word from him and had more than once.

And out of all of that, Serena still refused to believe things wouldn't get better.

My phone vibrated against my leg, and I looked down to see a text from Jesse about getting together for a night out at some local bar. Shaking my head, I tossed the phone aside and mumbled, "Too late, pal. I'm half a bottle ahead of you."

A few minutes later, I heard a knock at my door and even though I knew Jesse would be standing there with a million reasons why I should go out trolling women at some hole in the wall bar, I figured I'd answer it anyway. Maybe he could take my mind off my problems for at least a little while.

I threw open the door and saw Serena standing there barefoot in jeans and a black sweater with sleeves that hung down over the middle of her hands and made her look even smaller than she was. The look on her face told me something had happened, so I quickly pulled her into my apartment and closed the door.

"What's wrong?" I asked as adrenaline pumped through my veins, instantly killing my buzz.

"I needed to see you. I can't stay in that apartment any more. I'm going crazy and I started to think about doing something," she said, wincing like she was in pain.

I held her by the shoulders and searched her eyes for what that meant. "What do you mean doing something? Doing what?"

Serena looked down toward her bare feet. "Don't make me say it, Ryder. I'm ashamed that I'm so fucking weak that I'd even think about doing that again."

A sick feeling settled into my gut. I knew what she meant. The memory of finding her naked in that bathtub bleeding to death right in front of my eyes raced through my mind, and I shook my head violently to push the thought away.

I couldn't think of her doing that again.

"Don't ever say that, Serena. Do you hear me? Never," I said, my emotions spilling out in my words.

She winced again and turned her head, as if she expected at any moment to be hit. "Don't yell at me. I didn't want to do it. I just said I thought about it."

I cradled her face and kissed her, loving the feel of her soft lips against mine. I'd missed that so fucking much.

"I'm sorry. I just can't think of you doing that again. It hurts too much."

A single tear slid down her cheek as her lower lip quivered. "I thought I could stay so strong, Ryder. I want to. I want to be the person who said all those things when I was lying in that hospital bed. I meant every word. I did. But now that I'm back in that apartment where everything happened, I don't know. It's like little bits of my strength chip away every day I'm there. I'm afraid I'll wake up one of these days and there will be none left."

I pulled her to me and held her close as she began to cry. I'd wanted her to be strong too, even if I hadn't wanted to go along with her plan to get revenge on Oliver.

She sobbed against my chest as I asked, "Did he do something to you? I want you to tell me."

If he did, I wasn't sure I could hold back from doing what I wanted to do to him.

Serena shook her head and looked up at me as she dried her eyes. "He says the same thing all the time. He threatens to hurt the two of us if he ever finds out who I was with. But he's had some big acquisition at work to deal with, thankfully, so I haven't had to see him much at all."

"That's good, at least. I hate thinking about him there with you. I lay in bed at night worried I'm going to hear sirens at any minute and I'm going to race over there and find you—"

I couldn't finish that sentence. Every damn night I dreaded hearing those sirens because I knew she'd be dead if I heard them. And then I'd have to live with the fact that I hadn't protected her when she needed me most.

"He doesn't care enough about me to try again, Ryder. It wasn't me he wanted to hurt."

Pushing down my emotions about him intentionally killing our child, I took her by the hand and walked over to the chair. More than once this past week, she and I had cried all the way to the soup kitchen about losing the baby. I didn't want to cry anymore. I didn't want to think about him or her anymore.

I pulled Selena onto my lap and wrapped my arms around her, loving just having her next to me. Something about feeling her against my body made everything else in life fade away until it was just the two of us. It had been like that ever since that first night we got together years ago, and still all it took was having her with me to make my world livable again.

To make me believe in the dream.

Lightly tracing her finger along my jaw, she looked over at the half-empty bottle of whisky on the table and asked, "Why do you drink so much?"

"To forget."

She gazed into my eyes. "Does it work? Because if it does, I want to drink too. I want to forget."

I shook my head. "No, it doesn't work. It just makes me think more."

"Then why do you do it?"

Sliding my hand through her hair, I stopped and twisted a section around my finger. "Because after I spend hours sitting here alone every night thinking of how much I'd hate myself if you were hurt and I wasn't there to protect you, the alcohol finally knocks me out and I can at least get a few hours of sleep."

Serena pressed her lips together. "I'm sorry. If only I was as strong as I want to be or even if I was like Janelle, you wouldn't have to worry all the time."

Just the thought of being with her sister made me smile, and her mood brightened immediately. "What's so funny?"

"Me with Janelle. That would never happen."

Searching my face for more of an answer, she finally said, "I told you what she thought you were brought here to be. Remember? She thought you were here to be a stud and swore to me she'd never sleep with you."

I slid my hands down Serena's arms and folded the cuffs of her sleeves. "The other night she was singing a different tune, but there wasn't going to be any way in hell I'd ever sleep with her."

When I'd finished fixing her sweater, she placed her palms against my cheeks. "But you'd sleep with me. Did you want to before I came to your room that night?"

Thinking back to those early days when I was

new at the estate, I said, "I don't know. I wasn't sure what to make of you. I just knew Janelle was a bitchy little rich girl. But you seemed different."

Her eyebrows raised and she smiled. "Different, huh? Why's that?"

"Your big brown eyes always seemed to be looking at me, and I wasn't sure what you were seeing. Or what you wanted to see."

Serena ran her finger along the collar of my dress shirt and shyly admitted, "You were so foreign compared to everyone here. I wanted to know everything about you, but I didn't know how to do that. So I watched you whenever I could."

"So I was foreign? What if I had been like everyone you were used to?"

She kissed me sweetly, sliding her tongue along the seam of my mouth. "I don't think I would have cared if you were exactly like everyone here with the way you look."

Stuffing my hand into her hair, I pulled her to me and whispered against her lips, "So that's why you always seemed to be staring at me."

"I wanted you from the moment I saw you in that tub," she said with a sexy grin.

"All beaten up?" I asked, remembering how I looked all black and blue and swollen from the fight days earlier.

Serena nodded. "Yes."

We sat there together in silence as memories of that time so long ago made me smile. Finally, she said, "I needed this tonight, Ryder. To see you and see you smile. Thank you."

"You're all that makes me smile anymore."

She snuggled up to me, nestling her head in the space between my shoulder and my jaw, and I couldn't imagine feeling happier than I felt at that moment. For as much as I loved when my cock was inside her, the mere act of holding her as she sat curled up on my lap satisfied my need for her tonight.

After a few minutes more in silence of my apartment, I said, "Tell me what it's going to be like when we escape this place, Serena."

Sighing, she kissed my neck and sat up, and in the dim light I saw her eyes open wide with excitement. "It'll just be the two of us and no one else. And we'll spend every night in each other's arms and Sunday mornings we'll sleep in late. There will be nobody telling us who we have to be ever again."

"I want to believe that all can happen. I can't tell you how much I want to believe."

"It's all I think of when I lie in bed at night, Ryder," she said, gently running her hands through my hair. "If I didn't have that future to dream about, if I didn't have moments like this, I'd have nothing to live for."

Even though I didn't want to hear her say things like that, I knew just what she meant. If all I had was my life there but I didn't have her or the promise that someday we'd be away from there together, I'd want to stick a fucking gun in my mouth and blow my brains out.

"I won't do anything to hurt myself, though. I promise. I wouldn't put you through that again, Ryder."

I stroked her cheek and cupped her chin as I realized how beautiful she looked at that moment. I didn't tell her that if she did leave me here alone, I wasn't sure I'd live another month without her.

"I love you, Serena. Don't leave me here without you. I couldn't take it if you did."

"I won't. We're all we have. You and me. And one day, we'll leave this place behind and all the horrible things we saw here. We'll go somewhere, just you and me, and make a life we want."

Chapter Six

Serena

AS MUCH AS I hated to leave Ryder's, I had to if I wanted to still keep us a secret. So after kissing him one last time and promising him this wouldn't be our life forever, I crept back to my apartment with the plan to be in bed when Oliver finally got home.

My blood ran cold when I turned the corner to head into my apartment and saw him leaning against his blue BMW, his arms folded and a triumphant smile on his horrible face.

I'd been caught.

"Out late, Serena? Coming from Daddy's office? Oh, but that can't be since I checked and he's nowhere to be found tonight. The guards at the gate told me he left an hour ago. So where were you?"

My mind raced as I worked feverishly to construct a lie he couldn't see through. "I went out for a walk in the garden and then went to the main house for a bite to eat since my father had told me the cook had made lamb special for him today."

Oliver's gaze traveled down my body and

stopped at my bare feet. Grimacing at my lack of shoes, he said in a low voice, "I'd think your feet would be wet if you went out for a walk in the garden at this time of night, but they look bone dry. Want to try again?"

I began to walk past him to get into the house, but he grabbed my arm around my bicep and squeezed it tightly, bringing tears to my eyes. Leaning in close to me, he whispered, "I can smell him on you. Back to fucking him already?"

"Let go of me!" I cried as I attempted to pull away from his hold, only to have him tighten his grip on my arm until my skin burned. "You're hurting me, Oliver. Let go!"

"I knew that kid wasn't mine. That's why I had no problem getting rid of it. And the first chance I get, I'll get rid of the guy who's been fucking my wife too."

The mere thought of Oliver, with his scrawny body and small hands, going up against Ryder made me laugh in my husband's face. "Just try to get rid of him. He'll kill you where you stand. You don't know who you're dealing with, dearest husband, so let go of me and accept that I've got you just where I want you after what you did."

Fear filled his beady little eyes, and he pushed me away as hard as he could. Stumbling across the concrete driveway, I steadied myself and shot him a look before heading into the house. He could think whatever he wanted. If he thought Ryder was going to disappear that easy, he had no idea who he was.

That meant he didn't know who I'd been with.

Thankful for at least that, I undressed and climbed into bed, hoping to avoid Oliver for the rest of the night, like usual. In the state he was in, I didn't want to risk another fight with him. I may not live through a second one.

I closed my eyes and thought about that life I'd promised Ryder we'd someday have. I'd thought about it so many times I could picture it down to the last detail. We'd live in a cozy house with a yard for a dog and our kids and a white picket fence in the front. During the day, I'd take care of the babies while he worked somewhere doing an honorable job that didn't involve fighting or hurting people. Then at night, we'd sit on the back porch and he'd hold me in his arms as we looked up at the stars, counting our blessings as we thanked God for helping us escape this place.

It was what I thought of every night before I fell asleep, and sometimes I dreamed about that little house with the green grass and could almost smell the flowers I'd plant every spring down the front walkway. Yellow daisies or some other happy looking flower that told anyone who saw them that our house was full of love and joy.

We could be happy. I believed that, even though I struggled to remember more than a few days of my entire life I could truly say were happy. A few of them involved my mother, and then for a long time, all I had were days filled with questions why she'd left and lies my father told me to keep me in line.

The rest of my happy days were because of Ryder. That first night he invited me into his room. The times we spent talking as we lay on his bed, as close as we were now but still innocent. The night I went to his room with the candy I'd spent all afternoon making just for him and the sensuous feeling of his lips on mine for the first time.

Every moment I got to be near him when I came home from the hospital after my suicide attempt. For the first time in my life, I'd had something that felt normal. I knew no one else would ever think of what he and I were then as normal, but when we sat down to eat breakfast and walked around the grounds each afternoon, each of us cared that the other person was right there.

My mind always travelled to that night when the world thought my husband and I would be happily celebrating our marriage, and instead Oliver left me alone and I turned to the only person I knew would understand.

The only person I wanted to spend that night with.

Had our child been conceived then as we made love, finding one another's body and soul after I'd been given away to another man?

I choked back tears as I thought about the child we'd never have. Had it been a girl I could have dressed in pink and tied ribbons in her hair? Or had it been a boy who would have taken after his father and grown up to be strong and protective of the woman he loved?

We'd never know. Oliver had made sure of that.

And now I planned to make sure he'd pay for what he did. I just had to stay strong, no matter how hard that seemed.

I heard him walk into the bedroom and instantly my body tensed like it did every night when he came home. Sleeping next to the man who'd tried to kill me, the man who'd taken my child from me, sickened and terrified me.

He stopped at the foot of the bed and said in a low voice, "I don't know what you think you're going to do to me, Serena, but it won't work. If your father believed it was me, he would have killed me by now, just like he killed my brother."

I knew who had killed Jacob. My father may have ordered his death, but he hadn't gotten his hands dirty. The man Oliver thought to go up against had been the one to do it.

And if my father ever decided my husband was

to die, the same man would kill him. And I wouldn't shed a tear.

I remained silent as Oliver continued to stand there just beyond my feet. His breathing seemed labored, like he had to work to control himself, and I fought the urge of every cell in my body to curl up into a ball to protect myself.

"There's no proof of who attacked you, so whatever that little act in the hospital was, I'm not worried."

The shakiness of his voice told a different story. Oliver knew it was only a matter of time before I'd figure out how to exact my revenge.

Flush with excitement about how cornered I actually had him, I pushed the covers down off my shoulders and sat up to face him. Instantly, I saw the fear in his eyes, but there was something else in them too I couldn't quite put my finger on.

Not anger. No, whatever he felt wasn't anger. As I stared up at him standing there looking at me, I realized what I saw in his eyes beside the fear that someone would find out what he did.

He knew. I didn't know how he'd found out, but he knew who I'd been with.

"The truth always comes out, Oliver. No matter how hard you try to hide it, the truth is always there waiting for someone to see it."

Arching one eyebrow, he nodded as the corners

of his mouth crept up into a smile that reminded me of my father's. "Do you remember that night when your brother brought your shoes to you? I told you I didn't want you to be around him anymore."

"Then you should have made that clear to my father because I've never stopped seeing him in my father's office, when he drives me to the soup kitchen, and even when I have dinner at the main house. He is my brother, after all."

I didn't know where Oliver was going with this. Whatever he planned, I didn't want to be sitting down when it started, so I threw off the blankets and stood up, my legs shaking as fear wound through me.

"What do you think the world would think about Robert Erickson's daughter fucking the boy he claims is his adopted son, Serena? Your father is an important man who rubs elbows with politicians and billionaires in his business dealings every day. Do you think he'd approve of you and Ryder?"

And there it was. The truth, finally. The reality of someone other than me and Ryder referring to us as anything romantic hit my ear oddly. The way Oliver said his name, practically hissing when it came out of his mouth, made what we were sound wrong.

"I don't know what you're talking about. Both he and I told you. He's like my brother, and my father considers him his son. I even think he plans to leave his businesses to him. So I'd be very careful accusing Ryder of doing anything, Oliver. He's the golden child even more than Janelle and I are."

"I know what's been going on. You two haven't been as clever as you thought. I saw you coming from his apartment tonight, and when I tell your father what I know, Ryder won't be the golden child or anything else anymore. I have too much information on Robert Erickson for him to make the same mistake he made with my brother. You see, I'm far smarter than you ever gave me credit for, dear Serena."

There was no point in arguing with him about this. He'd called my bluff, and the one thing I hadn't thought of had done in my plan for revenge. I'd never thought of the possibility that he'd be ballsy enough to go up against my father.

I knew how his attempt to blackmail my father would end. Anyone stupid enough to try that found themselves dead. The problem was before Oliver died, he'd ruin any chance for Ryder and me to have that life I dreamed of for us. Ryder may have been my father's pet project, but I doubted he'd be okay with us together.

He'd caught us once before and I was sent away to another continent for two years. This time I feared Ryder would be the one sent away, never to come back. And then my father would simply find me another husband who suited his business interests.

If I thought I could kill Oliver myself, I would have right there in that bedroom. I knew better, though. I wasn't strong enough to take care of him.

Gathering every bit of courage I possessed, I walked past him to grab my purse and hurried out of the apartment as he called out, "Go ahead, run to him. This will be your last night together because tomorrow he'll be the latest name on your father's hit list."

My mind began to spin out of control. Could I head off Oliver's attempt to speak to my father by getting to him first? Maybe. But what would I say? Would I finally admit it was my own husband who pushed me down the stairs?

No. Even if I reached my father first, when Oliver told him what he knew, Ryder and I would still suffer. It wouldn't be enough to just pre-emptively cut him off at the pass.

Oliver had to be taken care of or everything Ryder and I dreamed of would be lost.

I ran into the main house and up to my old bedroom, locking the door behind me as I searched for the cell phone I used to contact Ryder. My hands trembling so much I could barely type out the words, I messaged him with a desperate plea.

Meet me in my old bedroom now! It's an emergency!

Pacing back and forth across the carpet, I waited for what seemed like hours for him, but finally, I heard a quiet knock on the door. I opened it to see his eyes open wide in terror and pulled him in before quickly closing the door.

Ryder grabbed my arms and examined my wrists. "Are you okay? I thought you did something again."

I shook my head and took a deep breath. "No, it's nothing like that. He knows! Oliver knows! He just told me he plans to tell my father about us. He can't do that, Ryder. If he does, my father will send you away. Or he'll kill you. He won't stand for lying to him. People who betray him suffer."

He brought my hands to his lips and kissed them. "Slow down. Tell me what happened."

Looking up into his green eyes, I tried to find some sense of calm in them, but it was no use. I knew Oliver planned to follow through on his threat as early as tomorrow. Whatever we did, we had to do it that night.

"He knows about you and me, Ryder. Oliver knows. He told me he's going to tell my father. I thought maybe if I got to him first I could tell him what Oliver did to me, but that won't work. As soon as Oliver tells him, everything we want and dream of will be taken away from us. He needs to be dealt with tonight."

For a moment, Ryder looked stunned, like someone had slapped him across the face. He opened his mouth to speak, but nothing came out. Finally, he said in a quiet voice, "You know what you're asking me to do, don't you, Serena?"

I did. I'd wanted my revenge and to keep Ryder from doing anything to Oliver, but he left me with no choice. If he told my father, it wouldn't be me sent away this time. It would be Ryder who'd pay.

"I'd do it myself, but I can't. I'm not strong enough. You're the only person who can do this. It's for us, for the future we want. For the baby he took from us."

The surprise faded from his expression, replaced by a look I'd never seen on him. His eyes contained nothing as he looked at me now, like he had gone ice cold inside.

In a voice so calm it sounded like someone else speaking, he said, "You don't have to convince me. Stay here and go to sleep, and when you wake up all those dreams you have for us will still be there."

He placed his hands on the sides of my face and kissed me sweetly, and I believed every word he said. He'd saved my life twice before, and now he'd protect me when I needed him most.

"I love you, Ryder," I said as his hands slid from my face.

"I love you, Serena. Now leave this up to me and

know I would never let anyone hurt you."

He walked out of the room, and I exhaled like I'd been holding my breath from the moment I walked down that staircase to marry Oliver and now could finally breathe again. Ryder would protect me. He'd protect us and our dreams.

And someday, we'd have the chance to escape that place and find that little house with the white picket fence and the back porch where we'd sit together and look up at the stars.

PART TWO

Chapter Seven

Serena

STARING OUT FROM behind the black veil pulled down over my face, I sat on the wooden folding chair on the freshly cut green grass next to Oliver's gravesite and watched a man crank the handle of a machine to lower the casket into the hole in the earth. His mother sitting two seats away from me wept uncontrollably, sobbing into her handkerchief about losing both her sons in one year, and his father held her hand as he struggled to maintain his composure.

To my left, my father sat staring straight ahead, as if seeing someone put in their final resting place engrossed him. His face remained emotionless the entire time, even when Oliver's mother began wailing when the casket disappeared out of view into the ground.

I knew Ryder stood somewhere nearby, never far away from my father. I yearned to look around and find him to give me that sense of security he always provided, but I felt his gaze on me as I sat there emotionless watching my late husband go into his grave.

He'd never cared one bit for me and would have been sitting just like I was at that moment if our roles were reversed, so I felt no guilt as I hid dry-eyed behind my veil and silently prayed for the funeral to end so I could return home and begin my life again with the man I loved.

The man who had saved me from having to live another moment with Oliver.

The minister spoke a few last words before walking over to me to once again express how sorry he was at the untimely death of such a young and vibrant soul. I simply nodded, afraid if I opened my mouth the truth would come tumbling out.

"My daughter has had a very difficult time. I think I should take her home now," my father said as he grasped my arm. Looking past me, he said to Oliver's parents, "My deepest sympathies on the loss of your son."

His mother continued to cry while we walked away toward the road where the car waited for us. We said nothing on our way there. What could be said? I had no idea if my father knew what had happened to Oliver, and I didn't care.

I'd never wanted to marry him. My father had wanted that. And now my husband was gone, and I'd be damned if I was going to be shackled to another man simply to suit my father's business interests ever again.

I sensed Ryder nearby and turned to see him walking behind us, his focus entirely on me. A tiny smile broke the serious look he wore and told me he was as happy to see me as I was to see him.

If only we could talk and hold each other instead of having to pretend neither of us cared the other was so close.

AFTER A RIDE filled with nothing but more silence back to the estate, I couldn't bear not being near him for any longer. When my father and Ryder stopped in front of his office, I said, "I think I want to be alone. It's been a very tiring day."

I just hoped Ryder understood my hint and would be able to escape soon.

To my surprise, my father shook his head. "Unfortunately, even on the saddest days, business must be dealt with. I don't think it will take long, though."

"What do you mean?" I asked, confused about what part I could have in any of his business.

He guided me into his office as Ryder followed. "We have matters to settle concerning your husband's death, Serena. I wish it didn't all have to be dealt with today, but that's the way of the world."

I looked over at Ryder and saw him standing

stony-faced in his position near the bookcase on the far wall. All I wanted to do was lie in his arms and listen to him tell me about the time when we'd finally get to escape this world of my father's, and now after enduring days of mourning for a man I felt nothing for, I had to be part of some business deal my father wanted to finalize.

"Dad, it doesn't seem in bad taste to conduct business today?" I asked, praying to God some tiny shred of decency existed inside him.

He poured himself a drink and sat down behind his desk. Grinning like I said something amusing, he pointed toward the red leather chairs in front of me. "Sit, Serena. This isn't usual business. We have a will to deal with, so as soon as Oliver's lawyer gets here, we'll start."

I couldn't believe my dearly departed husband had ever liked me enough to leave me anything of worth in his will. Then again, since his brother was dead too, maybe his will would give me something.

Not that I wanted anything from him. I had my freedom. There was nothing else of worth he could give me.

"Doesn't that usually happen later?" I asked as I reluctantly sat down.

My father shook his head as his face twisted into a look of near disgust. "I made sure to contact his attorney as soon as I heard he died. No time like the present."

Clearly, my father wasn't in mourning about Oliver's passing. I waited for him to continue speaking, but he opened up his laptop and his fingers began tapping at the keys, so I sat silently wishing for all this to be over and sneaking glances at Ryder as we waited for the lawyer.

A short man with glasses and wearing a brown suit too big for his frame showed up less than an hour later clutching an old leather briefcase. Mousy looking, he looked flustered as he waited for my father to wave him into the office. Robert Erickson had that effect on people.

After they exchanged pleasantries, Attorney Max Frendle sat down beside me and withdrew a stack of papers from his battered briefcase. "Mrs. Landon, as your deceased husband's attorney, I must inform you that you are the sole beneficiary of his will."

Every word after Mrs. Landon got lost in my brain as I tried to grapple with being called that one last time. I'd never liked having anyone refer to me as that. It always made me feel subservient. While I didn't enjoy being called Serena Landon, at least when people called me that I felt like I was my own person and not just the wife of some man I'd been forced to marry.

"Unfortunately, the art appraisal business he and his brother ran until his death is all but bankrupt since they misspent their money. I'm afraid there's not much left for you to receive after all is said and done."

All the better. I never wanted anything to do with Oliver or his business.

My father, on the other hand, looked genuinely disappointed in my dead husband's lack of business acumen. Wearing a deep frown, he shook his head slowly as the lawyer explained how little the appraisal house would give him.

"What a terrible day it has been for my daughter. First, she had to bury her husband, and now as a young widow, she hasn't even been left a sufficient amount to live on. Thank God, she has family to support her."

I cringed at hearing my father refer to supporting me. Out of the corner of my eye, I saw Ryder's eyes narrow as my father pretended to be that wonderful father figure he loved to have the rest of the world see him as.

Oliver's attorney attempted to paint a rosier picture, though. "For what it's worth, the business is a solid one, other than the debts that must be paid, so Mrs. Landon can look forward to profits in the future."

None of this interested me. I wouldn't get to directly benefit from the appraisal business anyway. My father had been the one who wanted it, and now that Oliver was gone, he'd get it.

His business completed, the lawyer left and my father poured himself another drink, clearly pleased with how things had gone. "That wasn't too painful, was it?" he asked with a broad smile.

"You mean painful like having to live with a man who never cared about me? A son of a bitch who never once attempted to show me an ounce of kindness or warmth? That kind of painful?" I asked.

Looking past my father as he sipped his bourbon and branch, I saw Ryder's eyes grow wide in surprise at my words. My father didn't look surprised but confused, though. Furrowing his brow, he returned to his seat.

"What do you mean by that? Are you still holding onto those teenage girl fantasies of what marriage is supposed to be like? I would have thought you'd grown out of those by now."

"He pushed me down those stairs, Dad. There was no intruder who tried to kill me. Just my husband."

My father's mouth dropped open in shock, and for a long moment, I wondered if he'd say anything. When he finally spoke, he didn't seem to believe me.

"Oliver? That squirrely husband of yours did that?"

I leveled my gaze on him, refusing to let him think I'd made up this story. "The man you decided I needed to marry was nothing but cold toward me. On my wedding night, he left me alone to go to his brother's house. He hated me."

"Well, he couldn't have hated you that much. You wouldn't have been able to get pregnant if all he felt for you was hate."

The silly grin on his face irritated me. I wanted to tell him the truth of who the baby's father was, but I knew better. This was a long game I was playing with my father. Someday I'd tell him the truth, but not now.

For now, I'd have to ignore his grinning.

"How nice of you to make a joke about me losing my baby, Dad. First, you shackle me to that bastard, and now you think it's funny to make jokes about my miscarriage that only happened because he threw me down a flight of stairs and then kicked me as I lay in agony at the bottom."

The smile slid from my father's face, and with a groan, he tipped his glass up to his mouth to take a drink. It gave him time before he said, "I didn't know, Serena. I never would have figured Oliver for a man who abuses women."

"Not women, Dad. Me. One woman. He abused one woman. His wife," I snapped, tired of my father's willingness to give Oliver the benefit of the doubt.

For the second time in minutes, I'd shocked my

father. He sat back in his chair and groaned as his dark eyebrows drew in like angry black slashes.

"I'm willing to tolerate many things, but hurting one of my daughters is not one of them. I would have had him taken care of if I knew, Serena. Why didn't you tell me when I asked you what happened in the hospital?"

Sure I couldn't tell him the truth about wanting to exact my revenge on Oliver without giving away that Ryder had been the one who helped me get away from Oliver, I quickly devised a lie. "The man was my husband and he was standing right there when you asked me what happened. I knew I'd have to go back to living with him once I left the hospital. What did you expect me to do?"

"I'm sorry, honey. I had no idea. If I did, I would have taken care of him like he deserved," he said somberly before finishing his drink and pouring himself a new one.

My father so rarely expressed genuine kindness that his apology surprised me for a moment, but I knew I couldn't forget my pretending was to ensure Ryder and I were safe. Forcing a smile, I said what I knew my father would want me to say.

"He deserved a lot of bad things, but I'm glad you didn't have to kill him, Dad."

My kindness wasn't lost on him, and he smiled at me. "You were too sweet for him, Serena. I should have known that."

I waited nervously for him to begin making plans for my second marriage, but his mind stayed on Oliver. "I wonder who would have wanted your husband dead since I've doubted it was just some robbery gone bad at his office as the police claimed since the very beginning. And now that you're telling me there was no intruder who attacked you, I'm doubly curious."

"Why?" I asked, suddenly terrified by his curiosity.

"Well, when I thought there was a possibility that some attacker had broken into your home, it made sense that someone would have done the same to Oliver at his office, but since he was the one who attacked you, that theory makes no sense."

As he thought about this, I snuck a look at Ryder and saw fear in his eyes that my father's suspicions could lead to something very bad for us. So quickly, I scrambled to come up with a believable reason why someone would want Oliver dead.

Someone other than me.

"Dad, the lawyer said that Oliver and his brother frittered away the appraisal business's money. We don't know what that involved. They could have gambled it away, and you know as well as I do that gambling often involves loans and getting into people for large sums of money. Maybe that happened and when they couldn't pay, whoever they owed got their money another way."

My father chuckled. "What do you know about gambling, Serena?"

"I watch TV. People get into trouble with gambling all the time, don't they? You know, hit men, concrete shoes, sleeping with the fishes kind of stuff?"

His chuckle exploded into a full-fledged laugh, and he threw his head back. "I forget how funny you can be, Serena. I'm not sure any of that still happens other than in the movies and on TV."

Happy I'd been able to distract him, at least for a few minutes, I smiled. "Well, maybe they don't, but I'm sure while Oliver and his brother were blowing all their money, they made some enemies. Maybe one of them decided Oliver had crossed him one too many times."

Clearly skeptical, he sighed and nodded his head. "Perhaps. Well, whatever happened, I'm glad he got his just desserts, no matter who gave them to him. It's been a long day for you. Go home and relax."

I knew when my father wanted me to leave, so I walked around his desk and kissed him on the cheek like a good daughter should. "Thank you, Dad. It has been a difficult day, so I think I will."

"Good idea, honey."

I shot Ryder a knowing look to give him the sign

that I wanted him to find a way to come see me, but in return I received the same stony look he usually wore while he stood guard in my father's office. Hoping he understood my hint, I headed out into the hallway and then turned around to ask my father a question.

Peeking my head into his office, I asked, "Dad, will you be here all night?"

He looked up from his laptop and smiled at me. "I plan to go out as I usually do. Do you need something before I do?"

I shook my head. "No. I just wondered since it's just the two of us again."

His gaze darted over toward Ryder and then back at me. "Don't you mean just the three of us again?"

Suddenly, I couldn't help feeling self-conscious. Did he know about Ryder and me? Did he know Ryder was the father of the child Oliver had killed? Did he know Ryder did just as I asked and fixed everything so I never again had to fear another night in the same apartment as my husband?

With as much control as I could exert on my expression, I tried to remain casual and looked over toward the man who I owed my very life to. "That's right. I'm sorry, Ryder. I didn't mean to imply you weren't here too."

As my father watched, Ryder smiled warmly.

"It's okay."

"There we go. One big happy family," my father said with one of his crocodile grins. "Now run along and take care. You have the rest of your life ahead of you starting tomorrow."

Something in the way he said that unnerved me, but I didn't want to stick around to hear any more of his cryptic messages.

"Goodnight, Dad. Goodnight, Ryder."

I left his office and once again hoped to see Ryder leave right behind me. Waiting in the back hallway, I poked my head around the corner and watched to see him. After nearly ten minutes, he finally walked out of my father's office and saw me waiting.

Waving him toward me, I said in a hushed voice, "Come here."

He smiled but then looked around to make sure no one was watching before hurrying to join me. Gently, he pushed me back into the hallway out of sight.

"How are you? Are you doing okay?" he asked as he cradled my face and stared down into my eyes with a look of worry.

I covered his hands with mine, loving the feel of his touch on me. It had been days since I got to enjoy him next to me. Closing my eyes, I whispered, "I'm fine now."

Reveling in just being with him, I tried to push the rest of the day away and focus only on Ryder. When he was near me, I always felt safe and protected. Now that Oliver was gone forever, I hoped I'd finally get to be with the man I loved.

No more running around and hiding how we felt about one another. I wanted the world to know I loved Ryder and he loved me and that love had endured ugliness and meanness, but it had endured and grown stronger through all we'd been forced to suffer through.

I felt his lips gently brush mine before he whispered, "We can't risk anyone seeing us. You have to go, Serena."

Opening my eyes, I shook my head. "I don't want to. I want to spend the night in your arms and fall asleep with my head on your shoulder like we used to."

Ryder looked around and then quickly kissed me. "I'll find a way to get to your place. Give me a few minutes. Your father seems preoccupied, so I might just get lucky and not have to do anything for him for the rest of the day. Go and wait for me."

I drew him to me for a kiss full of all the need I had for him, and when he pulled away and mouthed, "I love you. I promise I'll come," I reluctantly left to go back to the apartment that I now had all to myself.

Chapter Eight

Ryder

WHEN A HALF hour had passed and Robert hadn't called me back into his office, I hoped to God whatever had been occupying his attention kept doing it and headed out toward Serena's apartment. I needed to avoid the cameras positioned outside the living quarters area of the estate, so I made my way around the back of Serena's townhouse. I found the cellar door open and crept up the very stairs that fuck Oliver had thrown her down.

She stood with her back to me looking out the kitchen window at the courtyard. Coming up behind her, I wrapped my arms around her waist and kissed her softly on the neck just below her ear.

"I missed you. It was so fucking hard watching you sit through all that today and not being able to help you get away from all those people."

Serena turned in my hold and looked up at me. "I stared out from behind that veil and didn't feel one thing. Not for him. Not for his parents. Not for my father. All I wanted to do was run to you and beg you to whisk me away from all of it."

"It's over now. He's gone, and he'll never hurt you again."

She stood on her toes and kissed me softly. "Because of you. I owe you my life so many times over, Ryder. You're my savior."

I pressed my forehead to hers and whispered the only truth I knew about us. "I would do anything to protect you, Serena. I'd give my life for you."

"Don't even think that," she said, hugging me tightly and pressing her cheek to the spot over my heart. "I couldn't go on if you weren't in the world. I wouldn't want to."

Tilting her head back so she had to look at me, I gazed into her beautiful dark eyes. "I promise you, Serena, I'm not going anywhere. They'd have to drag me out of this life to make me leave you."

"I laid in bed for the past few nights hating that you were so close by but still I couldn't have you next to me. I'm tired of playing these games. I'm not married anymore, so what would anyone care if you and I were together?"

As much as I wished it was that easy, I doubted it ever could be. Not with Robert still living. His need to control everyone in his world, especially Serena, meant we'd never get to be together without his blessing.

And the chances of him giving that seemed unlikely, at best.

"I don't care what anyone thinks, Serena. All I care about is that I love you and you love me. The rest of the world can disappear for all I care."

"But do you think we'll be able to be together now?" she asked, her eyes so full of hope that I hated what I knew to be the truth.

"It doesn't matter. We're together and we love each other. That's all that matters."

She slid her hands up under my suit jacket and slid it off my back. Holding it up to her face, she closed her eyes and inhaled deeply as she pressed the collar to her nose. "I wish I had this with me the past few days. It smells like you. Your cologne and the way your skin on your neck smells like a man should smell. Masculine, strong, powerful."

I watched her revel in the scent of my jacket and loved how sensual she was. Since the night I met her, she'd been that same soul who seemed purer than anyone else I'd ever met. I loved that about her. A tiny thing like the smell of my cologne made her smile.

She was too good for me, but I didn't care. I needed that sweetness and goodness she brought into my life, and I wouldn't give it up for anything.

Opening her eyes, she smiled up at me. "I bet you think I'm being silly, but I read somewhere that of all the senses, the sense of smell can trigger some of the most powerful memories of them all."

"Oh yeah? What memories does smelling my suit jacket trigger?" I asked, teasing her even as she charmed me.

Serena inhaled the scent of my jacket again and smiled. "That first night you wore a suit in front of me. Do you remember that night? I taught you how to dance downstairs in the guest room. Remember?"

"I remember," I said as the memory of that night settled into my brain. "You looked so beautiful that night. You were in that little dress and that old guy who's friends with your father kept grabbing your ass as you danced with him."

Her mouth turned down into a pout. "That's not what I was talking about."

I slid my hands around to cup her ass and pulled her to me. "That's not all I remember, though. The wine cellar. How incredible you felt in my arms. How long I'd wanted to feel your body pressed against mine."

"I love that memory, even though you were a huge tease that night," she said, frowning.

Kissing her hard, I stuffed my hand into her hair and tugged gently. "No looking sad in front of me today. I want to see you smiling when I'm around."

Her tongue slid across her lower lip and she grinned up at me. "I always smile when you're around, Ryder. Even when I'm mad at you, I'm still happier when I'm with you than I am when I'm not."

"Oh, yeah? Why's that?"

"Because I love you more than life itself."

"Not because I rock your body when I fuck you?" I asked as I slowly thrust my hips forward to press my already hard cock against her.

She looked down and ran her hand up the front of my pants, thrilling me with her touch even through the fabric. "Definitely because of that too."

I pulled her hair hard as my need to be inside her coursed through me, making my body ache. All day, I'd been close enough to reach out and touch her but couldn't, and now that she was in my arms again, I craved the feeling of having her like no other man on earth could.

Her fingers slid inside the top of my pants, grazing the tip of my cock and sending a jolt of electricity through me. I bent down and kissed her neck, reveling in the flavor of her skin on my tongue. The mixture of her natural taste and the vanilla body wash she used filled my mouth and nose, exciting me.

I sunk my teeth into her earlobe before whispering, "God, it was torture being next to you all day and not being able to hold your hand or tell you I was there."

Serena scratched her nails across the back of my

neck and moaned. "I knew. I always know when you're nearby."

Lifting my head, I looked down at her dark eyes staring at me. "I wanted everyone to disappear so I could take you into my arms and get you out of there."

She slid her tongue along the seam of my mouth and a tiny moan escaped from her lips. "I know. I'm sorry that you had to go through that, but he's gone now, Ryder."

I knew Oliver's death changed nothing with her father, but at that moment, I didn't want to think of anything but Serena and how much I needed to be buried balls deep inside her. Whatever Robert would do from this point on, I didn't care. All I cared about was Serena.

Slowly, she lowered herself to her knees and pulled my cock out of my pants. Looking up at me with a wide-eyed look full of innocence that had no place between us at that moment, she took all of me into her mouth until I butted up against the back of her throat. Warm and wet, the tip of her tongue flicked against the base of my shaft, making my eyes want to roll back into my head in ecstasy.

But I didn't want just that. I needed more than to just watch her get me off. I needed to see her come as I fucked her with all the desire that existed inside me.

Gently, I pushed her off me, and with a pout she sat back on her heels, her hand still palming my damp cock. "What's wrong?"

"Come here."

I pulled her up so she stood in front of me. "I want more. I need to feel you around me."

Our hands fumbled with our clothes, and in seconds she stood naked in front me and I stood in my pants barely clinging to my hips. Lifting her, I positioned her just above my ready cock and pushed her back against the wall.

"I want anyone who looks into your eyes to know you aren't fucking mourning that son of a bitch. I want them to see that sparkle in them I see when you moan my name as my cock fills you."

As I spoke, she whimpered and dug her heels into my lower back. "I want them to know how much I love when you fuck me. How I love the feel of you inside me. And how I don't want any other man ever again."

The head of my cock slid into her wet pussy, and inch by inch I filled her until our bodies joined together completely. She was tight and hot and it took everything in my being not to jackhammer into her like a fucking animal. All the rage at Oliver and Robert and every other bastard who'd kept us apart roiled in my brain, but she didn't deserve to feel that from me.

She deserved better than that. She deserved to be adored and worshipped.

And that's what I intended to give her.

Her hands clutched at the back of my neck, pulling me to her, and I kissed her long and deep like everything I'd ever needed existed in that one kiss. Slowly, I slid my cock out of her snug cunt and then even slower I eased back inside her body. I wanted this to last forever, just the two of us together as we gave one another the pleasure we'd never found anywhere else but with each other.

She sunk her teeth into my shoulder and then whispered, "Oh, God, when you go slow like that, it's like the sweetest torture, Ryder."

"I want to take my time and fuck you until you can't stand and I have to carry you to bed," I groaned as I slid my cock back inside her.

Serena moaned as I hit that spot I knew made her feel incredible. "I don't care how you do it. Fast, slow, just don't stop. Don't stop," she begged.

She didn't have to worry. I couldn't stop if I wanted to.

Her cunt squeezed my cock every time I retreated from her, as if her body didn't want to lose that feeling our joining created, and gave me the most unbelievable sensations that for a second I didn't mind leaving her.

But every time that feeling was fleeting, and I

was back to missing how her body felt around me. Serena consumed my every thought, my every need, just as she had since the first moment I touched her all that time ago.

I buried myself inside her one last time, staying where I found the only physical pleasure in my days and nights, and leaned against the wall as I came. Her thighs closed around my waist, trembling against my sides, and she came as she kissed me like I truly was what she called me.

Her savior.

Her mouth took from me as my cock filled her, our tongues mingling as we tumbled over that ledge into sublime pleasure that for at least a few minutes pushed everything and everyone in the world away and let us be nothing but completely happy. Finally, she collapsed against me and lay her head on my shoulder with a sigh.

For a long time, we said nothing, each of us silently reveling in the other person next to them. When Serena finally spoke, I heard the concern in her voice.

"Tell me we'll still get away from here, Ryder. I need to hear you say it today. That we'll someday soon leave this place and go somewhere just the two of us."

I turned my head and saw the fear written all over her face. Those beautiful dark eyes stared into mine as she waited to hear me tell her what she so desperately wanted to know.

That I'd do what I always promised.

Easing out of her, I lowered her to the floor. I cradled her worried face and smiled. "We will leave here, Serena. We'll go to the mountains and find a place away from the rest of the world where the two of us can live away from the ugliness of this house."

She covered my hands with hers. "I need to believe that, Ryder. I can't stay here much longer."

"There's no reason you have to now. We can go. I don't have a lot of money since your father likes to say he's paying me when he puts money into an account only he can get to, but I have a little saved up. I don't know if I'll ever be able to give you a home like this, but what I promise I will do is give you everything I can."

"I don't need what I have here. I've always had a beautiful home and never felt like I belonged. I want to feel like I belong somewhere."

I knelt down in front of her and wrapped my arms around her waist as I pressed my cheek to her. "You belong to me, and wherever I am is where you should be."

Serena gently ran her hand over the top of my head. "I belong to you. I always have. And wherever you are is where I want to be."

I stood and kissed her softly. "Are you going to

stay in this apartment or go back to your room at the main house?"

She looked around at the place she had shared with that fuck of a husband and frowned. "I don't want to stay here. I only came back here after the funeral because I wanted to make sure we had someplace we could be alone. I feel nothing for this place."

The misery she'd had to endure there filled every word, and I hated it. Taking her into my arms, I held her to me and whispered, "I'm sorry, Serena."

"Why?" she asked, looking up at me like what I said hurt her.

"I should have gotten you away from here before your father made you marry that fuck. If I had, you would have never..."

The rest of my sentence got stuck in my throat.

Serena pressed her finger to my lips and shook her head. "You tried to convince me. I didn't go. That was my mistake. You saved me from a life with him. I could never ask any more of another soul in this world. You have nothing to be sorry for, Ryder. You saved me."

I kissed the tip of her finger and wished I could believe I'd done enough. Pressing my hand to her belly, I said, "If I had made you leave..."

Again, I couldn't bring myself to say if I had gotten her away from him, our child would still be growing inside her. What I didn't do haunted me more than what he did.

Cradling my face, she kissed me and whispered against my lips, "Don't do this to yourself. You aren't to blame for anything that happened."

"I can't help it. The sight of you lying at the bottom of those steps in a pool of blood makes me want to hate something. I can't hate him anymore, so that leaves only me."

"Then hate me for not listening to you when you said to leave this house with you that night. Hate me."

The thought of that made my heart feel like someone had it in a vice. I couldn't hate Serena. How could I hate the very soul who made life worth living?

I grabbed her by the shoulders and held her in front of me. "Don't say that. Don't ever even think that. I couldn't hate you. You're the only thing in this world that keeps me human. If it wasn't for your love, I'd be nothing but the fucking animal your father wants me to be."

She took my hands in hers and placed a kiss on my knuckles. "Then hate him. Hate my father for marrying me off to that bastard. Hate him for what he makes you do for him. Hate him like I do."

I took her in my arms to hold her against me. "No more talk about hate tonight. I don't want to talk about hate with you. Only love."

"I love you, Ryder," she whispered sweetly against my chest.

I kissed the top of her head, feeling the softness of her hair against my lips. "I love you, Serena."

"I wouldn't be alive without you. Never forget that."

As we stood there in each other's arms in that apartment where Oliver had tried to kill her and had succeeded in taking our child away, I had once again saved her just in time, but the truth was I wouldn't be alive if it weren't for Serena. I might exist and look like I was alive, but I would have been dead inside long before now if I didn't have her.

She made me want to live like I hadn't wanted to since I had a home and my parents. And now that I felt that love again, I'd protect it with my life, if necessary.

I'd do whatever I had to do to get her away from Robert and that world where love couldn't exist. I'd promised her I would, and if I died trying, I'd see her free from this place.

Chapter Nine

Ryder

SERENA'S HAIR TICKLED my nose, waking me from a sound sleep. I looked down my body to see hers entwined with mine. Her tanned and smooth left leg rested against my left thigh, and I couldn't help running my hand over her skin.

She lifted her head off my chest and looked up at me with a smile. "Good morning."

"It is," I said, returning her smile with one of my own. "Anytime I get to spend all night with you is a good thing."

Shimmying up my body, she kissed me and dipped her head to nuzzle my neck. "I guess you have to go, right?"

As much as I didn't want to even think about leaving that bed or her, I knew Robert would start to unravel if I didn't make it to his office for nine o'clock. The last thing I wanted was to deal with him like that after spending such an incredible night with Serena.

I nodded. "Yeah. You know how he is."

Serena looked up at me and grimaced. "I know. Just tell me we get to leave here soon and you leaving now won't be so bad."

I'd thought about how hard it would be for us to get away as she drifted off to sleep hours before, but now in the light of day, all those ideas amounted to nothing but self-imposed obstacles. Oliver was gone, so we had nothing to stop us now.

"We'll go tonight. I'll text you the details later, but for now, be ready for when he leaves to go out."

Stunned at my announcement, she sat up and stared down at me with a look of shock in her eyes. "Tonight? Oh, my God! Ryder, this is really happening, isn't it?"

I smiled and brought her hand to my lips to kiss it. "Yeah. It's happening. We'll leave tonight. We won't have much to live on and it's going to be hard for a little while, but we'll be away from here, and that's all that matters, right?"

She threw her arms around me and hugged me. "Yes! That's all that matters! I love you, Ryder. I don't know how I'm going to keep this secret all day. I'll have to hide out here so I don't blow our cover."

Cradling her face, I kissed her on the forehead. "I need you to promise me you won't say a thing. This only works if nobody but us knows. I don't want to take a chance of your father finding out."

"I know. I won't tell a soul. I want to leave here

more than you know, so I won't mess this up."

"I love you, Serena, and when we're away from here, you're going to see how happy we can be."

She hugged me once more before jumping out of bed. "I love you. Oh, I have a million things to do before we leave. You better go so he doesn't think something's up. I'll be waiting for your text."

Watching her naked body as she trotted away into the bathroom made me want to grab her and pull her back on top of me for another round of lovemaking, but we'd have all the time in the world for that once we got away from there. For now, she was right. I needed to get to Robert's office before he suspected anything.

✧   ✧   ✧

JESSE STOOD OUTSIDE the office staring straight ahead across the massive grand entryway like some kind of stone statue. Likely he'd been sent out by Robert for saying something stupid that had irritated him, but he seemed far more somber than usual when he saw me.

"You in the doghouse for something?" I joked as I stopped in front of him.

He simply shook his head but didn't say a word as he avoided looking at me. Since Jesse was usually a huge talker, I had a feeling he'd gotten himself in real trouble. Poor guy. He really was a decent human being, although sometimes I wondered if he had hay for brains.

"Okay, I guess I better get in there," I said as he continued to stare straight ahead. "See you later, Jess."

I stepped into Robert's office and the door slammed behind me. My brain raced with the idea that Jesse had just closed me in, but why? Before I could figure out the answer, I saw Robert stand from his desk and felt a fist slam into the back of my head. I staggered forward toward the red leather chairs as another blow hit me, this one even harder.

Hands grabbed me and threw me into a wooden chair against the wall I didn't remember ever being there before. My back slammed against it as the hands held me down so I couldn't move.

"What the fuck?" I barked in Robert's direction as he came around the desk slowly to stand in front of me.

His mouth spread into that crocodile smile that never failed to terrify me. Staring down into my eyes, he said, "I just want the truth, Ryder. That's it. The truth."

Once again, my mind raced to understand what was happening. Did he find out about Serena and me? Is that what this was about?

I moved to stand, but the two men holding me down pushed me back hard against the chair.

Swiveling my head to look at them, I sized up my chances at escape. Definitely unlikely. Both were giant with thick necks and arms like tree trunks. They looked like the type of guys who fucked people up for kicks, if the rabid look in their eyes was any indication. I knew I couldn't overwhelm either without having the other one get me.

"What's going on, Robert?" I asked, even as I knew what his answer would be.

"I just want the truth. You've never lied to me, have you, Ryder?"

The look on my face likely told him the truth. I'd lied to him about Serena since practically the night I arrived there. He'd caught us that one time and punished us by sending her away and having me nearly pounded into the ground, so he knew I'd lied to him at least once.

Or maybe that wasn't a lie so much as it was me breaking his cardinal rule. Whatever it was, he'd exacted his revenge quickly and painfully on both Serena and me.

"What's this about, Robert?" I asked, hoping he'd stop the cryptic shit and finally tell me why he had the two behemoths standing behind me holding me down while he just stared at me and smiled that fucking psychopath grin.

"I guess we know the answer to that question. Maybe I should ask another one and see if you can answer that one. Who do you work for, Ryder?"

Unsure if that was a trick question, I tried to figure out what he was going for as the two guys behind me pressed down harder on my arms, holding them tightly to the chair and sending waves of pain through my shoulders. Did he think I'd been doing work for someone else? The mere idea was ridiculous.

"You, Robert. I work for you."

The crocodile smile faded just a little, and he took a step toward me. Looking down, he smiled broader again, but I had the sense it was forced now.

"And what is your job you do for me?"

I had no idea where he was going with this, but I answered, "To some people, you say I'm security. To people in business who owe you money, I'm the long arm of the empire you've built."

My answer seemed to please him. He nodded his head and stepped back away from me. "Some people would think that's a smartass answer, but I don't. Do you remember the first night I met you and I told you I thought you were pretty fucking cocky?"

"Yeah. I remember you thought I had reason to be cocky then too."

"You did. You had brass balls, son. Still do, it seems."

Even though the goons still had a tight hold on me, I felt like something in Robert had relaxed, so I took a chance and asked, "Robert, why do you have two guys holding me down so you can ask me these questions? They're not necessary. You're my boss. Ask me anything and I'll tell you what you want to know."

His eyes narrowed to slits, and he looked over my head toward the two men, gesturing for them to release me. I stretched out my arms to get the blood flowing in them again as Robert returned his attention to me.

"So you work for me? I like hearing that, Ryder."

The ominous sound of an unspoken threat under those words told me he didn't like anything about me at that moment. I'd already assessed my chances of getting out of there in one piece if he set the two giants on me and decided my odds weren't good. I hadn't entirely gone to pot in the time I'd been working for Robert, but even in good shape I wasn't enough to handle two guys both larger than me.

"Yeah, of course I work for you. Always have since the day I walked through the front door."

He shot the two guys another look and then leveled his gaze on me. "Then why did you get rid of Oliver? Who ordered that? Because I didn't."

Suddenly, I realized what this was all about. He thought I had taken care of Oliver for someone else and I was working for him.

"Oh. It's not what you think, Robert. I'm not working for anyone else."

In a flash, the two guys had a hold of me and Robert slammed his fist into my face, jamming his knuckles into my eye socket with a punch that sent my head flying back against the chair. Before I could say another word, he hit me again just as hard in the eye a second time.

"Who ordered it, Ryder? Who ordered the hit on Oliver?" Robert bellowed so loud the words echoed off the walls of his office.

I wasn't going to bring Serena into this. God only knew what he'd do to her if I admitted I'd killed Oliver for her. So I said nothing and braced myself for the next shot to my head as the pain in my eye radiated down my cheekbone.

"You don't have to say it. I already know. Serena. I should have known at some point I'd have to deal with your little infatuation with each other. I thought sending her away for two years would take care of it, but I see that didn't work."

If he thought I was going to simply admit I'd done it for her, he had no idea how wrong he was about what we felt for each other. It hadn't been simple infatuation since before he sent her off to Italy.

"Robert, he was a fuck. He choked her and pushed her down the stairs. It's no loss."

As soon as the words were out, I knew my mouth had gotten me in trouble again. His face turned red with rage, and he barked, "Only I can order you to kill someone! Only me!"

I opened my mouth to say something to defend Serena, but from the side a fist hit my jaw with such force that it felt like my fucking teeth all shifted in my head. Another fist hit the right side of my face, pounding into my cheekbone that still ached from when Robert nailed me in the eye.

From there, the two beasts that had been holding me down went to town on me. One would slam his fist into my face while the other one focused on my gut and chest, pummeling me so fucking hard I couldn't breathe.

The metallic taste of blood filled my mouth after a few shots, and I couldn't see out of either eye once the guy on my left began to shove his fist into them repeatedly.

All the while the two of them beat the hell out of me, I heard Robert say over and over, "Only I can order you to kill someone! Only me! No one else. Not even Serena!"

He was like a man possessed, and he watched his two goons fuck me up, smiling every so often when they got a good shot in and I cried out in pain. By the time they finished with me, I couldn't even sit up straight from the searing pain of broken ribs and my face hurt like someone had hit me with a fucking sledgehammer.

At some point they must have stopped, but by then I'd slipped into unconsciousness. I think it was after the guy beating my face began slamming my head off the back of the chair.

I OPENED MY eyes and felt a rush of unbearable pain tear through me. They'd dumped me on the floor just inside my apartment and left me there, unconscious and for all they knew, dead.

Not that I wouldn't have done the same thing. I had done exactly that many times for the very man who'd had me beaten within an inch of my life.

As I lay there with the hard floor pressing into my aching body, a terrible thought settled into my brain. What had Robert done to Serena for her part in Oliver's death?

I lifted my head to begin getting up and got my shoulders about two inches off the floor before the pain became too much. Stupidly, I tried to take a breath, but that was cut off by the stab of agony from my broken ribs. Crying out, I gritted my teeth and prayed to God it would go away or kill me, but whatever happened, I just wanted the pain to end.

Tonight I was supposed to take Serena away from this terrible place, but once again, her father had made sure that didn't happen. I didn't know if he'd caught wind of our plans or just found out that I'd gotten rid of Oliver, but the end result was still the same.

We were stuck here, and as I lay on the floor hating everything about Robert Erickson and his fucking world, I couldn't see us ever getting out.

Pain ebbed and flowed over me in waves, sometimes starting at my eyes and other times in my ribs. It didn't matter where it started because once it did, it immediately became unbearable. I faded in and out of consciousness so many times I lost count. When I first opened my eyes, the sun still streamed through the window, but at some point I must have passed out because when I opened my eyes again, everything was dark around me.

My phone vibrated against my hip, but no matter how much I wanted to see if Serena needed me, I couldn't move to grab it. Over and over, it signaled someone wanted to contact me, but all I could do was wait until the vibration stopped and hope to God she was okay.

As I lay there, I knew I should be angry enough to kill Robert when I could walk again, but that thought never stayed long in my head. Every time it popped up, another thought joined it, reminding me of all that he'd given me since bringing me to this place two years ago. I should have wanted to make him pay for what he'd done to me and Serena, but somehow my brain couldn't get past the fatherly feelings I harbored for him, as ridiculous as that sounded.

How could I ever forgive him for having me beaten within an inch of my life for killing a man he likely would have ordered me to kill eventually anyway? What kind of fucked up person was I? He'd never truly treated me as his son. I'd always been a pawn he liked to parade in front of people when it served him and his thug when he needed to make a point to people who thought they could cross him.

I'd never been anything more to him, but now as I lay there in agony because of him, I still couldn't bring myself to want to kill him. Leave this place? Fuck, yeah. Never look back. Yep. But not kill him.

Someone else he fucked over would take care of him. I'd always believed that. Some part of me hated him for what he did to Serena by sending her away and then forcing her to marry Oliver even when he knew she'd rather die than do that. For her, I'd never doubted I could kill him or anyone else.

But not for me. Not even now as I lay there broken in pieces by his command.

A noise outside my door roused me from the misery of my pain and my thoughts, and I struggled to turn my head to hear who it was. For a long moment, I heard nothing and became convinced my mind was beginning to play tricks on me, but then the sound of a faint knock filtered down to where I lay.

I groaned out the word hello but far too low for whoever was outside to hear. I tried to speak again, louder this time, but still I doubted they'd hear me.

Another knock sent my spirits soaring. I had to find a way to let them know someone was in here.

With all the strength I could muster, I slammed my hand down on the floor next to me. Not as loud as I'd wanted, but I hoped the person on the other side of the door could hear it.

"I'm here!" I croaked out far too quietly. "Come in!"

The person knocked once more, and then I heard the sound of them jiggling the doorknob. I just hoped to God it was Serena and not Robert or his bruisers.

"Ryder?"

Happier than I thought I could be feeling like a team of horses were pulling me apart, I breathed a shallow sigh of relief at the sight of Serena poking her head in through the door.

"Ryder, are you here?"

"Serena, I'm here," I said with all the volume I could give my voice.

She looked down and saw me, and instantly I knew how bad I looked by the horrified expression on her face. Throwing the door open, she rushed in and knelt at my side.

"What happened to you? Who did this?" she asked as her gaze ran up and down my battered body.

I took her hand and held it like it was the only thing keeping me tethered to the earth. "I'm so glad you came looking for me. Was that you texting me for the past few hours?"

Gently, Serena touched my face, and I flinched in pain. "Oh, Ryder. What happened to you?"

"I'm sorry I didn't get to message you. I've been busy lying here on the floor for a while."

Her dark eyes filled with tears. "Don't joke about this. Who did this to you? Does my father know?"

I didn't want to burden her with the truth just yet. It meant more to me to have her there by my side. Knowing she was safe at least took the pain of worrying about her away.

"Did anything happen to you today?"

She shook her head. "No. Why? What's going on, Ryder? Why are you asking me that when you're lying half-dead on your living room floor? Why won't you tell me who did this to you?"

I couldn't keep the truth from her forever. She'd have to find out that her father knew everything. But what would he do now?

Chapter Ten

Serena

MY HEART BROKE at the sight of Ryder bruised and bloodied there on the floor next to me. His right eye was completely swollen shut, and the left eye wasn't much better, but at least he could see out of that one. His right cheekbone looked like someone had pounded on it with their fist repeatedly until it was nearly as swollen as the eye above it. Dried blood from where it had trickled out of his mouth stained his chin and jaw. And by the way he cringed every time I even got close to his shoulder and his side, I suspected whoever had done this hadn't limited their anger to his face.

"Ryder, can you get up? If you can get to the couch, I can clean you up and get you some ice so some of that swelling can go down."

He winced at my mention of moving and let out what sounded like an excruciatingly painful sigh. "I don't know. I think I've got some broken ribs, and my shoulder might be dislocated. I can probably walk, but getting to a standing position is going to be the problem."

"I can just sit here with you then," I said. "I can bring everything you need right here."

Shaking his head, he gave me a tiny smile. "No, I can't stay on the floor forever. I need to get up."

Every word sounded like it was being dragged out of him. I didn't know how he'd ever make it across the room to the couch, even with me at his side.

He closed his eyes and groaned loudly as he slowly rolled over onto his stomach. I wanted to reach out and run my hand down his back, but I knew it would only make him hurt worse. When the pain subsided, he eased up onto his hands and knees and let out a low groan.

"Just tell me when you want me to help you up," I said, trying to sound chipper and supportive even as I struggled seeing him this way.

Hanging his head, he took a few shallow breaths. "I'll meet you at the couch. Go get some ice and some water. Actually, forget the water. Bring the whisky."

"Are you sure? I can help you get there."

He shook his head but didn't look at me. "No. I'll be fine."

I knew he was too proud to have me help him, even though he obviously needed help. I wasn't sure if I'd see him back on the floor when I returned from the kitchen, but I hurried off to gather up the things he needed.

Even though I found the whisky and ice quickly and even got a bottle of Advil and a wet washcloth to clean his face, I didn't go back into the living room for nearly five minutes, as much as I wanted to just in case he needed my help. I knew him well enough to understand he didn't want me seeing him beaten and broken like this.

What I wanted was to know who had done this to him and why.

"Serena, you can come out now," he said in a low voice that barely made it to the kitchen.

I walked in and saw him leaning back against the couch with a look of utter agony on his face. Hurrying to his side, I moved to place the ice pack on his cheek but stopped.

"I don't want to hurt you. Where do you want me to put the ice?"

He held out his hand. "Just give it to me."

Gingerly, he put the ice on his face so it covered his right eye and cheek and asked, "Did you find the whisky?"

Nodding, I held the bottle out in front of me. "Yeah. Do you want me to pour you a glass?"

He shook his head and took it from my hand. "Nope."

I watched him slowly twist off the cap before he

tilted the bottle to his lips and took a gulp. He swallowed hard and groaned before taking another drink even bigger than the first.

"Another ten or twelve like that and I might be able to handle this pain," he said in a gravelly voice as he put the ice pack back against his face.

"I need to clean around your mouth. There's blood there. I don't want to hurt you, though."

He looked at me and gave me a smile. "You couldn't hurt me any more than I already am. Do your worst."

Dabbing the washcloth against his skin, I cleaned the dried blood from where it had stained around his mouth and on his chin as he leaned back with his eyes closed. I wanted to ask him again who was responsible for hurting him like this, but I didn't.

Instead, I simply cleaned him up and helped him tip the bottle toward his mouth when he wanted a drink. But after about ten minutes, I couldn't keep silent anymore.

"Are you going to tell me what happened? Did you fight again like you told me you used to?"

He simply shook his head and took another gulp of whisky.

"Who could do this to you? No one can handle themselves like you, Ryder. What happened?"

I didn't get an answer to those questions either,

but he smiled and said, "One man didn't do this."

"More than one man jumped you? Is that what happened? Where? Where did this happen, Ryder?"

He let out a slow sigh and lifted his hand to cradle my cheek. "You know who did this, Serena."

I couldn't believe that. Shaking my head, I tried not to hear what he said. "No. Why? Why would he do this? You're his favorite."

Ryder pulled me to him and kissed me sweetly on the lips. "I told you I'd look back on that day I first kissed you and know I'd pay for it. He knows about us."

I recoiled in horror that my father had him beaten because he cared for me. "Oh, Ryder! He did this because of me?"

"No, no. I didn't mean that, Serena. He didn't have those guys beat me up because we're together. He had them do it because of what I did to Oliver."

The more he explained, the more I didn't understand. My father disliked Oliver enough to order him killed himself, so why would he punish Ryder for doing just that?

"My father as much as said he would have taken care of Oliver for what he did to me. What does it matter who did it or why?"

Ryder shook his head and smiled. "It matters because you asked me to do it, not him."

"That's crazy. I'm his daughter."

I hung my head as the reality of what had happened sunk in, but Ryder gently lifted my chin so I had to look at him. "He knows about us, Serena. I think that was part of why he had me beaten."

His swollen face looked so awful I nearly broke out in tears. "I'm so sorry. I never imagined he'd do this when he found out. I always thought he would find out, but I didn't think he'd do anything like this to you. I just figured he'd send one of us away again and that would be it. Then we'd have to find a way to be together. I never meant to do anything to hurt you, Ryder."

"Shhh. I don't regret a thing. I'd gladly give my life to be with you, so a beating by two of your father's thugs is nothing. I'll be fine."

He winced as he said the word fine, and I knew he was anything but. Bringing his fingers to my lips, I kissed them and pressed my cheek into his palm. "I never wanted you to suffer for being with me. You're the only thing that makes life worth living most days. I would do anything to make sure you weren't hurt because of me."

"Serena, I've been beaten ten times worse when I used to fight. I'll be okay. I just need to have some more whisky and close my eyes for a few minutes."

He took another swig from the bottle and handed it to me. He looked exhausted, so I set the bottle on the coffee table and helped him lean back on the couch. Mumbling something about how much he loved me, he closed his eyes and fell silent before drifting off to sleep a minute later.

I watched as his chest barely moved as he breathed, his body protecting him from pain with every inhale and exhale. Never before had I seen him so beaten, yet still he wanted to protect me, to be with me no matter what cost to him.

My father's actions would have consequences. If it was the last thing I did, I'd make him pay for hurting the man who had saved my life more times than I deserved.

I SLIPPED AWAY while the whisky gave Ryder some relief and let him sleep. Heading down to my father's office, all I could think of was how much I hated him for what he'd done. All my life, he'd pushed around everyone I cared about. This time he'd gone too far.

One of his goons stood guard at the door, and as I marched toward him, I wondered if he was one of the men who had beaten Ryder. Staring him down, I pushed past him and walked into my father's office before he could even try to stop me.

"I want to talk to you," I announced as I stopped behind one of the chairs in front of his desk.

My father looked up from his laptop and cocked a single eyebrow, like my being there intrigued him for the moment. "Are you feeling better today, dear?"

"I would be if I didn't know you had Ryder beaten half to death."

Instead of saying anything in response, my father stood and walked over to the bar to make his usual drink. His back to me, I heard him slowly drop three ice cubes into his glass and then pour the bourbon and water over them. I knew this technique of his, though. I'd watched him do this very thing many times before when he wanted to control a situation.

But I wouldn't let him control anything anymore. Not me and not Ryder.

"I know what you're doing, and it's not going to work. You can draw out making that damn drink of yours all you want. I have no intention of allowing myself to become relaxed because you made me wait. Trust me, my anger is going to increase if you keep dragging your feet."

He turned around and looked at me, that one eyebrow still cocked. "I don't know what you're so upset about today, Serena, but I can assure you that whatever it is, I'm not doing anything other than getting myself a much needed drink. Would you like one?"

"I'd like to know why you would have your thugs attack your favorite, Dad. That's what I'd like."

Returning to his desk, he sat down and took a

sip of his drink. "I haven't attacked you at all, and since you're my favorite, Serena, I can't imagine what's got you so upset."

Rage built up inside me until I felt like I was going to explode. Me, his favorite? How ridiculous! Did he think I was stupid?

My eyes narrowed to angry slits as I glared at him. His grey hair, so perfectly slicked back, and his face so many people thought of as handsome now made him look like a real monster more than ever before.

"Please don't insult my intelligence, Dad. I've never been your favorite. First, it was Janelle because you saw so much of yourself in her, and then it became Ryder once he arrived here. I've never been anything close to being the favorite in this house. So why don't you explain to me why you had your favorite beaten?"

My mention of Ryder by name made his mouth tighten into a straight line. "My business requires many things you might not like, Serena. You should stay out of it."

Suddenly, my anger exploded out of me. "You're a coward! You had him beaten to show that you control him, but you're a coward. That's not control!"

My father bolted out of his chair and stared at me with eyes flashing his rage. "Ryder is mine and mine alone to command! Only I have the power to order a man's death at his hands! Only me!"

I stepped back as the sound of his bellowing took me by surprise for a moment. I'd expected him to be furious when I stood up to him, but I hadn't expected that level of anger at me or Ryder.

But I wasn't about to back down.

"So that's what this is?" I screamed. "A power play against your own daughter?"

"You had no right to order him to take care of Oliver!" he bellowed in return. "Ryder works for me."

"I didn't order him to do anything. He knew what Oliver did and didn't want to see me hurt again. I told him how Oliver was acting when I returned home from the hospital, and I asked him to help me. You're just angry that he's with me, aren't you?"

For a long moment, my father simply looked at me like he didn't know what to say. Maybe he thought I didn't know, or maybe that look signaled his disbelief that I had actually admitted the truth about Ryder and me right there to his face. Whatever the reason, my admission stunned him for a second.

Far calmer than just a minute before, he said, "I told him the night I brought him here he wasn't to touch either one of you girls. He's lucky I didn't beat him before today for what he's done."

"He hasn't done anything wrong. He's saved my life every day for months. He had to watch me marry another man and still loved me as much as I love him."

"Love? Is that what you think this is between you two? You have no idea who he is, Serena. You're so naïve. Who do you think is the person I turn to when I usually want someone beaten like that? Who do you think takes care of the Olivers in this world for me? Your beloved Ryder."

He smirked like anything he said could surprise me. I knew who Ryder was. I'd known for a long time. The girl who watched him wide-eyed and infatuated as he lifted weights in those days right after he came to the house had disappeared when she was sent away. I knew from the moment I saw him dressed in a suit and working as one of my father's men who he was.

And I loved him anyway.

"I know all about Ryder. I'm not a little girl anymore, Dad. I've lived my life surrounded by your men. You didn't think I knew what you'd made him into when I came back here and saw him working for you?"

My father snorted in disgust as he sat down behind his desk again and reached for his glass. "What I made him into. You have no idea, Serena. He was an animal long before I found him."

I braced my hands on the back of the chair in front of me and felt the coolness of the leather against my palms. "I know what he was then too. I know everything about him, and I still love him. So I won't allow him to be beaten again."

Grinning that crocodile smile I hated, he said, "Well, I'll do you one better. I won't have to beat him again because he won't be with you ever again."

Just hearing him threaten that made my heart skip a beat. My mouth grew dry at the mere thought of losing Ryder, but I stayed strong and said, "You won't do that or you'll never see me again, Dad."

"I know you, Serena. Your heart will keep you here for him because you'll need to find a way to keep being with him. You're like your mother that way. Always the dreamy-eyed romantic."

He stared up at me like he'd uttered something that would stun me, but those days were long gone. "I'll leave here faster than you can even imagine and never look back. And he'll come find me because he loves me as much as I love him. Never underestimate the power two people can have when they join together, Dad. You can either agree to what I want or never see me again. That's my final offer."

My father slowly lifted his glass to his mouth and sipped his drink before taking a deep breath. "So those are your terms? I'm to just allow you and Ryder to be together?"

"And to make sure you never hurt him again, I want him as my bodyguard. He'll work for me from now on."

Shaking his head, he frowned. "No. Ryder is mine. I brought him here and he works for me."

I knew he likely wouldn't relent on my demand that Ryder be my guard, but I still had to try. That didn't mean I planned to just give in, though. If I didn't stand my ground now, my father would think he won.

So I turned and began walking toward the door. "Goodbye, Dad."

I took two steps before he gave in to my bluff. "I won't stop him from being with you, but he answers to me. He stays as one of my men."

The slight shaking in his voice told me he believed he could lose both me and Ryder if he didn't agree to us together, but I still worried about what he'd do in retaliation to the man I loved. My father didn't give in easily, so he must have something on his mind that could hurt Ryder.

I slowly turned around and tilted my chin up. "He's never to be hurt again. If he is, I swear to God my leaving will be the least of your problems."

The crocodile smile returned, like he'd won something in our test of wills. I had a feeling this wouldn't be the last time we faced off like this, but for now, I'd take what I'd gotten.

He took another sip of his drink and folded his arms across his chest. "You're so much like your mother, Serena. Everything is about love. I'd hate to see your life turn out like hers."

I knew a threat when I heard one, but Ryder wasn't like my father and I wasn't like my mother.

"Janelle is more like Mom, to be honest. I think I'm more like you, Daddy. In fact, if I were you, I'd worry about that."

His smile faded away, and I left him sitting behind his desk as he opened up his laptop again. Ryder and I had won. For now. But I wasn't a fool. Good rarely won out over evil in Robert Erickson's world.

I knew that all too well.

But as I walked back to Ryder's apartment, my hands shaking after all that had happened, I swore my father wouldn't do to me what he'd done to my mother and sister.

Chapter Eleven

Ryder

THE THROBBING IN my head felt like someone with a jackhammer tunneling into my fucking brain. I'd been beaten up before, but now I didn't seem to be getting any better and it had been nearly twelve hours since Robert and his goons had fucked me up.

Curious about the time, I tried to sit up to turn the light on so I could find my phone, but halfway there I had to lie back down. Even if my head wasn't banging like a bass drum, my broken ribs weren't going to let me just move around willy-nilly for a while.

Through my one eye I could actually open, I looked around for Serena but didn't see her. Had she left? Or had Robert done something to her too?

A sudden rush of terror raced through me, and I tried to sit up again to go find her. I couldn't let him hurt her. Sharp pain stabbed at my sides, but it didn't matter. Nothing mattered if he hurt her like he'd hurt me.

Staggering to my feet, I steadied myself and tried to see in front of me, but with one eye only half working, seeing much of anything wasn't happening. With my first step, I grazed the corner of the coffee table with my shin, and another level of pain added to the rest I felt. I didn't care. As long as I found Serena, I didn't care how much it hurt.

Every movement of my body resulted in new agony, but I made it to the door. Exhausted from just crossing the room, I sagged against the wall as my brain urged my body on and my heart seconded the idea, but my body couldn't follow through.

I stood there wanting to run to Serena's apartment to see if she was there and safe, and all I could do was hold myself up and pray to God my legs didn't give out and send me crashing to the floor.

What if he did something to her? I'd seen Robert exact his revenge on others before me. Ruthless only scratched the surface of what he was to people who betrayed him, and that was exactly what he believed she'd done by having me take care of Oliver. He wouldn't just let her get away with it. He never did.

Even I would get more than just the beating he'd had those guys give me. This was only the beginning. I knew that, and I could handle it. Whatever he did, I'd deal with it.

But Serena had already had to deal with too

much. She didn't deserve having more misery piled on top of what she'd gone through with Oliver. I wouldn't let Robert hurt her anymore.

The sound of footsteps outside my door brought me back to the pain torturing my body, and I waited to hear a knock on the door. Instead, it opened and I saw Serena walk in.

"Ryder, I'm back," she whispered softly as she headed toward the couch.

"Serena, I'm right here," I croaked out behind her.

She spun around and stared at the door. "Where? I just came in. Where are you?"

"Right here. Next to the door."

"What are you doing off the couch?" she asked as she came toward me and took me in her arms.

God, she felt so good. "I didn't know where you went, so I wanted to go find you to make sure you're okay. Where were you?"

She began to walk me back into the living room. "Lean on me. Let's get you to the bed so you can lie down."

Ten agonizing steps later and I was flat on my back in my bed. Serena brought me a glass of water, but all I wanted was more whisky. Water wouldn't touch the pain, but whisky would at least deaden it a little.

"You need to drink something, Ryder," she said

as she tried to position the glass near my mouth.

I pushed it away. "I need to drink something that's going to take the edge off. Water won't do that."

She sighed and frowned before putting the glass on the night table. "You shouldn't have gotten up. You probably made things worse for yourself."

"All I could think about was finding you and making sure he didn't hurt you too."

"He wouldn't do anything like this to me. My father's brand of torture for me runs in a different direction," Serena said as she cradled my cheek.

"Did he do something?"

I knew he eventually would. It was just a matter of time.

Shaking her head, she leaned in and kissed me softly on the lips. "He tried, but don't worry. It's all good now."

Serena had a way of seeing goodness where none existed. Nothing was all good now, except her with me. Everything else was shit, just like it always had been.

"What did he try? Did he say he was going to send you away or was it me this time?"

"Shhhh. I don't want to talk about this now. All I want to do is take care of you like you've always taken care of me when I needed it. I think I might have some painkillers in my room at the house. I can go get them so at least the worst of it will disappear."

She moved to leave and I caught her by the arm. "No. Don't go. The pain's not too bad now. I'd feel better if you stayed right here."

Leaning over, she turned on the light next to the bed. As soon as I saw her eyes open wide, I knew how bad I looked. I'd seen myself a few hours after fights. Even after those I'd won, I sometimes looked pretty fucked up.

"It's okay, Serena. It looks much worse than it really is. I'll be fine," I said in an attempt to reassure her even as the pain in my ribs brought tears to my eyes.

"Oh, Ryder. I'm so sorry. I promise this will never happen again," she said, fighting back her own tears.

I pulled her mouth to mine and kissed her again. "Don't make promises you can't keep."

"But I can," she said with the kind of smile that never failed to melt my heart.

"No, you can't. Your father isn't going to just let me go on this. Not this time. I'm worried what he's going to do to you too."

"He's not going to do anything. He's sworn to me that he won't ever do this to you again, and he's accepted us together. So, you see, you don't have to worry. It's going to be okay."

I couldn't believe my ears. Robert accepted that

Serena and I were together? No way.

Looking up at her face so filled with optimism, I hated that I had to doubt her, but I knew him all too well. Whatever he'd said, he wasn't good with me being with Serena, and things were definitely not okay.

"What did he say and how exactly did he say it?"

She smiled and shook her head, like my questions were mere silliness. "Do you think I honestly don't know my father, Ryder? I've lived with him all my life. Long before you got here, I saw exactly the kind of man he was. I'm not naïve. I know not to trust everything he says, but I'm telling you he's accepted us together and promised you'd never go through this again."

"Why would he do that?"

"Because if he didn't, he was going to lose both of us, and he knew that. I'd leave and then you'd leave to be with me. My father is a lot of things, but he's not stupid. He knew when I said I'd leave this place if he didn't promise me you'd be safe that I wasn't bluffing."

I still didn't believe Robert had accepted anything. It wasn't in his nature.

"Was he smiling when he said he was okay with me and you together? Because if he was, I'm guessing I'll be dead by tomorrow morning and you'll be locked away in some home by the end of the week," I said sadly.

My question made her giggle. "You mean that smile he wears when he looks at you like you're prey?"

I nodded, surer than ever that nothing was okay. "The crocodile smile. It's the one he puts on right before he devours another person's soul."

"He might have been smiling, but it's going to be fine, Ryder. I even tried to get him to let you be my bodyguard instead of working for him, but that's where he put his foot down. I did get the promise that he'd never hurt you again and you and I could be together, so all in all, I think negotiations went pretty well, don't you?"

Never before had I seen Serena so confident about anything concerning Robert. I still worried he'd do something to us, but for the moment, at least she looked happy.

"So he knows we're in love?"

She kissed me again and whispered against my lips, "Madly, truly, and completely in love."

I cupped the back of her head to keep her there and kissed her again, this time sliding my tongue into her mouth. She moaned softly and teased my tongue with the tip of hers before sucking it between her lips.

"We're going to be fine, Ryder."

"I wish I could believe he was okay with us

together like you do."

"No more talk about him tonight. I want to take care of you, so what do you need? Just tell me and I'll get it for you."

"Nothing. Just stay here," I said as I pulled her close to me. "I just want to lay here with your head on my shoulder like we used to back when I was in the guest room."

She lay down beside me and carefully positioned herself next to my body so she could do as I wanted. The gentle scent of her shampoo filled my nose, and I stroked her hair, loving the feel of her there with me. If only we could stay there and never have to leave that room again, we'd be safe.

"I love you, Ryder, and I'm so happy we don't have to hide anymore. Everything's going to be okay. We don't even have to leave now. We can just be together right here."

My heart sank. Maybe we would be okay, but the dream of leaving had been with me for so long that hearing we never would made me sad.

And I didn't believe for a second that staying at that house would ever end up good for us.

"You don't want to go anymore?" I asked as disappointment settled into my brain.

She heard it in my voice and looked up at me. "All I ever wanted was to be with you. Now that we can be, we don't have to go anywhere. Isn't that a good thing?"

"That means I'll have to keep working for your father. Are you okay with that, with who I have to be in his world?"

I watched the hopefulness dim in her dark eyes and knew the answer. The problem was she didn't even know all of what I'd had to become just to fulfill Robert's orders. She thought I was some thug, but I was so much more than that.

So much worse.

"I love you, Ryder. I don't care what you are for him or what you've had to do. I only care that you love me."

"You once asked me what kind of father our child would have when you found out I was the one who killed Oliver's brother. Now you're okay with me being that man?" I asked, afraid of her answer but needing to know.

She looked away and lowered her head. "I didn't mean it that way."

"What way, Serena? I'm that same man lying here now who was standing in that room with you that day. I'm exactly what you thought I was."

"I don't want to talk about this now," she said and shook her head. "Whoever you have to be to the rest of the world doesn't matter. I know who you are."

I tilted her chin up so she faced me. "Who am I,

Serena? What do you think working for him has made me?"

Her dark eyes turned a watery brown, but she didn't look away. "I know what you do. What you've done. What you'll have to do in the future if we stay here. I don't care. All I care about is that you love me and I love you. That's all that matters."

"Why do you want to stay here now? If I'm going to have to still be that man, I need to know why."

She said nothing for a long moment and winced like what she had to say hurt her, but then she said quietly, "I want to find my mother. If I find her, we can go. I promise. I just can't leave here knowing she's out there somewhere and the minute I go he'll hurt her."

From that first night I met her, Serena had never given up on seeing her mother again. I'd never heard Robert refer to her even once, and I wondered if she was even still alive. He'd used hurting her as a threat nearly every time he wanted to control Serena, but that didn't mean he wasn't bluffing.

"Did he say something about her today?"

"No. For the first time, he didn't threaten to hurt her if I left. I think he knows that won't work with me anymore."

"Why?"

She took a deep breath and let it out slowly

before laying her head back down on my shoulder. "Because I'm not afraid of him anymore."

I closed my eyes and hoped everything she believed would come true. That Robert was okay with us together and I wouldn't have to endure another beating. That he saw her strength and respected it. That we would be safe.

But my gut said none of that would ever happen.

Chapter Twelve

Ryder

I SANK INTO the hot water until it covered up to my chest and closed my eyes as the heat slowly eased my pain. More than a week after Robert had me beaten like a misbehaving dog, my side still ached every time I moved, but the rest of my injuries had begun to ease up and my face didn't look like the Elephant Man's anymore.

So today was the day I got to return to work for the very man who'd done this to me.

"I wish you didn't have to go back there already," Serena said quietly from beside the tub.

Turning my head, I opened my eyes and smiled, hoping that if I pretended everything was all right that she wouldn't worry. "Me too. It's been a nice little vacation we had here. Well, except for feeling like a bus drove over me and not being able to be with you."

She pressed a kiss onto my lips and slid her hand through my wet hair. "I remember the first time I saw you all beaten up soaking in a tub."

The smile she wore looked so sexy. If it wasn't for the fact that half my torso wasn't in working condition, I would have pulled her right into that tub with me.

"I remember that. I hurt like a son of a bitch, but as soon as I saw you, all I could think of was how happy I was you came to find me."

"Then it was your shoulder," she said as she slid her hand up my arm as it rested on the side of the tub. "I guess things don't change much, do they?"

"Nope. It seems like your father is always having me beaten one way or the other."

"Was it this bad when he did that after finding us together that night he sent me off to Italy?" she asked, her eyes full of concern for me.

Chuckling, I shook my head. "He made sure to find the biggest guy the circuit had ever seen. There wasn't a chance in hell I'd be able to beat him. The guy pounded me into the ground, just like Robert wanted, but I guess I'd have to say it was worse that time."

"Why?"

"Because there was no chance I'd see you once I felt better."

Serena's eyes narrowed in anger. "I'm sorry, Ryder. You must think you should have never come to this place."

Cupping the back of her head, I pulled her

mouth to mine to kiss away that idea. Looking into her eyes, I told her the truth. "Never once. I've never regretted coming here two years ago. Seeing you every night made whatever I had to do for him worth it."

"How bad your life must have been before you came here then. You've had to go through so much because of me."

I sat up out of the water and slowly turned to face her. "You? No. Your father's to blame, not you. None of this is because of you. Don't ever think that."

She lowered her head and quietly said, "I never meant for you to suffer because of me, Ryder. I hope you know that."

"Of course I know that. Look at me, Serena."

Keeping her head down, she said, "I know what you're going to say, and it doesn't change the fact that all of this happened because you're with me. Don't say it hasn't because it has."

With my finger, I gently tilted her chin up so she had to face me and saw her dark eyes filled with sadness. "I would go through this a hundred times more if it meant you and I got to be together. I've been fighting since I was fifteen. I can take a beating. As long as he doesn't hurt you, I'll take it as many times as I have to."

A tear rolled down her cheek. "You shouldn't

have to take it at all just to be with me. I wouldn't blame you if you told me this was too much. Now you have to go back to work for the monster who did this. I have to stay here, Ryder, but you don't."

I cradled her face in my hands and kissed where that tear stopped. "Yes, I do. You're here, so I have to stay here."

Serena leaned forward and kissed me. "Do you hate me for staying here because of my mother?"

Shaking my head, I tried to dry her cheek with my thumb but only made it wetter with the bath water. "I hate a lot of things, but not you. Your father, this world of his, seeing you unhappy. Those things I hate, but never you."

"I need to find out where she is, Ryder. If I could find her and know she's safe from him, I could leave here with you and then we'd be happy. I told you I wouldn't care if we didn't have a dime to our name, and I wouldn't. I don't stay here because of the money."

"You're not Janelle, so I know you don't stay here just for that. No woman who prefers to watch a movie in bed over a night out cares that much about money. Don't worry about us staying here for a little longer. Whatever he does to me, I can handle it. I promised you I'd protect you, and that's what I intend on doing."

With that sweet naiveté that still existed in her,

she said, "He gave me his word that he wouldn't have you beaten again."

I didn't believe that for a second, but I didn't want her to worry, so I smiled. "See? You have nothing to worry about then. He'll probably just stick me with some job none of the other guys would want. Maybe stable boy?"

Confused by my joke, she shook her head. "What do you mean? We haven't had horses in years."

"Just a joke. When I first came here, I worried that's what he was going to make me do in addition to fighting to be able to live in such a beautiful house."

Giggling at my lame attempt at humor, she stood and looked down into the water before looking up at me. "If those ribs of yours weren't still hurting, I'd climb in there with you."

I opened my arms to welcome her in, even though I knew moving even a little would hurt like a motherfucker. I didn't care. I'd take the pain to feel her body pressed against mine as I slowly slid my cock inside her.

"I told you. I can handle the pain," I said with a wink.

Serena crouched down next to the tub and slid her hand down between my legs to palm my cock. The feel of her hand around me after days of not being able to touch her made me as hard as a rock in seconds. I lifted my hips off the bottom of the tub to glide my cock over her skin, closing my eyes to hide how bad the pain shooting through my side felt.

"Mmmm, maybe I was wrong," she whispered as she began pumping me. "Maybe you are doing better."

With each stroke of my cock, her hand delivered pleasure that mixed with the pain shooting across my ribs and made the top of my head feel like it was about to blow off. I groaned low and deep every time her palm grazed the base before sliding up slowly to the tip, my brain involved in a tug-of-war over how much I wanted her to continue and how much I wanted to come so the pain would subside.

She kissed me long and deep, slipping her tongue into my mouth to tease me. I buried my hand in her hair and held her to me, moaning against her lips, "Don't stop, baby. Fuck, don't stop."

I felt like someone was stabbing me in the side over and over, but I didn't care. Ecstasy overwhelmed the agony.

"You look like this hurts," she whispered. "Are you sure you want me to continue?"

Looking up at her, I saw the concern written on her face. "I don't care how much it hurts. Just don't stop. This feels so fucking good. I need something to think about when I have to be away from you today."

"Okay. Then lean back, relax, and enjoy yourself," she said with a smile.

I did exactly that and let her jerk me off as I fantasized about the next time I'd be able to be inside her, my cock sliding in and out of her tight cunt as she moaned how much she never wanted me to stop.

"You look so masculine lying there so completely focused on your cock, you know that?" she said as she lingered her hand on the tip.

Opening my eyes, I looked down at the beautiful sight of her touching me and smiled up at her. "I'm actually thinking about how good it's going to feel when I get to fuck you again."

"Oh yeah? How good?" she asked as her hand slid down to cup my balls to give them a single gentle squeeze.

"Oh, God…I'm going to make you come so hard with my mouth on your pussy, and then I'm going to bury my cock in your cunt and fuck you until I fill you up. And when I'm done, you're going to beg me to fuck you again."

Serena kissed me hard as I began to come and whispered against my lips, "And you will because you know how happy I am when you're inside me."

Groaning as my balls emptied all over her hand, for a precious few seconds I felt no pain, just the pure ecstasy of coming that pushed aside every ache in my body. I inhaled a deep breath for the first time in days and let the air out slowly, relishing how good it felt.

But then the pain rushed back, and I doubled over in agony. Pushing Serena's hand away, I fell back against the tub.

"Are you okay? I didn't mean to hurt you, Ryder. I'm sorry."

I saw the horror in her eyes and shook my head. "No, it's okay. At least for a few seconds, nothing hurt. The problem is when the pain came back, it came back with a vengeance. I'll be good in a minute or two."

"Coming isn't supposed to hurt," she said with a sexy smile.

"Broken ribs do their best to put a damper on sex."

Leaning over the tub, she kissed me sweetly on the lips. "Do they put a damper on you going down on me?"

I smiled at the thought of tasting her on my lips again. "No, I think that could work."

"Good. When you get back from work today, I'll be waiting in your bed."

As she walked out of the bathroom, my cock started to get hard again at the mere idea of her waiting for me. "Be naked. If it's a bad day, I'm not going to want to bother with clothes."

"Naked it is," she yelled in from the bedroom.

"Naked, wet, and dying to feel your mouth on me."

As always, I'd be counting the seconds until I saw her again.

✦　✦　✦

ROBERT SAT ALONE in his office when I arrived, so I knocked on his door since I wasn't sure I would be welcome there anymore. He may have promised Serena he wouldn't have me beaten again, but that didn't mean he still thought of me as someone he could trust.

He looked up from his laptop and stared at me, his dark eyebrows rising into his forehead like he was surprised to see me standing there. "Ready to get back to work again?"

I nodded but still didn't enter his office. I didn't know what I expected, but I didn't want to push my luck and overstep my bounds on my first day back.

"You can come in, Ryder. Nothing's changed."

Everything in his demeanor said otherwise, and my broken ribs seemed like strong evidence that things had definitely changed between us. I walked in and took my position against the bookcase on the far wall as he continued whatever he was doing on his laptop.

He may have wanted me to think nothing had changed, but something in the air felt different. If I knew Robert, he liked the idea of me wondering when the other shoe would drop. It gave him power over me, something he'd always enjoyed in that sick way of his.

After fifteen minutes of waiting for him to say something, I began to wonder if having me waiting on pins and needles was exactly what my job would be. Sort of free amusement for a sadist.

Not that I expected an apology for what he'd done to me. He'd never apologized to Serena for any of the horrible things he'd done to her, and nothing made me believe he felt any remorse for having me beaten within an inch of my life.

I'd betrayed him, and he'd punished me for it. To Robert, it was as simple as that. You were either loyal or not. I'd made the mistake of being disloyal, and he'd made me pay for it.

The question was just how long he would make me continue to pay. I didn't care as long as I was the one paying and not Serena.

Finally, he looked up from his laptop and nodded. "We've got a big day ahead of us. I want you to accompany me to a meeting I have with Tamsin Industries. Are you up to it?"

His gaze slid down my body to where his guys cracked my ribs, and I instinctively winced in pain. "I'll be fine. Whatever you need, I'm good."

That familiar crocodile smile spread across his face. With a chuckle, he said, "This meeting ought to be enjoyable. My company is planning a hostile takeover, and this is Tamsin's last chance to give in before I begin turning the screws. I love these kinds of meetings. There's nothing like squeezing the life out of someone when you know you can."

I knew how much he loved that kind of power and wondered if Serena and I would ever be safe again as long as we stayed at that house. The sooner we got out, the better, before we were the ones he was turning the screws on.

Pretending that I didn't believe he was talking about lording his power over me or his daughter, I smiled and said, "You're going to own the entire mining industry soon."

He dismissed my flattery with a wave of his hand. "Oh no. Tamsin isn't mining. It's pharmaceuticals. It's best to always make sure to have more than one iron in the fire."

What I knew about Robert's actual businesses added up to very little. He usually kept me involved in the illegal parts of his empire, so trying to discuss anything about his mining interests or his planned hostile takeover of a pharmaceutical company left me with little to say.

But I had the sense he had more on his mind, so I did my smile and nod routine and prepared to fake listen to him brag about his business expertise. When he didn't continue talking and returned his attention to his laptop, I had to admit I was thankful. I still didn't feel entirely comfortable there with him, but at least silence meant he wasn't threatening me or Serena.

After a few minutes, he closed his laptop and leaned back in his chair. "You know, I gave my daughter permission to be with you. Do you know why?"

Not a single answer I came up with sounded like anything I should actually say out loud, so I merely shook my head and remained quiet.

"I like you, Ryder. I always have. I didn't want to have you beaten like I did. It pained me to hurt you. I think of you like a son in many ways. The son I never had. But I didn't have a choice. You betrayed me, so there had to be consequences."

For a moment, I considered asking why he was allowing Serena and me to be together then, but I decided now wasn't the time for being cocky. Better to let Robert just talk since he didn't look like he was finished quite yet.

"I guess in hindsight I should have predicted this would happen. I mean, after catching you and Serena that night in your bedroom before I sent her to Italy, I guess it was just a matter of time. I thought she'd outgrown you when I saw the two of you together at Janelle's wedding, but I should have known better. Once Serena cares for someone, that love never dies. I can say that for her."

"We never meant to make you angry by being together," I said quietly, feeling like I needed to explain myself in some way.

He looked past me toward the top of the bookcase and chuckled. "I wasn't angry. I knew she never loved Oliver, and I guess in retrospect, that marriage never had a chance."

I wanted to say he was as much to blame for that marriage being a failure as we were, but I didn't. Maybe it was the pain in my side practically bringing tears to my eyes as I stood there, or maybe it was the feeling that there was no point in trying to explain to Robert that forcing someone to marry someone they didn't love wasn't right.

Suddenly, he returned his focus to me and knitted his eyebrows. When he began speaking, it felt like he was intentionally taking his time so I understood his point. "I'm going to warn you. Sleep with one eye open, son. If it was Janelle you were with, I'd say you've got it made. She's entirely predictable and easily placated. But Serena is nothing like her sister. There's something in her I can't put my finger on. She's like her mother, and to this day, I still can't explain why she did the things she did. Serena's not ruled by logic, and those kinds of people don't live by the same rules we do. Watch yourself."

Whatever rules he thought I lived by, nothing I

based my life on resembled what he believed in the least. He didn't know Serena because he'd never seen her as anything but something to use and manipulate for his own gains.

That her heart ruled her was one of the reasons I loved her. I said nothing in response to his warnings and merely continued to smile as the truth began to sink in. Robert not only didn't understand her.

He didn't believe that we could actually be in love.

Chapter Thirteen

Serena

ALL DAY I worried about what my father could be doing to Ryder now that he was back at work for him. Robert Erickson prided himself on his skill in breaking people, and even though he'd promised me Ryder would never be beaten again, I knew in my heart he'd do something to make him suffer.

Sooner or later, he'd drop the façade and show his true self once again.

As I thought about what he'd do, I heard the door to Ryder's apartment open and hurried to see how he'd fared on his first day back. My heart raced at the idea that he might be hurt even worse than before, but as I watched him slowly walk toward the living room, he seemed to be okay.

"Hey, I thought the deal was you'd be waiting for me naked in bed. I've been looking forward to that all day," he said with a smile, wrapping his arms around me and pulling me close.

I tilted my head to look up at him and thought I

saw a dark area under his left eye. "What happened? Did he go back on his promise already?" I asked as I gently ran my fingertips over his cheek.

Ryder took my hand in his and brought my fingers to his lips in a kiss. "I'm fine. He didn't do anything. It was just a regular work day, strangely enough."

"Nothing? What did he say about what he did to you?"

"Nothing. He acted like everything was the same between us. Like he didn't have his two goons rough me up right there in that office."

"I don't trust him. That sounds like how a psychopath acts."

Bending down, Ryder kissed me sweetly and smiled. "Oh, he's a psychopath. I have no doubt about that. For now, though, he seems to want to pretend like we're okay and he has no problem with us being together."

I placed my head on his chest over his heart and sighed. "So now we get to wonder when he'll strike again. Sounds like the work of a psychopath."

"Don't worry," Ryder whispered against the top of my head. "Whatever he does to me, I can handle it. As long as we're together, I can take anything he dishes out."

Looking up, I saw that sweetness I loved in him as he gazed down at me like all of this was perfectly normal for a man in love to deal with. "You shouldn't have to, Ryder. I bet if you knew our life would be like this, you never would have let me into your room that night I came looking for you."

Pressing his forehead to mine, he whispered, "I still would have."

"So about that whole naked waiting for you thing. Give me a few seconds and I can make that come true."

His hands drifted down my back to cup my ass before he gave it a gentle squeeze. "Just long enough for me to down some whisky and take the edge off the pain in my ribs. I'll meet you in the bedroom."

Before he turned to walk away, I stopped him and asked, "Are you sure you're up to it? If you're in pain, we can just relax tonight."

Ryder grinned in that sexy way I knew meant he'd actually looked forward to coming home to see me naked in his bed. "I'm a red-blooded American male. Trust me. A few broken ribs aren't going to stop me from pleasuring the woman I love. Even if my jaw was wired shut, I'd still be game to go down on you."

"That sounds truly awful," I said with a chuckle as the image of that ran through my head. "Nothing like looking down and seeing a man gritting his teeth near your lady bits."

He ran his tongue along his lower lip and

winked at me. "See? It could be much worse. Now get in there and get naked. I want to see you ready and waiting for me when I come in."

"Oooh, I love it when you get all bossy with me."

With his forefinger and thumb, he gripped my chin and tilted my head back to kiss me. "Good, and I'm starving for you, so I'm going to devour that beautiful pussy of yours."

When he said things like that, a sweet ache formed inside me, like the mere description of what he'd do to me made me want him even more. I watched as he slowly walked toward the kitchen to get his drink and loved the way even when his body was racked with pain, he could still be so focused on me and my happiness.

Slipping out of my jeans and sweater, I placed them on the chair in the corner of the room and lay down. I wriggled out of my panties and bra, tossing them across the room to the same chair, and waited just as he'd ordered—naked and ready for him on his bed.

Ryder appeared in the doorway and smiled a grin so wicked I felt myself get wetter just looking at him. He'd removed his tie and unbuttoned the top two buttons on his black dress shirt, making him look so fucking sexy.

"You look beautiful there just waiting for me, like the perfect woman all for me," he said in a low voice that hit me deep inside.

Slowly, he walked over to the bed, and I saw that intensity in his green eyes that never failed to make me feel desired. His gaze remained focused entirely on me, never wavering as he stared at my body like I was something to be worshipped.

"It seems unfair that I'm the only one undressed here," I said as I reached out to tug him by the waist of his pants to bring him closer.

With a smirk, he shook his head. "Nope. Tonight I get to be spoiled by enjoying you completely."

"I don't think you're the only one who gets to have a good time since you'll be doing all the work."

He slid his hand down between my breasts and shook his head. "Trust me. It's not work to go down on you."

My nipples tightened from his touch on my skin, sending waves of pleasure down my body straight to my pussy. It never failed to amaze me how hands so violent with others could give me so much happiness. Hard and rough, they had broken bones and bloodied people, but when they touched me, his hands brought me to sensual heights no other man's ever could.

"We might have to make some adjustments tonight. My ribs are killing me," Ryder said as he climbed onto the bed, grimacing in pain.

"How about instead of you down below me you can just lay there while I'm on top of you?"

He sat back on his heels and nodded. "Sounds pretty lazy for me, I know. Ordinarily, I wouldn't need to, but they're hurting like a son of a bitch tonight."

I patted the sheets next to me. "Lie down and take it easy. You're still doing all the work, so you won't hear any complaints from me."

Slowly, he lowered himself to the bed and looked over at me. "Don't worry. I promise this won't affect my performance, ma'am."

"No worries here, but how about you stop referring to me like I'm your district manager?"

Ryder smiled at my joke. "Now that's a job title. District manager of eating pussy. Eastern region."

Kissing him lightly on the lips, I giggled. "Imagine that on a job application. How do you want me to do this? I don't want to cause you any more pain, and I have a feeling if I move the wrong way, that's exactly what's going to happen."

"Just don't sit too far down on my chest. Don't worry. If you get too close, I'll push you up."

I sat up and shook my head. "This might be the sexiest thing I've ever done."

My sarcasm wasn't lost on him. "Trust me. Once my mouth settles in and does its thing, you're going to forget all about this preliminary stuff."

In the most indelicate way ever, I flung my left leg over him and knelt above his face. Looking down, I tried to feel sexy instead of intensely awkward. "Interesting view, huh?"

His gaze traveled up between my legs and then my body to focus on my face. His hands cupped my ass, and smiling, he said, "It's beautiful. Like a flower ready to bloom."

"That's so poetic, Ryder."

He rolled his eyes. "I read it once. Now be quiet and let me work my magic."

I pretended to zip my lip as he gently flicked his tongue over my clit. Waves of pleasure washed over me, and the feel of his fingers teasing the inside of my thighs, so close to where I craved his touch, made me roll my hips in the hope he'd give me what I craved.

My fingers tightened in his hair with every stroke of his tongue over my needy pussy, and when he sucked my clit between his lips, I tugged hard to keep him right on that spot. His mouth and how he used it on me felt sublime. If he stopped now, I'd beg him to give me more, willing to trade anything to keep his mouth on me.

"Oh, God…Ryder, that's it…don't stop…please, don't stop…" I whimpered while his tongue focused on my pussy and he fucked me with his fingers, sliding one and then two inside me.

I looked down to see him smile as he stared up at me, watching my reaction to what he was doing to me. His mouth took me to the very edge and then eased me back as only he could do. Over and over, I watched him use his mouth so expertly, like he understood exactly what would give me the most pleasure and how to prolong it just by knowing my body as no one else did.

My release began to uncoil inside me, and I pulled hard on his hair. "I'm almost there. Oh, right there. That's it," I moaned as he sucked hard on my clit and pumped his fingers into me.

Seconds later, I felt the familiar, sweet sensation of my body surrendering to him. I rolled my hips and he held me tightly to his mouth, lapping up everything my pussy offered.

When I finished, I sagged against his chest, my hands barely able to hold me up as they clutched the headboard. Beneath me, he wore the expression of a conquering hero.

"You look completely satisfied with what you did there, you know that?" I said, looking down at him.

"There's nothing like making a woman come so hard she rides your face like a bucking bronco," he said, practically gloating.

"That's a sexy image." Lifting my leg, I eased it over his chest and sat down beside him. "I hope I looked better than some rodeo rider.”

He turned his head to face me and chuckled. “I didn’t see any fringe, so I think you definitely looked better than a rodeo rider.”

I kissed him, tasting myself on his lips, and cradled his face in my hands. “It’s not every man who can make a woman come like that and make references to fringe on rodeo costumes. You’re truly a Renaissance man.”

“Your Renaissance man.”

“All mine. And I’m all yours,” I answered, never more sure I loved him as completely as I ever could love someone.

He remained quiet for a few minutes as I recovered from the pleasure he’d given me. Finally, he said, “I don’t want you to worry about what’s going to happen, Serena. I’m going to take care of everything. I promise.”

I trusted him more than anyone else in the world. He’d saved me more times than I deserved, and I knew he’d do everything in his power to ensure my safety.

But as much as he loved me, I worried he was no match for what my father would do.

“Just promise me whatever happens, you won’t give up on us.”

He winced like what I said hurt him. “I won’t ever give up on us, Serena. He can do whatever he wants. It won't matter. As long as I'm breathing, I'm going to love you. That's all there is to it."

When he said things like that, I almost believed we'd be okay.

"I love you," I whispered against his lips before kissing him again. "I don't know what I'd do without you."

He tucked my hair behind my ears and kissed me back. "You won't ever have to know because I'm going to love you for the rest of my life."

I placed my head on his shoulder, loving the feel of his strength beneath me. Like we used to when he first came to the estate, I closed my eyes and let myself drift off, knowing he was right beside me making sure nothing bad happened to me.

Chapter Fourteen

Serena

A S WINTER SETTLED in, bringing with it colder weather and longer nights, Ryder and I slowly let the rest of the world know we were a couple. Instead of hiding out in his apartment to be together, we took those walks he dreamed of, holding hands as we made our way through the garden or the streets of the city when we drove into Baltimore to shop or have dinner.

I had a feeling showing everyone we loved each other made him even happier than it made me. I was used to living in secret. I'd done it most of my life. But Ryder liked to be more upfront about what he cared about. Sneaking around had always made him miserable.

The reaction from the rest of my father's men ranged from disinterest from the older ones to curiosity from the young guy named Jesse. Not that either of us cared what they thought.

My father at times appeared to seethe when he saw us together, but he never said a word about it after that day when he promised he'd never beat Ryder again. I didn't pin all my hopes for happiness on that one statement, but as time went on and he didn't retaliate against either of us, I wanted to believe things had gotten better.

Emboldened by this, I lay in Ryder's arms as we slept in late on a Saturday morning and decided the time had come to find my mother. I knew my father would fight me on my choice, but I couldn't continue to pretend to be all right knowing she was out there somewhere and might want to know me as much as I wanted to know her.

I stared up at the ceiling above Ryder's bed and thought about what I'd say to her when I finally got to meet her after all these years. Would she be happy to see me? Would I be who she hoped I'd become or would she wish I was more like Janelle?

As these thoughts rambled around my head, Ryder nuzzled my neck and whispered, "You look a million miles away. You okay?"

I looked over at him and saw concern in his sleepy expression. "I'm fine. I was just thinking."

He kissed me on the cheek and wrapped his arms around me to pull me close. "Okay. You want to tell me about it?"

"You know I want to find my mother, Ryder. I got some money from Oliver's will, and I know you and I could use it toward us getting away from here, but it's important to me that I finally see her. I want to hire a private detective to find her for me."

My words were met with silence.

Turning toward him, I saw the drowsiness fade from his expression, replaced with concern. Was he upset I didn't want to use the money to help us leave this place?

"I know you want us to leave here, and you're right. I thought we could stay when my father agreed we could be together, but we should go. I just can't continue knowing she's out there and I can't have a relationship her because my father wants to keep her from me. Or maybe it's that he wants to keep me from her. I don't know. I just know not having her in my life all these years has left a hole inside me that will never go away if I don't try. Even though I'm blissfully happy with you, Ryder, there's still that part of me that misses my mother."

Shaking his head, he quietly said, "You don't have to explain yourself to me. I've accepted that we probably won't leave here. Robert's been almost nice these past few weeks, so maybe we don't have to."

I hated hearing him sound so defeated. Cradling his face in my hands, I pressed a kiss to his lips and said, "Don't say that. We will. I want that place you talk about in the mountains where it's just the two of us. I don't want to spend the rest of my life in this place like some kind of caged animal who's allowed to roam freely as long as my owner knows exactly where I am and what I'm doing. I just don't want to go on not knowing my mother."

Ryder nodded and smiled. "You know, when you tell him, he's going to fight you on this. Are you up to that?"

"I won the last round. Maybe I'll win this one too."

His eyebrows rose to show his disbelief. "You like to live dangerously, don't you?"

"No. I just have a strong sense of justice, and his keeping my mother from Janelle and me all these years isn't right."

"Maybe not telling him until you've found her might be better?"

I thought about it and had to agree. Plus, if I told him before the private detective found her, he might do something to ensure I never found her. "Okay. That's what we'll do then. When I know where she is, we'll tell him."

"We?" he asked with a smile.

Pushing him onto his back, I lay my head on his shoulder. "Yes, we. This is about us, so we it is."

He pressed a kiss onto the top of my head and whispered, "Okay, we. For now, I say we stay right here and enjoy a few more minutes of sleep."

His arms holding me tightly to him grew slack, and I looked up to see he'd fallen back to sleep. But I couldn't sleep because the very idea that sometime soon I'd see my mother made my mind race with thoughts about how wonderful it would be to once again be her daughter in more than just my dreams.

✧   ✧   ✧

"Serena, I want you and Ryder to come down to my office."

My father's demand for us to join him on the very evening after I'd spoken to the private detective about finding my mother sent my mind into a tailspin. Had I mistakenly hired someone who knew my father, or even worse, worked for him? Had he told him my plans and now he intended to put a stop to them before I even had a chance to find out where she was?

As my hand holding the phone began to shake, I nervously asked, "Is something wrong?"

"Just be in my office in an hour. I assume you're with him since he's not at work, so that shouldn't be a problem."

I barely got the word okay out before he ended the call, leaving me wondering if all my plans had been dashed already. Setting my phone on the coffee table in front of me, I leaned back and took a deep breath before letting it out slowly as I tried to calm myself.

"I don't have to ask who that was. He's the only

person in the world who can make you look that way."

Forcing a smile, I turned to face Ryder next to me on the couch. "What way?"

"Terrified."

And in a single word he encapsulated my entire life with my father. But I wasn't that teenage girl who worried every time he called me into his office anymore. I'd stood up to him before, and if I had to, I'd do it again in an hour.

"He wants to see us in his office. We've been summoned."

Now worry settled into Ryder's face, and he frowned. "Do you think he found out about you hiring someone to find your mother?"

"I don't know, but I don't care. He can be as angry as he wants. I just hope he doesn't do something to make sure I can't find her. That's my only concern."

Ryder nodded. "I wonder why he wants me there with you. That makes me think it's about something else and not about you looking for your mother."

What he said made sense. Heartened by the mere possibility that my secret hadn't been revealed, I smiled and kissed him. "Thank you."

"For what?"

"For always helping me see the bright side."

Instead of smiling back at me, he knitted his

eyebrows and I saw concern in his eyes. "Whatever he has to say to us, don't worry because I'll be right by your side. Nothing he does, no matter how bad it is, can hurt you with me there."

Taking his hands in mine, I brought them to my lips in a kiss. "I know, and I can't tell you how much I love you for that. I'm not afraid to go to see him with you there by my side."

His expression lightened, and I finally got that smile in return. "Good. Maybe he's going to tell us he's decided to move in with his girlfriend and we can have the house all to ourselves."

I laughed at his optimism, sure that wasn't what my father wanted to see us about. But no matter what he wanted to say, we'd be fine because we had each other.

MY FATHER'S OFFICE seemed darker than usual as we walked in and sat down in those red leather chairs in front of his desk. He stared at me for a long moment and then turned his attention to Ryder, flashing one of those smiles that never failed to make my stomach twist into knots.

"You look good, son. I guess all those bones healed."

"I've taken worse beatings before. You should know that," Ryder said flatly.

"That I do." My father stopped for a moment

and then said, "So I guess Serena knows about what you used to do for me."

Ryder simply nodded, but I felt the need to answer. "I know all about it, and it doesn't change how I feel about him, if that's what you're getting at."

My father shot me a glance but returned his focus to Ryder. "All the better. I wasn't looking forward to explaining that to her anyway. I should have guessed there'd be no secrets between you two."

Neither of us said a word. I felt Ryder take hold of my hand and a sense of calm came over me. Nothing my father could do could hurt us.

He stood from behind his desk and walked over to the bar to make himself a drink. With his back turned to us, he said, "I'm glad we can be so open about everything now, and Serena, I think you knowing about my business with Ryder will make what I have to say go much smoother."

"Oh? Why?" I asked, suddenly concerned about this announcement of his.

Turning around, he smiled at me and returned to his seat. Unlike usual when he spoke to me, it felt like he was hesitating, as if he wanted to take his time to find the right words for what he had to say.

With every second that passed, my anxiety ratcheted up another notch until my hands became drenched with sweat. I squeezed Ryder's as if to remind myself that no matter what words came out of my father's mouth, I wasn't alone.

No matter what he did, Ryder would protect me.

He placed his glass down on his desk and when he spoke again, he sounded almost chipper. "So that little ugliness between us got me thinking, and I think your talents are being wasted on merely convincing people to pay their debts, Ryder. Don't you?"

"My talents? What would those be?"

"What got my attention in the first place. Fighting. So it's time we start utilizing those talents again so we both benefit."

Leaning forward, Ryder let go of my hand and stared in shock at my father. After a few moments, he asked, "You want me to fight again?"

"You have no money to speak of, and if you're going to be with my daughter, you need to bring something to the table other than the fact that she likes you," my father said with a sneer.

"Loves him," I said, correcting his mistake in characterizing how I felt about Ryder. "I love him."

Without even looking at me, my father continued, "Which makes it even more important that you have something to offer her. So you'll be fighting from now on. I've contacted Floyd, and he's setting up a fight in three weeks."

I had no idea what to think about what my father was proposing, but as I watched Ryder's mouth drop open in shock, I knew it wasn't good.

Leaning back, he shook his head. "I haven't fought in over two years. Three weeks won't be enough time, and you know it. You're setting me up to get my head crushed in again."

I waited to hear my father say he'd give him more time, but instead he said, "You can either fight in three weeks or you can leave this house tonight. Your choice."

Ryder stared straight ahead, and if my father's ultimatum rattled him, he didn't show it. Barely loud enough for me to hear, he said, "Three weeks then."

Clapping his hands, my father smiled. "Good! I look forward to seeing you fight again."

I couldn't believe my ears. None of this was good. He just blackmailed the man I loved to get his way and send Ryder back to fighting, even though he damn well knew he wasn't ready to face anyone in three weeks.

"No! Ryder and I won't be held hostage by you anymore," I said as I jumped up out of my seat. "You're practically making sure he gets hurt, and you promised me you wouldn't do that again."

My father narrowed his eyes to slits and sternly corrected me. "I promised I wouldn't have him beaten again, and I won't. He has three weeks to get in shape. What he does in that time is up to him."

Ryder stood up and grabbed my arm to stop me,

but I continued to protest my father's cruelty. "Why are you doing this to him? He's done nothing but do your bidding ever since he returned to work."

"Don't, Serena. Let's go," Ryder said, pushing me toward the door.

Looking back at my father, I saw him smirk like acting this way toward Ryder pleased him to no end. "Listen to your boyfriend, sweetheart. He knows I'm not bluffing."

I slipped out of Ryder's hold and stormed back to stand next to my father's desk. Glaring down at him, I said, "You think you can just send him away and I won't leave with him? You're crazy. I wouldn't stay here for one damn second if he wasn't here. In fact, you should thank him because he's the only reason I'm still here."

My father stared up at me the whole time I said what was on my mind, never even blinking once as he listened to the truth of how I felt about being there in that house and around him. When I finished, he slowly lifted his glass to his mouth and took a sip of that damn bourbon and branch shit he liked to drink, all the while smirking like he had all the power.

That he did for the moment didn't matter to me. Someday he wouldn't. And on that day, he'd see what his hatefulness and cruelty had created.

Swirling the ice in his glass, he grinned. "That's

always been your Achilles' heel, Serena. You care about others. Maybe you'd rather I threaten your mother instead of having Ryder fight? Okay. How about we make it your choice? Ryder fights or your mother suffers. It's up to you."

My emotions threatened to explode out of me in a mixture of rage and hurt from how powerless I felt standing there as he smiled up at me waiting for my choice of which person I loved would be hurt. I hated him, and as I forced back the tears so he wouldn't be able to enjoy how miserable he made me, I silently swore I'd never forget this moment.

"Serena, don't," Ryder said behind me as he gently tugged my arm so I'd join him.

I looked back and saw him standing there, his eyes full of the same hate I knew mine held, and I knew he'd never let me choose to have my mother hurt. I loved him all the more for that, but I'd never forgive myself if he suffered for me once again.

Without even bothering to look at my father, I turned and followed Ryder out of the office. He took my hand in his and squeezed it as we silently walked toward the hallway to the south wing and his apartment. Once again, my father had found a way to make me see that only a fool would believe they could find happiness in his world.

I'd been that fool for weeks, blissfully trusting he would let Ryder and me live in peace. Now, as my hate for him threatened to choke me, I tried to remember it was only a matter of time before the private detective gave me some information on my mother and I'd be able to see her again.

And once she and I were reunited, he could threaten all he wanted. I'll have beaten him at his own game.

Chapter Fifteen

Ryder

SERENA HAD NO idea what her father had just done. I'd been out of the game for over two years. Working as his muscle had often required me to get physical with guys, but nothing like fighting on the circuit. He knew that. He knew even though I worked out daily, it wasn't anywhere near enough for me to be ready to face any guy in a fight in just three weeks.

And still the fucker did it.

I sat down on the couch and tried to pretend everything would be okay. I'd told her so little about my time fighting that maybe she'd believe that I could get in shape to fight whatever behemoth Robert found for me in less than a month.

She leaned her head on my shoulder and whispered, "I'm sorry, Ryder. I don't know why he's doing this. I thought maybe he might have found out about me looking for my mother, but he didn't seem to. I don't know why he suddenly wants to punish us again now."

Closing my eyes, I let myself enjoy the feel of her next to me. "Because that's who he is. Who knows? Maybe he's still punishing me for what I did to Oliver. Maybe this is because I went behind his back with you. I don't know. All I know is that this is who he is."

"We. What we did."

I turned to look at her and saw those dark eyes so gentle and sweet staring up at me. "You know what? I can't wait to meet your mother because I have to know how someone so good could come from someone so evil. It must have been because of her."

Serena beamed at my mention of her mother. "I can't wait either. I just know when I get to talk to her, she's going to say she's wanted to know me and Janelle all these years. I have to believe my father's been telling the truth when he says I'm like her. He thinks it's a bad thing, but I don't."

I kissed her on the forehead. "You're gentle and kind and nothing like him. He doesn't understand someone like you. All he knows is how to be vicious. It's all he is."

Her smile faded as a look of concern crossed her face. "So about this fight? You'll be able to handle it, right? You work out every day and you still look as good as you did when you came to the house back then."

Forcing myself to appear like none of it worried me, I nodded. "I'll be fine. I'm not too rusty, and I'm a couple years older now. I'm like wine. I get better with age."

She studied my expression for a moment and then innocently asked, "Is that really how it works?"

"Sure. I definitely wouldn't have wanted to go up against someone my age when I was eighteen. I would have gotten my ass handed to me."

I'd never lied like that to her. When I first came to the estate, I'd avoided telling Serena what I did for her father, but never in all the time I'd known her had I lied so completely about anything until that moment. I just couldn't be the reason she spent the next three weeks worried sick about this.

But I knew better than to think the past two years had given me any advantage in a fight. I may have been in good shape, but I wasn't in fighting shape, and that would mean the difference between holding my own in the ring and getting beaten worse than Robert's guys had done to me.

"So what do you have to do to be ready for this fight?" Serena asked, her eyes full of curiosity. "Is it like when you first came here?"

I smiled at her mention of that time. She'd followed me around for days back then, spying on me around corners as I worked out, her dark eyes wide as she watched me do what I had to so I didn't get my ass handed to me in the next fight. The memory of her so curious about me seemed so innocent for all we'd gone through since then.

Pulling her close, I kissed the top of her head and held her to me. I didn't want to face her when I lied again. "Yeah, pretty much. Training is basically the same no matter what, so it'll be fine."

The uncertainty in my voice came through loud and clear to me, but I didn't know if Serena heard it. I waited for her to say something, my brain scrambling to come up with a lie she wouldn't be able to see through.

Serena looked up at me and smiled. "Is there anything I can do to help? If you want, I can stand next to you while you work out and say encouraging things. You know, sort of like a cheerleader."

I shook my head and laughed at how cute she could be. "You don't have to do that. I don't think anyone has ever offered to do that for me."

"Well, I saw it in the Rocky movies when that old guy helps Rocky train, but I don't really want to yell nasty things at you, so I figured maybe I could be more of a cheerleader than like the old man."

"To be honest, I think you'd be more of a distraction than anything if you were standing next to me while I train," I said before dipping my head to kiss her on the lips. "But thank you."

"I could get a cheerleader uniform. You know

the kind. A little skirt that barely covers my ass," she joked. "And an even tinier t-shirt that says Team Ryder. What do you think?"

The image of Serena dressed in that settled into my mind, and I smiled. "I think the other guy is going to have an easy time caving my head in if you do that because I'm not going to be getting any training done if you're anywhere nearby in an outfit like you described."

She slowly dragged the tip of her tongue across her bottom lip as she looked up at me. "Well, we wouldn't want that to happen, so I guess no cheer-leader outfit."

"There will be time for that after the fight," I said, winking at her.

Looking down, she traced her fingernail over my chest and quietly said, "It's going to be okay, right?"

"Yeah. Don't worry. I've got this handled."

Serena nodded and smiled up at me, but I knew it was forced. "Good. I know you'll do great and then we can go back to our life."

Everything inside me pushed me to tell her this was going to be our life from this point on. Robert wasn't going to just let me fight once and then be done with me. Win or lose, I was back in it again.

I didn't say those words, though. I just hoped Serena found her mother soon and then we could both leave this place.

FOR THREE WEEKS, I trained harder than I'd ever done before. Floyd agreed to help me get back into fighting shape, even though he risked the wrath of his boss for doing it. I saw the fear in his eyes every time I stood to fight the sparring partners he brought in. He knew what I knew.

That two years away wasn't going to be made up by some training in three weeks, no matter how hard I pushed myself. He could throw every guy he found at me and I could practice twenty hours a day, and it still wasn't going to be enough.

The day before the fight, he sat down next to me as we waited for the next fighter to get to the warehouse. I sat on that same rusted metal chair I'd been sitting on when Robert Erickson walked into my room and announced he'd bought me like some used car he wanted to fix up. In those two years, I'd faced everything he pushed on me like I'd faced everything life had dealt me since that night my parents died.

But this felt different. This felt like something I might not be able to handle.

I knew that doubt could be my downfall in the fight that would happen in that very building just twenty-four hours from then. I'd never doubted myself when it was just me fighting for my life.

That's how I'd seen it.

Fighting for my life. For the chance to have more

than just the pain and suffering that The Pit offered if I could only make enough to pay Floyd off and get away from this shithole.

And now, after seeing what having money could do for someone, I was right back there like the stray that I truly was.

Floyd pulled up a chair and sat down next to me, kicking a broken piece of concrete out of the way with his foot. Never close, we usually had very little to say to one another, but in the past few weeks, I'd seen a side of him I'd never known existed back when I worked for him. Back then, he'd been more like that old guy Serena described from the Rocky movie, but now he seemed pensive whenever we were alone, like he had something on his mind he wanted to share.

Clearing his throat, he said, "I really believed I'd never see you back here again, kid. I figured after that fight with that gorilla Mr. Erickson had me go find, you'd be done. Then I found out you went to work for him and I thought to myself, 'Well, he's got to do what's right for him,' you know? But I figured you'd find your way around that world and do just fine."

I turned my head to look over at him as I sat hunched over resting for my next sparring partner. "I thought I did just that. I guess I was wrong."

He hesitated for a few seconds and shook his

head. "What happened? Why does he want you back here fighting after two years away?"

Shrugging, I tried to pretend like I didn't know what this whole thing was for Robert. I knew, though. This was his way of showing me how unworthy I was to have Serena. He wanted her to see I was nothing but that stray he brought home two years ago, and no matter how well I cleaned up or how well I seemed to fit in with his world, I was still less than an Erickson.

Even though he insisted on referring to me as his adopted son from time to time.

"Maybe he thinks I get better with age," I said with a fake smile and hoped to convince Floyd I wasn't scared half out of my fucking mind at what I'd face in tomorrow night's fight.

"Yeah. Maybe," Floyd said with the same forced joking tone in his voice.

Our conversation over, I hung my head and closed my eyes as I focused on the hope I'd seen in Serena's eyes every time I told her everything would be fine. She asked at least once a day, and each time I pulled her close to me and kissed the top of her head so I wouldn't have to face her when I lied.

Everything wasn't going to be fine. Far from it. If I was lucky, I might make it out of this fight as badly hurt as when Robert had me beaten that day in his office. If I wasn't, I'd be looking at a nice stay in the hospital or worse.

Shaking my head, I tried to clear my mind of the worse.

"You know, Ryder, I didn't want to find that guy for him," Floyd said in a low voice. "I didn't have a choice."

His words came out slowly, like he didn't want to say them. I didn't blame him or anyone but Robert for that fight. Floyd wasn't lying when he said he didn't have a choice.

None of us did in Robert Erickson's world.

Looking over at Floyd, I saw what he had to do still bothered him after all this time. "You were just doing your job, man. We all have our roles to play, and that was yours. No hard feelings. Hell, I went to work for the guy after that, so I guess I must have been okay with things with him too."

A look of confusion settled into Floyd's face. "Yeah, why did you? Did you still owe him something?"

I thought back to that day when the doctor said I could leave the hospital and remembered thinking I had nowhere to go. I couldn't come back here to the warehouse since Robert owned that, so where could I go and what would I do for money? I doubted he'd be willing to let me fight for anyone else.

Those realities didn't leave me with many options. I could go back onto the streets and deal with the addicts and homeless I'd be stuck living with in the shadows. I'd done that before Floyd helped me out with the room in the warehouse, so I could have chosen that.

But I'd had a taste of a better life, and I didn't want to return to living in those piss stinking alleyways where every minute was a struggle to exist.

So I took Robert up on his offer to work as security for him, knowing full well that wouldn't be what I'd be doing. Once you see how good life can be on the other side of the tracks, you don't want to go back to where you used to be. Even doing his dirty work was better than returning to that life I'd had before.

Shaking my head, I answered Floyd's question truthfully. "Not really. I just didn't see any other way. He told me I wouldn't have to fight anymore, and I believed him. And for a long time, he lived up to that deal. I guess that's all changed now."

"I hear rumors, you know? Rumors about a girl and things like that with you. Is that why you're back here?" Floyd asked, worry hanging off each word.

He'd always warned us fighters not to let women ruin our lives. I'd assumed that was more sour grapes about his own life and not really career advice.

"She's more than a girl," I said as I sat up straight in my chair. "Her name's Serena, and she's everything to me. I'm back here for her."

Floyd nodded, and I saw by the knowing look in his eyes he understood who Serena was. He didn't say anything about her, but he knew.

When he finally spoke, he asked in a hesitant voice, "So she's like her father with the fighting?"

I dismissed that with a wave of my hand. "No way. She's nothing like him. She's good and sweet, and there's a gentleness to her I've never seen in anyone else in the world. She has no idea how hard this fight is going to be for me."

His eyebrows raised, like he couldn't believe what he was hearing. "And you're here for her? Sounds like suicide to me."

"I didn't have a choice. When the woman you love needs you to lay it all on the line for her, you do it without a second thought, no matter how bad things might get for you."

Floyd rolled his eyes. "I always had a feeling there was more hero than villain in you, son. So you're doing this for the love of a woman. Still sounds crazy to me, but if anyone can do this, I'm betting it's you."

I patted him on the shoulder for the vote of confidence. "Thanks, man. Now I guess we just have to hope he doesn't bring in another goddamned behemoth to fight me and I might get out of this in one piece, more or less."

"I don't know who he has lined up for you. He hasn't given me the card yet. He knows I've been working with you, so I'm not surprised he's keeping it to himself. Maybe he'll have you fight one of the guys I've run past you in the last three weeks," Floyd said hopefully.

"Yeah, maybe. If that's the case, I might be okay."

Robert wouldn't be putting me up against any of Floyd's guys. Nope. He was going to bring in someone who could hurt me so the message he wanted to send would come through loud and clear.

This stray was good enough to call his son in front of his friends, and he was good enough to do his dirty work, but he wasn't good enough for his daughter.

Chapter Sixteen

Serena

"WHAT TIME IS it? Why didn't you wake me up?

I sat up in bed, still trying to shake the sleep from my head. How long had I been asleep?

Ryder opened the curtains and pointed to the darkness outside. "It's around seven, Rip Van Winkle."

"That's Miss Van Winkle, thank you. Why does it look like you were going to leave without even saying goodbye?"

A sheepish look crossed his face, and then he smiled. "You looked so peaceful lying there, so I figured I'd just let you sleep and see you when I got back."

My head clear of the nap I'd taken, I understood what he meant. I didn't like it.

"I want to go with you tonight, Ryder."

He shook his head and winced like he was in pain. "No way. I don't want you anywhere near that place, Serena. That's no place for someone like you.

I'll see you when I get back. We can have a late dinner and relax together."

I swung my legs off the bed and walked over to hug him. Wrapping my arms around his waist, I pressed my cheek to his chest and heard his heart beating wildly. "I've seen seedy places before, honey. I'm sure it's not that bad."

Gently pushing me away, he held me at arm's length and shook his head again. "It's dank and nasty, but it's not what it looks like that worries me. I don't want you around the kind of people who go to these things. Just stay here and wait for me."

"Why? What kind of people are we talking about? My father goes to these fights, right? I can't imagine him in any place where I couldn't fit in. I'll be fine."

Ryder frowned and knitted his brows in worry. Cradling my face with his rough hands, he sighed. "You have no idea what your father's like, Serena. Trust me. This isn't the kind of thing you should be around. The crowds get ugly. Between the drinking and the drugs and the fights, it's no place for someone like you."

I covered his hands with mine and leaned my cheek into his palm. "I'm not some China doll you have to worry will break easily. I can handle this. I promise."

He stared down at me, doubt filling his green

eyes. "Not this. Please just trust me. Not this."

"You're scaring me, Ryder. What's this about? Why don't you want me to be there for you?"

Backing away, he turned away from me and said in a low voice, "I don't want you to see me like that, Serena. It's not how I want you to think of me."

I slid my arms around him and leaned against his back. So much larger than me, he made me feel small, but his strength made me feel brave.

"You don't have to worry about how I'll think of you because you're fighting. It's nothing to be ashamed of. I'll be the proudest person in that building watching you, win or lose. It won't matter to me."

Turning in my hold, he pulled me close and hugged me tightly to him. "Please, Serena. Don't do this. Stay here and wait for me. I don't want to fight about this with you."

I looked up and saw real concern written all over his face and his frown deepening. I didn't know what was worrying him, the fight or something else, but I hated seeing him like that.

"Okay, I'll stay here. I don't have to go. I'm feeling a little sleepy anyway, so I'll just wait here until you get back."

He smiled and nodded, but the worry never left his eyes. "Good. I won't be gone long, and when I get back we can watch some TV in bed, okay?"

"Okay." I kissed him lightly on the lips. "Do you want me to have anything for you when you get back?"

"No," he said, shaking his head. "Just you here waiting for me is all I need."

I knew he hadn't told me the whole truth about what would happen in the fight that night. The day before I heard my father discussing it as I passed his office on my way to the kitchen in the main house and the way he was talking about it, Ryder would need a whole lot more than just me after this fight.

For the past three weeks, Ryder had known it too, but he'd done his best to hide the truth from me. He wanted me to think this wasn't going to be much more than two men dancing around a ring for a few minutes while they threw jabs at one another, but I'd done a little research and knew underground fighting wasn't like that at all.

I loved him for trying to shelter me from the awful truth of what he would endure that night, but I knew better than to think just seeing my smiling face when he returned would be enough. I just hoped and prayed he wouldn't need much more than a hot bath to soak his sore body in and an ice pack or two.

Ryder slipped a black t-shirt over his head and turned to face me. With a forced smile, he said, "Wish me luck."

"You won't need it. You're going to do great

tonight."

He kissed me, his lips lingering on mine like he didn't want to leave. Holding my hand, he backed away until he had to let go of me and walked out of the apartment.

As the door clicked shut, I whispered, "God, please let him be okay tonight. Don't let my father win."

I didn't care if Ryder beat the hell out of the guy he went up against. I didn't care at all about this stupid fight. I just wanted my father to finally understand that no matter what he did and no matter how many obstacles he threw in front of us, Ryder would do whatever he must to make sure we were together.

As the minutes ticked by to the time I knew Ryder would be fighting, my stomach twisted into knots from my fear that he wouldn't come out of this okay. What if my father had found someone bigger and stronger to ensure he lost? Would Ryder be able to defeat someone like that?

I didn't know. All I knew about this kind of fighting was what I'd read online. Everything about it sounded barbaric and horrible. I couldn't imagine seeing two men savagely attack one another like animals just to entertain a crowd.

A knock at the front door tore me from my

thoughts about what he'd have to endure, and I answered it to find my father standing alone outside. He looked down his very straight nose at me, inhaling a deep breath before he let it out slowly.

"I was surprised to see you didn't go with Ryder when he left for his fight," he said in that way that told me surprise wasn't at all what he'd felt. I suspected disappointment was closer to the truth.

But why?

"He didn't want me to go. From what he says, it's no place for someone like me. Or you, for that matter, Dad."

My father narrowed his dark eyes until they were barely slits. "I think it would be good for you to see where your boyfriend came from."

"You mean the man you refer to as your adopted son? You think I should see where he came from? Why do you act like you're any better than he is? He fought and you ran the fights. Doesn't that mean that he was an employee all along? Is that what your problem is with us together? You'd rather me be with someone like Oliver who had money?"

"Get your coat, Serena. It's time to go."

His command left little room for more argument, and to be honest, I didn't want to hear his answers anyway. I also had a burning curiosity about seeing Ryder fight. My father thought it would make me turn away from the man I loved, but I knew better. It didn't matter what Ryder did before he came into my life.

All that mattered to me was who he'd always been to me once he got there, and nothing I'd see from his fighting would change that.

I did as my father ordered and followed him down to the limousine waiting for us outside the garage. We said nothing to one another the entire way there. I stared out the window as the car rolled into a section of Baltimore that seemed to be an endless line of old warehouses near the docks. I'd never spent time in this part of the city, only once making a wrong turn and ending up here on my way to meet some people in Inner Harbor. It wasn't the type of place a young woman in a sports car should be alone at night.

The car came to a stop, and I looked out the window to see busted windows and graffiti covering the brick exterior of the building in front of us. A light flickered on and off inside a room on the main floor giving the place an eerie feeling I hadn't expected.

I turned to look at my father and asked, "What is this?"

Matter-of-factly, he answered, "A building I own, but people like Ryder call it The Pit. It's where fights are held."

"And this is legal?"

His mouth turned up into a smirk, and he shook his head. "Legal or illegal. Doesn't matter here. Watch where you step when you get out. There's glass and other things you don't want to cut yourself on all over the ground."

He leaned forward to tell the driver to wait for us there and then got out of the car without another word to me. I opened the door and saw garbage and glass like he'd warned me about, and as I walked toward the building, I saw syringes strewn about, evidence that his claim of legal or illegal, neither mattered here was right.

I swallowed hard thinking about Ryder spending his days and nights here before he came to the estate. This was no place for anyone to live.

My father led the way around to the side of the building, and we entered through an old metal door that slid open with a terrible scraping sound to reveal a dark hallway with a single dim light at the end of it. It reminded me of a horror film I'd seen a few years ago set in an abandoned factory where a killer tortured teenagers he found before dismembering them and hanging the body parts on meat hooks like fleshy trophies for him to admire. Every victim walked down a hallway just like the one we were in before they met the man who eventually killed them.

I only watched that movie once, but I still had

nightmares about it.

"Nice place, isn't it?" my father asked in a teasing voice.

"Well, you own it. Maybe some lights would be nice," I snapped back as my shoe crushed a piece of glass I suspected had once been part of a lightbulb.

"Lights draw attention to things. Better to keep things in the dark," he answered curtly before stopping at a second sliding metal door.

He turned to face me, and I barely made out the contours of his face it was so dark. "If I were you, I'd stay close, Serena."

His cryptic warning only served to make me more terrified of what I'd see when that door opened, but I didn't want him to know how frightened all this made me. Working to sound casual, I said, "I didn't want to be here in the first place, so I have no intention of wandering off."

"Good. Ready?"

I was anything but ready for what lay beyond that sliding metal door. All I could think about was how much this place felt like a real-life horror story and that the man I loved had actually lived here at one point and now was forced to return to fight because my own father wanted to punish him.

Why I still had no real idea. It could have been one of a hundred reasons. With Robert Erickson, you never knew exactly why he wanted to see you suffer. Sort of like that monster in that horror movie.

The door lurched open and on the other side sat a huge empty room. Dimly lit, it looked far less ominous than the hallway we just left. Chunks of concrete and metal lay scattered around the floor so I had to navigate a path behind my father, who seemed to know exactly where to walk. People milled about along the walls talking like they were in a bar or a restaurant and not some abandoned warehouse with the remnants of what the building used to be scattered around them.

In the distance, I heard the sound of a crowd yelling and cheering. My heart skipped a beat, and I suddenly found it hard to breathe. I knew this would be difficult for me after reading about what Ryder and fighters like him did in their matches, but being there and hearing those people screaming while two men beat up on one another felt too real and I stopped, unable to go on.

My father realized I'd fallen behind after a few steps and turned around to glare at me. "I told you to stay close. Come on. If you don't hurry, you're going to miss it."

I struggled to get my feet to move, but I caught up to him, even though I honestly didn't know if I wanted to see Ryder fight anymore. When it was some abstract idea I could read about and be horrified by, I thought I might be able to handle it, but now that I'd actually see him hurt another person, or even worse, be hurt, I didn't know if I could do it.

The lights in front of us flickered again as we left that big empty room and walked into a cavernous area of the warehouse. We passed a tiny walled-off area, and as I walked by, I saw some men waiting around for their fights and others bloodied and bruised who had obviously finished their matches.

But I didn't see Ryder anywhere.

The crowd grew quiet for a moment, and we drew closer to where it looked like over a hundred people stood watching. I couldn't see what they were looking at because I wasn't tall enough, though. Then I heard a man's voice announce the names of the fighters up next.

"Ryder Rhodes and Jake Turner. You're up!"

As I anxiously waited to see what this Jake person looked like, silently pleading with God to not let him be too big, the pounding of a drum beat and some song I'd never heard before boomed in the air around me to introduce him before it changed to a different song and a male singer's voice screamed, "I'm back!" and the crowd went wild again.

"You know the rules, so get out there and first one to give the signal loses!" the man shouted.

My heart slammed against my chest as I remembered reading these fights had no real rules like boxing or even MMA fights. I stood on my toes to see, but it was no use. The men around me were too tall.

As if my father had anticipated this, he waved someone over and instantly a man set a wooden bench down beside me and held his hand out to help me up onto it. The crowd began to holler and cheer as I tried to thank him, and when I looked out over the sea of people at the empty space in front of us, my breath caught in my chest.

Facing one another were Ryder and a man with a shaved head no less than six inches taller than him both dressed only in shorts and barefoot. Hulking and vicious looking with tribal tattoos all around his neck and up the back of his head, the guy looked like the kind of monster who belonged in a place like this.

Ryder stood looking at his opponent, sizing him up as the man walked around like he was stalking him. My heart clenched at the mere thought that in seconds I'd helplessly watch the man I loved be attacked by this beast. I wanted to scream out for him to get away and come home with me before he got hurt by the animal in front of him.

Afraid of what would happen next, I turned to see my father grinning like all of this pleased him to no end. He practically licked his chops at the possibility that Ryder would be injured right there in front of his eyes.

A greasy-looking man yelled something and the fight began. The giant who looked like a Skinhead charged at Ryder aggressively, like he wanted to end the fight in one swift attack. Ryder barely got out of the way of the man's fist, but after it missed his face it landed on his left shoulder with a loud thud of his knuckles against Ryder's muscle.

I knew it hurt by the look of pain that instantly covered his face, but I was thankful that he hadn't gotten hit in the other shoulder I knew had been injured before. The crowd around me booed loudly and screamed for the two of them to hit each other. The heartlessness in their voices chilled me to the bone. They didn't care who got hurt or how bad. They simply wanted their lust for pain to be sated.

The giant lunged at Ryder again, this time landing his fist squarely on his jaw. His head flew back and he stumbled away looking stunned by the shot. I held my breath while I watched the man chase after Ryder, not letting up his attack and hitting him twice more with punches to his face.

Why wasn't he hitting back? Was the guy too big or was Ryder too surprised to retaliate?

I screamed for him to hit him hard, as bad as the raving fans around me. "Get him, Ryder!"

But the guy kept coming, landing shots to his face and his chest, while Ryder continued to be on the defensive. Within the first few minutes, he'd already taken more blows than I suspected my father's goons had given him, but he still remained on his feet.

"Put him away!" screamed a drunken man in a denim jacket next to me, practically frothing at the mouth at the promise of a man being beaten for his entertainment.

My stomach roiled at the sight of such unhinged desire to see someone suffer. With every punch and every scream, I felt sick. My head began to pound, and finally, I couldn't hold back anymore and I jumped off the bench down to the ground, doubling over as I vomited onto that filthy floor.

Behind me, the crowd screamed for Ryder and the man to beat the hell out of one another, but I couldn't watch anymore. I threw up until there was nothing more in my stomach, and then I dry heaved until my sides hurt so badly I wanted to cry.

I couldn't stay there and watch the man I loved be attacked, so as soon as my body stopped trying to purge itself, I ran away. Ignoring the shards of glass and concrete, I hurried to that room I saw on my way in, praying I wouldn't be able to hear the horrible sounds of the crowd telling me Ryder had been beaten.

Two fighters stood talking in the middle of the room and turned to look at me when I entered. I didn't belong there, but I didn't care. I found the nearest seat, a metal folding chair that looked like it had seen better days, and tried to put all that ugliness going on just a few yards away out of my mind. My heartbeat pounded in my ears, thankfully blocking out the sounds of the crowd and the fight. Covering my face, I closed my eyes as tears began to flow down my cheeks.

"Are you okay?"

Looking up, I saw a young guy staring down at me with worry in his pale blue eyes. He seemed so fresh compared to the scene in the next room. Too fresh to be a fighter even though he clearly was dressed for exactly that.

I nodded. "I'm fine. Thanks."

He motioned with his chin toward where the fight raged on. "Too much for you to handle?"

The image of Ryder being pummeled by that monster ran through my brain, and I shuddered. "A little. I'll be okay in a minute."

"Okay. Do you want a drink of water? I wouldn't drink the tap water here, but you can have some of my bottled water," he said as he held out the bottle to offer it to me.

Parched from throwing up, I gladly accepted it, thankful for even a sip of liquid to pass my lips. "Thanks."

I took a swig of water and let it linger in my

mouth for a moment before swallowing cautiously, my throat raw from vomiting. Handing the bottle back to him, I thanked him again and said, "What's your name?"

"Dylan. And yours?"

"I'm Serena. I appreciate you being so nice to me. I guess I'm not really cut out for this kind of thing. Are you a fighter?"

He stood up a little taller and puffed his chest out. "Yep. Tonight's my third fight. I'm looking for my third straight win."

"How old are you?"

Looking around, he answered, "Eighteen."

Nothing on him said he had reached anywhere close to eighteen, from his baby face to the peach fuzz sitting above his lip he probably called a mustache to that innocence in his eyes. No, he definitely wasn't eighteen.

Before I could challenge him on that fact, I heard someone just outside the room bark out, "We need water and ice! Get out of the way!"

I turned around to see the greasy man who'd started the fight and another man carrying Ryder in. His body was covered in blood, and his head hung limp so his chin rested on his chest.

My heart stopped as I stared at him in horror. Had he lost the fight? Was he unconscious?

Chapter Seventeen

Ryder

FLOYD'S VOICE BOOMED his orders around me as I struggled to keep my eyes open. I knew I'd taken an ass kicking, but I wasn't sure if I'd won or lost. I hadn't showed the signal to give in, but that guy had fucked me up pretty good. Whatever happened, I lasted a hell of a lot longer than I'd thought I could after being out of the scene for over two years.

"Ryder…Ryder, can you hear me, son? Answer me if you can hear me."

I opened my eyes and saw him crouched down in front of me with a worried look on his face. Nodding, I croaked out, "I hear you."

"You must have a guardian angel watching over you, son. There's no way he should have given up after what he did to you. You must have gotten into his head, although I can't for the life of me figure out how when he spent the whole time pounding the fuck out of you."

His words floated in and out of my head, but I

"

understood the gist of them and smiled. "So I won?"

"Fuck if I know how, but yeah, you won," Floyd said shaking his head in disbelief.

"I wasn't going to give the signal. He was going to have to knock me unconscious, but I wasn't going to give up, Floyd."

Closing my eyes, I cringed from how much my body hurt. Two years away from fighting had taken its toll, and that behemoth motherfucker Robert found to pound the piss out of me made it a hundred times worse. But even though I felt like a truck had driven over me, I hadn't given up.

I wouldn't let Robert have the satisfaction of seeing me surrender. Not in this fucking fight in this shithole of a place of his and not with Serena. If he wanted me out of her life, he'd have to kill me because I wasn't fucking giving up.

Something cold pressed against my right shoulder, and I opened my eyes to see Serena holding an ice pack to my arm. Was I dreaming? Had I blacked out from the pain?

"Serena? Are you here?" I asked, reaching over to touch her hand to see if she was real or all in my mind.

She kissed me on the cheek and whispered, "I'm here, Ryder. You won."

"Why are you here? I told you I didn't want you to see me like this. This is no place for you."

"My father brought me to see you fight. I didn't see much, though. I'm sorry. I thought I could handle it, but it was so awful. How did you stand him hitting you all those times?"

Fucking Robert! What kind of father would bring her to this place? Son of a bitch! I didn't want her around this. She didn't deserve to be around these fucking animals who screamed for us to beat the fuck out of one another.

"I'll be okay. I can handle it."

"It looks a lot worse than it is," Floyd said with a chuckle. "That blood isn't his. He took a good beating tonight, but he busted up that guy's nose pretty good."

I looked down and saw my chest covered in blood. Smiling, I looked up and said proudly, "He must have been a bleeder because I didn't think I got him that good."

"He had you down on the ground, so I couldn't see what was happening, but it wasn't long after that he gave up. Did you say something to him?" Floyd asked as he wiped the blood off my skin.

Shaking my head, I tried to remember doing anything after he took me down. All I remembered was hitting the ground hard with all his weight coming down on top of me and me punching him as hard as I could because I was pretty sure I was fighting for my life at that moment.

"Ryder, where are you hurt?" Serena asked as she examined my shoulder. "Is it just your shoulder and where he hit you in the face?"

I didn't know how to answer her. Everything on me hurt. Every inch of my body ached with pain. But I didn't want her to worry.

"I'll be fine. I just want to get back home and soak in a hot bath."

From the doorway, I heard Robert say, "Two years and you still have it, son."

I turned to look at him as Serena grabbed my hand and squeezed it. "Yeah. I guess I do."

"Some people are made for this. Looks like that junkyard dog is still inside you," Robert said with a chuckle.

I wanted to tell him to fuck off. He'd set up this fight so I'd get my head crushed in, and I hoped he lost a ton of money when I didn't.

Instead, I just nodded and turned toward Serena. "You should go home. I don't want you around this. I'll follow you in a few minutes."

She shook her head. "No. I'll go home when you do. I want to stay and be here for you."

In her dark eyes, I saw a look of defiance. I knew Robert saw it too because he said nothing else before turning on his heels and walking away.

I touched her cheek and smiled at how strong she could be when she had to. "You know he's going to be furious you didn't go home with him."

Serena leaned in and gently kissed me. "He can be as furious as he wants. I'm pretty damn pissed off that my father brought in that animal to fight you."

"I'll be okay. I just wonder what he's going to throw at us next."

Cradling my face, she stared into my eyes. "I don't care what he does. Let's get you home and into that bathtub."

Floyd tapped me on the leg, and I looked down to see him smiling. "Maybe I was wrong, son. It wouldn't be the first time, and it won't be the last, I'm guessing."

He was wrong. Whatever I had to do to be with Serena was worth it. No matter how bad the beating I had to endure, I'd take it if it meant being with her.

Not many people in the world had shown me they were worth the effort, but she had. I'd sworn I'd protect her that night when I found her bleeding out in that bathtub, and I intended to live up to that promise. Whatever Robert or the world threw at us, I'd handle it to be with her.

✦   ✦   ✦

I EASED MYSELF back against the pillows and let the air out of my lungs slowly, all the while conscious of every ache and pain in my body. I may have won, barely it seemed now as I replayed the fight in my mind hours later, but it sure as hell didn't feel like I'd gotten the best of anyone.

Robert's handpicked opponent for me had been just what I anticipated. Big and out for blood.

And I'd suffered from the very deficiencies I knew I'd had since the moment he announced I'd be fighting in three weeks. Two years away from fighting had nearly crippled me at the beginning of training, and twenty-one days hadn't been enough to overcome that.

So I wasn't surprised when he came at me and I moved like my feet were encased in concrete. What I hadn't expected was how easily my mind slipped into that place it had always gone to when I faced another fighter in the ring. All the noises of the crowd faded away when that moment finally came a few minutes in after he'd hit me hard with a few shots, and after that, I was in the zone.

Unfortunately, the zone didn't trump my lack of training for all those months, and I was slower than I'd been a couple of years ago. Too much whisky and good food and not enough time in the gym made for a very different fighter. I overcame my slowness, though, so by the time he got me down onto the ground, I was that unbeaten champion I used to be.

I sighed, but it came out as a low groan that made me sound like I was some broken old man. Floyd had warned me when he first met me all those years ago that fighting would make me old before my time. A cocky sixteen-year-old, I thought he was full of shit, but now I wondered if he might have something there.

"Are you okay? You made a noise," Serena said.

Nodding, I forced myself to smile. "Yeah. I'm fine. Come here."

She sat down on the bed next to me and gingerly touched my shoulder. "Did he get you bad in this one?"

I looked down at where her fingers touched my skin. "No. Your father must have forgotten about my bum shoulder. Good for me, huh?"

Her hand slid down my arm, and she gently traced the outline of one of my skull tattoos. "You know, a couple of years ago, I wouldn't have believed he would ever do something like that. It sounds naïve, but I didn't think he was that kind of person. I mean, I knew he wasn't an angel, but things like this? Things like setting you up to get beaten? I wouldn't have thought he was capable of that."

The sadness in her eyes told me she still had a hard time accepting who Robert Erickson was. "It's okay. I told you. I'm tough. I can handle it."

She frowned and shook her head. "It's not okay. None of this is okay. I promise you when I finally find out where my mother is, we'll leave here and you'll never have to do anything like this again."

Her voice trailed off, and she looked away. "I don't ever want to see you fight like that again."

Even though lifting my arm felt like someone was pushing on it with all their weight, I turned her head toward me and forced away the pain to say, "I'm sorry you saw that. I never wanted you to see me in that place."

Serena's face twisted into an expression of sadness. "It was so brutal, Ryder. And all those people screaming for you and that animal to hurt each other like it meant the world to them. I've never seen anything like that."

I lowered my arm to my side and nodded at her description of the crowd. "I used to wonder who was worse—me for fighting or them for wanting to see us crush one another."

Her brown eyes grew wide with concern. "Don't ever think there's something wrong with you or anyone who does that. I didn't mean it that way. But to hear those people yelling for you to hurt another human being made me sick to my stomach."

Thinking back on all those nights I spent in The Pit, I couldn't understand how used to that life I became back then, but it was all I knew. I dreamed of better, but that's all it was. Dreams.

"That's not a world you belong in, Serena."

She shook her head and squeezed my hand. "Not just me. You don't belong there either. I can't believe you lived in that place at one time. All that broken glass and concrete all over the floor. I hate even thinking of you spending night after night in that place."

"Don't think of it then. It's all in the past. Now I'm here with you and we're going to figure out somehow to get us away from all this."

Serena leaned over me and softly kissed my lips. "Here where you belong."

Where I belonged.

I knew Robert would disagree with that claim. His attempt to show Serena that I was exactly what he called me that first night he brought me here—a stray—had failed. He thought she'd see me fight and be disgusted like her sister would be.

That she'd think of me as some lowlife who wasn't worthy of her love or her bed and he'd succeed in chasing me away. But that hadn't happened because he didn't understand her.

I never worried if she saw me fight that she'd turn away from me. That wasn't who she was. Serena cared too much, loved too much to just turn her back on us. I knew that.

What I didn't know was if I could be that fighter I'd been so long ago. Now that I knew I could be, I didn't fear what Robert threatened me with next. Let him throw fighter after fighter at me. I'd take them all on, and the more I fought, the more I'd win.

See, he didn't understand me either.

I SLOWLY OPENED my eyes as every ache and pain came rushing back into my consciousness. Turning to look at Serena, I found an empty spot where she was when I drifted off last night. The light coming through the bedroom window told me it was day-time, so why wasn't she next to me in bed?

The events of the night before rambled around my brain as I struggled to wake up. Each hit I'd taken in the fight replayed in my mind, and the corresponding hurt for each one registered as I gradually came alive again.

Fuck, I needed something to take the edge off the pain or I'd be no good until sometime around lunch.

I swiveled my head left and right to look for a bottle, but I found nothing. Not even a glass on the nightstand.

"Serena?"

"I'm in the kitchen. Give me a minute."

Something in her voice made the hair on the back of my neck stand up, so I eased myself out of bed one leg at a time and slowly made my way out to her. But she wasn't in the kitchen or in the living room.

"I thought you said you were in the kitchen," I said, confused why she would have lied.

"I meant the bathroom," she said in that same strange tone.

So she was lying about something and likely more than what room she was in. I walked as quickly as I could get my aching legs to go into the bathroom and found her standing in a pair of panties and one of my t-shirts with her back turned and looking at something. She covered it with her hand so I couldn't see.

"Serena, what's wrong? Why are you acting so weird?" I asked as I tried to peer over her shoulder to see what she was hiding.

She turned to face me but put her hands behind her back. "Nothing's wrong. I just got up early and had to go to the bathroom."

Her expression was riddled with guilt, but why? What had she done? "So why did you tell me you were in the kitchen?"

"I just got my rooms mixed up," she said, avoiding making eye contact with me. "It's no big deal, Ryder."

Before I could ask what she was hiding behind her back, she continued, "How do you feel? Are you sore? I can get you something to make you feel better. Why don't you go back to bed and I'll bring it in?"

As she spoke, I looked in the mirror and saw what she was hiding from me. I took a step toward her and reached around to grab a white plastic pregnancy test.

Holding it up between us, I leveled my gaze on her. "Why didn't you want me to see this?"

Serena hung her head and quietly answered, "Because I thought you might be unhappy."

I looked down at the result and saw two pink lines. Looking up at her, I asked, "Well, what does two lines mean? Yes or no?"

She grabbed it from my hold and sat down hard on the lid of the toilet. "It means yes."

"Yes?" I repeated as the answer sunk into my brain still muddled from sleep. "You're pregnant?"

"Yeah," she said, frowning as she nodded.

"You don't seem happy. Why?"

Without looking at me, she fiddled with her fingers in her lap. "I remembered how you reacted last time. I wasn't sure how you'd feel about this with everything going on."

How I'd behaved when she told me before she was carrying my child flashed through my mind, and I cringed at how much an asshole I'd been questioning if it was mine. No wonder she wasn't sure I'd even want to know about it now.

But things weren't the same as they'd been then. She wasn't another man's wife and we wouldn't have to hide the good news that we were having a baby.

I reached out to take her hands in mine and

pulled her up. Taking her in my arms, I hugged her to me. "I'm sorry I was such an ass then. I'm happy you're pregnant, Serena. I don't care what's going on with everything else."

She looked up at me and smiled. "So you're not worried?"

Cradling her face in my hands, I shook my head. "Worried about what?"

With a sigh, she said, "Everything. My father. You fighting. The fact that we're still stuck here. Everything."

I shook my head at each mention of the very things that could make our life together misery. "Nope. None of that worries me."

"And you're happy about the baby?"

"Yes. Very happy. Are you?"

She hesitated for a second and took my hands in hers to kiss them. "I want to be happy. I'm happy it's your baby. I just worry that something is going to happen that's going to make having this baby difficult."

I hated seeing her worried when this should have been one of the happiest days of her life. I wanted her to love the idea of us having a baby, not spend nine months concerned that at any moment her father would do something horrible to ruin it for her.

"I think it's perfect timing. You're going to find

your mother any day now, and then the baby will get to know his grandmother while you're getting to know your mother."

Serena smiled and then her eyebrows raised into her forehead. "Wait a minute. His grandmother? How do you know it's a boy? Maybe it will be a girl."

"That would be okay too. I don't care if it's a boy or a girl as long as it's healthy and you're healthy."

"You promise? I've spent my life living with a father who wanted sons. I'd never want a daughter of mine to go through that."

I kissed her sweetly and pressed my forehead to hers. "I promise. I'm not like him, Serena, so you don't have to worry. Girl or boy, it won't matter to me. I'll love him or her as much as I love you."

She slid her arms around my neck and hugged me. "Then I'm happy we're having a baby."

"Good. I don't want you to worry about anything. I'll take care of you and whatever comes up. You take care of our baby. Deal?"

Lifting her head off my chest, she smiled. "Deal. It's going to be okay, isn't it?"

I looked down into those dark eyes still with a hint of worry in them and nodded. "It's going to be more than okay. I promise."

As she sighed contentedly, I silently made plans to ask Floyd if he would be able to find me more fights. With a baby coming, I needed to make a lot more money as fast as possible so no matter what happened with Robert, we'd be able to leave so our child wouldn't grow up around the ugliness of his world. I'd won last night, and if I trained even harder than I had for the past three weeks, I knew I could win even more.

The undefeated champion who hadn't lost in nearly twenty matches still existed inside me. Now I needed to bring him back to life so I could provide for the woman I loved and our baby. I didn't want to be in the position where Robert would be able to dictate our lives anymore, and fighting would finally let me take Serena and escape this place.

We'd just have one more to leave when the time came, and I had to make sure we didn't lose that chance because I didn't do enough to ensure it happened.

Chapter Eighteen

Ryder

DURING THE DAY, the warehouse seemed devoid of the ugliness that it routinely saw at night when fights were held there. Sure, it looked just as bad with the broken glass and concrete lying all over, but until Serena mentioned that, I had never noticed those things. Or maybe I had back when I first came to the warehouse and I'd been there so many times since that they didn't even register anymore.

I made my way toward the back to a room where Floyd sometimes spent time in the afternoons, if he wasn't out finding fighters. I saw nobody as I walked through the main room that functioned as The Pit at fight time, but in the distance I heard what sounded like Floyd's old AM/FM radio he liked to listen to sports talk radio on. It always sounded more like static intermittently interrupted by someone talking, but he refused to give in and buy something from this century to listen to.

Sometimes when I lived at the warehouse, I'd sneak in at night and take the radio back to my room so I had something besides the sound of my own breathing and my thoughts to listen to as I fell asleep. It wasn't much, but even static made me feel like I wasn't completely alone in that big building.

Then in the morning, I'd make sure to return it to his makeshift office before he arrived so he didn't think I'd stolen it. Floyd and I weren't exactly great friends back then, but I knew better than to piss him off by taking that damn radio.

I peeked my head around the doorframe to see him sitting hunched over in the old office chair he'd had before I met him. The frayed fabric seat routinely seemed to possess a mind of its own, so when he sat down in it, sometimes he flailed around for a moment before getting his balance. It was funny to watch because he looked like a first timer on a pair of ice skates, and sometimes he landed on his ass flat on the floor.

"Hey, Floyd, what's up?" I asked, interrupting him as he listened to some guy talk about the Raptors and their shitty season so far.

He popped his head up from next to the radio and smiled. "Ryder, what are you doing here? I figured you'd be resting today back at Mr. Erickson's estate. You still live there, right?"

I took a few steps into the room and stopped at his question. "Yeah. Why?"

Turning the knob on his radio, he lowered the

sound just enough that all that came out of that dirty little white box was static and carefully spun around in his chair to face me. "No reason. He was none too pleased last night, so I wasn't sure if he lowered the boom on you and sent you packing."

I'd escaped Robert's wrath after the fight, and I hadn't seen him since. That meant that when I did see him when I got back to the estate, I better be ready because he'd likely be pissed.

Floyd didn't need to know any of that, though, so I brushed off his worry and smiled. "No, I'm still there. I imagine he has more fights planned for me, so why send away your gold mine, right?"

Chuckling, Floyd lost his balance as the chair took control and nearly tossed him onto the floor. Flailing his arms, he grabbed onto the old desk, sending the calendar from 2003 he'd never replaced skidding across the top, but finally steadied himself.

"You nearly made me fall out of my chair, son. Be careful how you talk about Robert Erickson around here. These days, he's the only show in town. Make him angry and you'll find yourself frozen out, gold mine or not."

I pretended not to care about Robert's overwhelming power in the local fight scene and shrugged. "I think you need to be careful of that chair, Floyd. That thing is going to kill you one of these days. You'll get bucked off and crack your damn head against that desk. And speaking of being careful, what was with the music last night? We used to have to keep the lights low so the cops wouldn't know what was going on here, and now the fighters get theme music?"

"Not anymore. Hell, Robert Erickson has the cops in his back pocket, so now he wants a little more show. I thought Aerosmith's Back in the Saddle seemed right for you. Did you like it?"

"I guess," I said, not sure how I felt about this new policy. The fights didn't need any help with the show part. They were already more circus than sport.

He looked around toward the desk like he was assessing the damage it could do if his chair decided to throw him and then turned back to face me. "No kidding, Ryder. I don't know about the other parts of your life, but in fighting, Erickson's the only show in town."

"About that," I said, hesitating for a moment, unsure I could trust Floyd.

It didn't matter, though. I needed to take the chance that I could if I ever wanted to make enough money to take care of Serena and the baby away from her father's estate.

"I want to fight more, and I was hoping you'd be able to find me some matches." I stopped and then added, "And I wouldn't want the boss to know about it. This would be between you and me."

He stared at me for a moment like he didn't understand the words I'd said, and then he slowly leaned back in his chair. When he knew it wouldn't throw him off, he answered, "Didn't you just hear me? Robert Erickson controls the fight circuit here. No if, ands, or buts about it. And don't even get me started on the between you and me business. If he found out I was arranging fights on my own for you, he'd have my head."

I understood Floyd's fear of Robert, but I couldn't let that stand in my way. I needed to convince him if I ever wanted to make enough money.

"There's got to be somewhere else I can fight, Floyd. You know about the fight scene for a hundred miles each way. There's got to be something. I need to make money and a lot of it. You'd be making out on the deal too, though."

He sighed and blew the air out of his lungs slowly. "This has to do with that girl, doesn't it? Erickson's daughter. Jesus H. Christ, Ryder, do you know what you've gotten yourself into?"

I knew all too well what I'd gotten myself into, good and bad. Nodding, I tried to get Floyd to focus on the fighting and leave the rest of it to me.

"I can travel. You say where and I'll be there. Come on. You know people. I know you do. And they can't all have Erickson's hand around their throats."

"Why don't you just ask your girlfriend for the money? As his daughter, she's got to be able to get her hands on all the money you two could need. She probably has a trust fund or something like that. All rich kids do, don't they?"

Shaking my head, I said, "No, she can't. It's got to be me."

Floyd smoothed his greasy comb-over against his head and sighed again. "I might be able to make some calls. I don't know. I can't promise anything. It would be a pretty far haul, though, because you'd have to get beyond the long arm of Robert Erickson, and that's no easy task."

His reference to the long arm of Robert made me smile. At one time, that's how I thought of myself as I acted like the muscle to enforce his demands on all those people I threatened for him.

"I don't know what the hell you're smiling about, son. This has disaster written all over it. What do you plan to do when he finds out? Because it's not an if situation but a when thing. He will find out, and when he does, God help you. I know what he'll do to me, but he seems to have a special place in his heart for you and when you do this, you're betraying him. I just want you to be honest with yourself."

Nodding, I knew he was trying to look out for me, but that didn't matter now. All that mattered was finding enough money to get Serena, the baby, and me away from her father. Whatever I had to risk meant nothing.

"It'll be fine, Floyd. Just find me some fights, okay? I'll make it worth your while, and I promise if anything happens and he finds out, I'll take the blame. I won't even mention you."

Floyd rolled his eyes. "Like he won't know. He's not stupid, son."

I walked around him and the possessed chair to find a sheet of paper and pen in the desk to write down the number of the phone Serena and I used back when she lived with Oliver. Handing it to him, I said, "Call me at this number only. Nobody knows about this one. As long as it's not on a night when I'm fighting for him, I'll be there wherever I have to go."

He scanned the number and then looked up at me with concern in his eyes. "Are you sure you know what you're doing, Ryder? I mean, she's beautiful. I get it. And she's crazy in love with you. That's clear. But she's Robert Erickson's daughter."

"I have to do this. Just help me, okay?"

"Okay. I'll see what I can do. If I find out anything, I'll let you know. Take care of yourself, son."

I shook his hand and before I turned to leave, I said, "Thanks, Floyd. I won't forget this."

He chuckled and rolled his eyes again. "Let's hope the two of us live long enough to forget all of this."

✧   ✧   ✧

WITH MY NEW job fighting for Robert again, I didn't know if that meant I got a reprieve from having to check in with him each morning. I hadn't before I left to meet with Floyd, and by the time I got back to the estate it was nearly one in the afternoon. Dreading having to talk to Robert but unsure if I didn't that something worse would happen, I walked to his office and hoped I'd find it empty.

Unfortunately, luck wasn't on my side and I saw him sitting at his desk staring vacantly at his laptop. Taking a deep breath, I prepared myself for anything he could throw at me and knocked on his door.

He looked over toward me with that same blank expression he'd worn while he stared at his computer, and for a few moments, he said nothing. Finally, he waved me in and said, "Just the man I want to see today."

I couldn't help but think that was a complete lie. After the fight last night, he'd been less than thrilled, probably because he put a nice chunk of money down on a bet against me. Part of me liked the idea of him losing big like that, but another part knew I'd end up paying for it in the end.

Taking a seat in one of the chairs in front of his desk, I worked to remain calm and look as casual as possible. Not that any of that mattered much. Whatever he felt toward me wasn't going to change just because I looked relaxed in front of him. It very well might make him all the more eager to torment me.

As long it was just me he wanted to torture, I could handle it.

"So how about that fight last night? I don't know, son. You have the magic touch, it seems, even after all this time," he said as his mouth spread into that all-too-familiar and terrifying crocodile grin.

My mind hurriedly wavered between cockiness and humility in the answer I had to give. I wanted to brag because I'd won a fight against the guy he put me up against after two years away from that world and three short weeks of training. I should have been able to brag, but something told me humility might be a better route with Robert now.

"I don't know about the magic touch," I said, not even convincing myself with that. "He gave me a good run for my money, but I guess I was just luckier than he was last night."

Robert's smile faded, and he squinted angrily across the desk at me. "Don't bullshit a bullshitter, son. I don't believe this humble pie act for one second. That fighter I met that night who was cocky as all hell is really the person you are, so don't bother to pretend you're someone else for me. I know better."

I shrugged, still unsure what he wanted from me. "Well, it wasn't an easy fight, and that's not being anything but truthful. He kicked my ass around that ring for a long time before I got the best of him."

Pursing his lips, he tilted his head left and right. "Now that we can agree on. He certainly did have your number for a majority of the fight. I'm afraid Serena didn't take you getting beaten up as well as I had hoped. She always was a bit delicate."

The idea of Serena as delicate almost made me laugh out loud. He had no idea how strong she could be when she wanted to. I would have thought her having me take care of Oliver after what he did to her proof of her strength, but Robert seemed to have forgotten that already.

"The Pit is no place for someone like her. I hope we can agree on that," I said and stared directly into his dark eyes to let him know I didn't appreciate what he'd done with that stunt bringing her there. That it hadn't worked was beside the point.

He remained silent for a long moment, his gaze fixed on mine, and then as if none of what we'd just said interested him, he announced, "I intend on having you fight from now on. I wasn't sure of my decision until last night, but after watching you, I think your talents are best served with fighting."

If he thought what he said should bother me, he had underestimated me and overestimated how much I liked working for him as his muscle. At least when I fought I could respect myself. It wasn't the best thing for me, but it was a hell of a lot better than threatening people on a daily basis.

That shit sucked the soul of me.

"Okay. When's the next one scheduled for?" I asked and enjoyed the look of surprise as it came over his face.

Had he expected me to be afraid or worried when he said I had to go back to fighting? He had no idea.

"I don't know yet. I have to say that I'm a little shocked you aren't fighting me on this. I thought you'd be unhappy going back to that life."

I shook my head and shrugged. "No. Like you said, fighting is where my talents lie. Why should I pretend that's not true? God gives each one of us a talent. Mine just happens to be beating the hell out of people in the ring. Now if you told me I had to go back to living in that warehouse, I'd be unhappy. That part of the life I wouldn't want. But the fighting? It's who I am, I guess."

Pleased with my answer, he nodded his head and smiled. "Smart man. Too many people in this world refuse to accept what they're good at."

"Not me. I know exactly what I'm good at. Just let me know when the match is. In the meantime, I'll be training hard for it. I've got an undefeated streak to keep up. One and counting."

My joke made a full laugh explode out of him. "You really are a cocky son of a bitch. Always have been. I should have seen that in these past months. I won't make that mistake again."

I stood to leave and smiled. "I hope you bet on me last night. That would have been a big mistake if you didn't."

His face quickly fell and his mouth turned down in a frown. "Yes, that would have been a mistake. Yet another I won't soon make again."

He didn't stop me on my way out of his office, and as I walked back to my apartment, I had to admit I felt pretty damn good with how this day had gone so far. My body still felt like a bus had hit me and then backed over me just for shits and giggles, but that would fade in a few days. In the meantime, hopefully Floyd would find me a fight so I could start making money to get Serena and me the hell away from this place and the long arm of Robert Erickson.

I got back just as Serena finished talking to someone on her phone, and as she pressed END, she hung her head. Had Robert done something because of that comment I made? Damnit, I shouldn't have been so fucking cocky!

Wrapping my arms around her, I took her into my hold and felt her trembling. "Hey, what happened? Whose ass do I have to kick?"

Serena laughed at my joke, but when she looked up at me, I saw that same sadness in her eyes I saw the first night I met her. "That was the private detective. He hasn't found anything yet on my mother. That wasn't what upset me, though."

"What was it?" I asked, wondering what this guy could have told her to make her so upset if he hadn't located her mother yet.

She let out a deep sigh. "He told me that it's possible she might not be alive and not to get my hopes up too high. Ryder, I can't believe she's dead. I can't. Not after finally being able to look for her now."

"Don't listen to him. He doesn't know anything yet, so he's just trying to cover his ass. He can't say anything for certain. It will be okay. He'll find her. I believe that."

Pressing her cheek to my chest, she rested her head there and sighed again. "I just want to hear some good news for a change. Is that too much to ask?"

I stroked her hair and smiled that I could be the one to give her that good news she so wanted. "Well, how about this? I'm not working for your father as one of his thugs anymore. He wants me fighting exclusively instead."

She looked up at me and knitted her brows. "I don't know if I should be happy or just more worried after what I saw last night."

Cupping my cheek with her palm, she tenderly ran the pad of her thumb over the spot just under my eye where that guy had gotten me good with a few punches. "I hate the idea of you fighting again, Ryder. What if you get hurt?"

I reveled in the feel of her touch on my bruised and battered face and closed my eyes to enjoy it. "I told you. I'm tough. I can handle it."

"I don't want you to have to be tough all the time," she said sadly.

Opening my eyes, I knew my news hadn't been good in her opinion. I couldn't tell her about what might happen with Floyd, but I wanted her to see my fighting again was a good thing.

"This is our first step toward freedom. Believe me, Serena, me back in the ring is good for us."

Her dark eyes opened wide at my mention of us finally being free of her father and this place. "How is it going to help us get away from here?"

I gently ran my hand over her belly and smiled. "I can't get into it all right now, but trust me. I'm going to do whatever it takes to get us away from here before the baby comes. I promise."

She wanted to ask more questions about how I'd do it, but I stopped her with a kiss, loving how her lips felt on mine. No matter what it took, I'd do this for her.

For us.

Chapter Nineteen

Serena

RYDER'S SECOND FIGHT came less than a week after his first one and even before he'd fully healed from the beating he'd taken at the hands of that monster of my father's. He practically begged me to not go back to that terrible place to watch him, but I couldn't bear to just wait at the apartment, not knowing if he was hurt and helpless to do anything.

My father stood at the back of the crowd like last time and said nothing to me as I took my position near him. Not that I wanted to spend even a minute with him since he decided risking Ryder on a weekly basis for the crowd's enjoyment was more important than any happiness I might hope for. Even seeing him made me so angry my hands curled into fists so tight my fingernails dug into my palms.

I marveled at the people around me as they yelled for the fighters to beat the hell out of one another. Drunk and high, they grew practically rabid as the night wore on, so by the time Ryder and his opponent's fight came up, the people around me were almost foaming at the mouth at the chance to watch one of them crush the other just a few feet away.

Any attempt to ignore the crowd's screams for blood would have been a waste of time, but even as I stood there listening to the madness around me, my heartbeat slammed in my ears from the terror racing through me at the mere thought that Ryder might be hurt this time.

He believed in his ability to fight, and it wasn't that I didn't believe in him. I just couldn't get used to knowing he had to pummel another human being so my father didn't throw him out into the streets. I wondered if living in the streets would be better. At least then we'd have our freedom.

But Ryder insisted fighting would be the way we'd get away from my father and everything that came with him, and I believed him. He'd saved me too many times for me not to.

A middle-aged, overweight man elbowed me in the arm and spilled his beer down the front of my shirt in his excitement at Floyd's announcement that Ryder's fight would be next. Turning his chubby red face toward me, the man grinned and slurred, "Sorry. I just got psyched at hearing my fighter is up next. I used to watch him a couple years ago when he had a nearly twenty fight undefeated run going. He was fucking good."

I stared at the man's corpulent face as he talked and wished I could be happy for his pride in Ryder's accomplishments back then. All I felt was revulsion, though. His lust for seeing people hurt one another for his pleasure sickened me as much as my father's did. The only difference between them was this man wasn't a billionaire who could order a man to put himself in harm's way because it gave him some sick thrill to throw his power around.

"Just watch him tonight. He's a beast!" the man said gleefully before he turned his attention back toward the ring.

Floyd let the crowd know that Ryder and a fighter named Seth would be up for that night's marquee match. Howls erupted from the men and women in front of me, followed by fist bumps and high fives as music like the last time thundered throughout the room.

I struggled to see what was happening without the aid of that bench from the last fight, but I didn't want to ask my father for anything, so I craned my neck and peered between the heads of everyone in front of me. In truth, I didn't want to see the fight. I just wanted to be sure that Ryder didn't get hurt, and if he did, that I was there by his side for him.

Amid the cheers and shouts for the fighters to hit one another, the fight began just as the other one had. Ryder's opponent rushed at him with the aggression of a wild animal that made my stomach tighten in fear he'd defeat him in just the first seconds of the fight. The guy looked like a man possessed, and I turned away, afraid to see the damage he'd do to Ryder.

When the crowd let out a collective cheer, I couldn't help but look to see if he'd hurt him, but when I let myself see what had happened, it was Ryder who had done the hurting, not that Seth guy, who now stood holding his bloody nose and mouth.

I waited to see if the fight would end, but instead I watched as Ryder lunged at the man, taking advantage of his weakness. Over and over, he landed punches to the very areas that were already injured until the man was covered in blood. Horrified, I wished for nothing more than for this to be over, but it went on for what seemed like an hour more until Seth gave up and Floyd announced that Ryder had won again.

He turned around to face the crowd in front of me, and the sight of him covered in that man's blood made my stomach turn. I couldn't reconcile the person I knew and loved with this creature, a man more barbaric than anything else. He smiled as Floyd declared him the winner again, and I saw he wore that same look that I saw when we were alone and he was genuinely happy.

My gaze met his for a brief moment before my

attention was directed to the man he'd just beaten. Bloody and defeated, he hung his head and hobbled away. I knew I should be happy that he had suffered and Ryder hadn't, but I wasn't.

At least not about that.

I turned to see my father grinning as Ryder walked past him toward the dressing room. Unlike the horror I felt at all I'd seen that night, my father looked blissfully happy at what he'd witnessed. If ever I'd thought I understood him, watching him enjoy these fights made me realize I didn't know him at all.

The crowd talked about the fight as I hurried to the room to join Ryder. I didn't want to hear any more of their assessment of his abilities. I'd seen the beast that man had claimed he was. I didn't need to know what else they thought of him.

He sat in that same chair as I found him in after the first fight, but this time he was alert and joking with another man who'd fought earlier. I walked in and waited for him to finish, and when he turned to face me, still wearing Seth's blood all over his chest, I had to stop myself from throwing up.

"Come here," he said, waving me over to stand near him.

I hesitated, and he looked down where my gaze sat fixated on all that blood. He asked the man for a towel and quickly wiped his skin, leaving faint traces of the evidence of his brutality behind.

"Better?" he asked with a smile as I slowly walked over to him.

"Yeah," I said, forcing myself to smile back at him.

"Floyd wants my help with something, so I'll get home as soon as I can, okay?" he said, surprising me with the news he wasn't coming home with me.

"Oh, I thought we would go together."

Taking my hand, he brought it to his lips and kissed my fingertips, looking up at me so sweetly I couldn't be upset with him. "I promise it's for a good reason. I won't be long, and when I get home I won't even be sore since that guy was practically no challenge at all."

I cringed at the memory of Seth being helped away. "Okay. I guess I'll go then."

Ryder stood and tenderly took my face in his hands, whispering against my lips, "I love you, Serena. Don't worry. I'm okay."

Closing my eyes, I willed my nose not to smell the putrid mixture of sweat and another man's blood that flooded over me. "Okay. I'll see you at home."

"Hey, what's wrong?" he asked before kissing me gently on the forehead. "Why won't you look at me, Serena?"

All I wanted to do was run away from the sounds and smells of that place, but I opened my eyes and tried to pretend none of it bothered me like it did. "I just feel a little tired. That's all."

He gently slid his hand over my stomach and smiled, but when I looked down I saw that man's blood had stained his fingers. Needing to get out of there, I quickly kissed him goodbye and hurried toward the door.

I barely made it out of that room into the hallway before I inhaled deeply, desperate for fresh air in my nose and lungs. I took another breath in and turned to leave, but out of the corner of my eye I saw my father and a female I'd never seen before. Blond and young, she had a cut-rate look to her.

Just my father's type, if his past choices in mistresses were any indication.

"Serena, did you get to see our champion?" he asked as they approached me.

"I have to go."

I took a step to leave when my father stopped me by grabbing my arm. "I want to introduce you to someone. Serena, this is Kitty. Kitty's an old friend of Ryder's."

Stopping dead, I looked back at the woman and studied her for a moment as he told her who I was. She reeked like she'd bathed in cheap perfume, its overly sweet odor hanging heavy in the air around her, and my stomach began to roil once more. Her face looked younger than mine, but something in her eyes said she'd lived a much harder life than I had.

Good. I liked the idea of Kitty, Ryder's old friend, living a hard life. What I didn't like was her being there to watch him fight.

I opened my mouth to ask exactly why she'd come there but stopped myself. I knew what my father was doing. First, he tried to make me dislike Ryder as a fighter, and when that didn't work, he now wanted to make me see the female he'd been with while I was in Italy.

But it wouldn't work. I wouldn't let him win.

Extending my hand to shake hers, I said with the biggest smile, "It's nice to meet an old friend of Ryder's. You must not have seen him in a long time."

Surprised by my comment, Kitty started to speak but nothing came out. Finally, my father spoke up and said, "You said you had to go? I think we're going to stop in and see our boy before we leave."

Kitty may have been flustered, but my father hadn't given up on trying to rattle me. It didn't matter. Ryder was with me, not some sad stripper.

"Nice to meet you, Kitty. Dad, tell Ryder I'll have dinner waiting for him when he gets home. I know how hungry he gets after these fights. Night!"

I spun on my heels and headed down the hallway to the door without giving my father a chance to say anything more. I knew his tricks better than anyone in the world. I also knew Ryder loved me, and no visit from some cheap girl hanging off my father's arm would change that.

As ONE HOUR turned to two and then three, I worried my father had done something to keep Ryder from returning home, but he finally walked through the door looking like a conquering hero from some hard-fought battle.

Tossing his duffel bag on the floor, he lifted me into his arms and kissed me like he hadn't seen me in ages. Setting me down on the ground, he asked, "How are you feeling?"

"I'm fine. I just had to get out of there," I said, hoping he didn't ask me why. I didn't want to say anything to ruin his triumph from winning that night.

"I know you don't like watching, but I won, and that's a good thing," he said with a look of genuine happiness in his green eyes.

"I know. It was just hard to watch," I admitted, hating that I felt that way almost as much as I hated seeing him hurt that man.

Ryder took me by the hand and led me to the bedroom. Sitting down on the edge of the bed, he lifted his shirt over his head and tossed it toward the chair in the corner. "See? I'm okay?" he said as he showed me his arms to prove he hadn't been hurt.

He pulled my hand to his chest and pressed it over his heart, but all I could think of was Seth's blood covering his chest. I knew my revulsion registered in my expression, and I didn't want it to, but there was nothing I could do to stop it.

I yanked my hand from his hold and pulled it away from him. The look on his face told me he didn't understand my behavior.

"Serena, what's wrong?"

"Nothing. It's nothing. Probably morning sickness. That's all."

The mention of the pregnancy made him smile, and he lowered his gaze to my belly. He gently placed his palm against it and said quietly, "I'm doing everything I can to make sure you and your mother are safe, little one."

But all I saw were those fingers that had been stained with another person's blood. It wasn't visible now, but that didn't matter. I saw it as clearly as I had back at the warehouse, and the memory made me want to run away.

My body tensed under his hand, and Ryder looked up at me with that same confused expression that had been in his eyes a few moments before. "What's going on, Serena?"

I hung my head and turned away, unable to face him. "I can't get the image of you hitting him out of my mind. All that blood…covering you and him…and then watching him limp away after you defeated him. All I can see is his blood on your skin."

Ryder stood and kissed me tenderly on the lips. "Ah. Okay, follow me."

He walked to the bathroom and stopped on the bathmat next to the tub to step out of his clothes. His body looked like it always did—beautiful, muscular, and hard with all those tattoos—and I knew what he planned to do, even though he'd obviously showered before he came home.

Stepping into the tub, he turned on the water and in seconds the steam fogged up the glass around him. I stood there wanting to show him it wasn't him that made me pull away. It was the violence and the blood.

I couldn't let him go on believing the very sight of him sickened me, so I undressed and stepped into the shower with him. He turned around and looked surprised for a moment before he set the soap down on the ledge and kissed me.

"I'm sorry, Ryder," I said after he pulled back and smiled at me. "I didn't mean to be so callous. That you'd do this means so much."

"It's a little soap and water. I'd do anything to make you happy, Serena," he said in a low voice as the water ran down his face.

"It's so much more," I answered, hoping I would

be able to explain how much this simple gesture meant to me. "I don't mean to be like this. I know there are a million other women you could be with who wouldn't have a problem with the fighting. They wouldn't have tried to kill themselves and then when you saved them, they wouldn't have been awful to you. I'm sorry I'm like this. I truly am, Ryder."

His smile never faded as I ran through the list of things I'd done. He gently pushed my hair off my forehead and cradled my face in his strong hands, staring down at me with that look of intensity I so loved to see in his green eyes.

"Don't ever be sorry for being you, Serena. I love you just like you are. I wouldn't change a thing about you, so don't think I would. I don't want any of those million women. I only want you."

I touched his hands and closed my eyes as my emotions began to overtake me. Hanging my head, I didn't try to stop the tears. I didn't know why I was crying, though. Was it because even after basically telling him what he did for us to be free sickened me, he still cared? Was it for how he made that man suffer while the crowd cheered for him like he was some kind of hero?

I didn't know. I just knew it felt good to cry. Ryder held me to him, and as the water streamed down over us, I marveled at how wonderful he truly was to me. After everything he'd had to endure to just be with me, he still only thought of my happiness.

"It's not so bad. Really," he whispered against my cheek. "Even the guy I beat is safe and warm in his bed by now. It looked worse than it was."

I opened my eyes and he looked down at me with that sexy smile that never failed to make me feel like I was melting inside. "I don't think I'll ever get used to it. I can't bear to think of you doing that. I can't explain it, but it physically hurts me to think of you in pain."

"It's just for a little while. Don't worry. I'm built for this."

"Don't say that. Nobody's built to be in pain, Ryder."

"I'll only do it long enough to make the money we need to get away and then I promise never again. Wherever we go, I'll get a normal job so you'll never have to worry about me being in pain again."

I ran my fingertips over his chest and down onto his stomach. "Please let that be soon."

"It will be. For now, I have something better in mind to focus on," he said as he gazed down at me with hooded eyes and licked his lips.

His mouth covered mine and his tongue slid between my lips in a kiss that succeeded at least for the moment in taking my mind off all the things troubling it. He moaned low and pushed his hips forward to press his hard cock against my stomach.

"I need to be inside you, Serena," he said in a deep voice as he slid his palms down my back to cup my ass.

Lifting me to waist-level, he gently pressed me back against the black marble tile wall and stared down at me like his every thought was of me. I moaned softly at the first touch of his cock, and then he thrust his hips forward to fill me in one incredible motion.

For a moment, he remained still, simply staring into my eyes with a look so powerful I couldn't look away if I wanted to. I didn't want to. I could have stayed right there looking into his eyes and been happy forever knowing I was the complete focus of this man.

I slowly dug my heels into his lower back, wanting more, though. I wanted to feel him slide in and out of me, fucking me like only he could.

He buried his hands in my hair and tugged, making pain skitter across my scalp, before he pulled back and plunged his cock into me hard and fast enough to take my breath away. Clinging to his neck, I held on, my hips seeking to match the rhythm of his as he fucked me.

"Tell me you still love me, even though you hate what I do," he mumbled low in my ear as he pumped his cock into me.

I pushed his head away and kissed him long and deep, hating myself for how I'd made him doubt my feelings for him. "Always, Ryder. It doesn't matter what you do. I'll still love you."

Over and over, he plunged his cock into my body, and over and over, I begged him to never stop, loving the feel of him fucking me as much there in that shower as I had from the first time he made me his.

My release washed over me, and I came hard on his cock before he came, filling me until it dripped down between us. I collapsed against his chest, content in his strong arms.

"I love you," I whispered against the wet skin of his neck before kissing the spot just below his ear. "Every single part of you."

He gently pulled me back so I could see his face. There in his eyes I still saw the intensity I adored in him. "I couldn't do it if I didn't have you and the baby as the reason. I need you to know that."

"I thought you loved it."

Ryder shook his head. "I love you. I love our baby. Fighting is what I have to do to take care of you. If it wasn't for you, I'd hate it just as much as I used to. It's only because I know it's a means to a much better end that I don't hate it now. But it's for you and the baby."

He set me down on my feet and knelt in front of me as he slid the soap along the inside of my thighs, cleaning me of all the traces of our time together. When he finished, he said nothing but turned off the water and wrapped me in a towel.

"I'll meet you in the bedroom," he said sweetly before kissing me softly.

When he and I were alone like this and no one else in the world intruded on our time together, I believed everything he promised would come true. That it meant he'd have to be that brutal man everyone else saw him as didn't matter.

All that mattered was when he was with me, he was the only person in the world I completely trusted with my heart and soul.

Chapter Twenty

Serena

FOR NEARLY FIVE months, Ryder trained constantly and when he wasn't training, he was fighting in matches my father arranged for him. Each night, he lay next to me with his hand on my belly as it slowly grew, the two of us sharing a secret no one else in the world knew about. We talked about my OB-GYN visits and decided we didn't want to know the sex of the baby until he or she was born. He told me about all the places we could go once he made enough money, and even though he never explained where he was making this money since I knew my father wasn't the source, I didn't ask, in part because I didn't want to know what he had to do to make it and in part because I wanted him to know I trusted him.

But I never stopped worrying that one of those nights he'd step into the ring and when he left, he'd look like Seth did staggering away in defeat.

Every day felt like the calm before the storm. My father seemed happy with his new arrangement with

Ryder, smiling in that way that didn't terrify me whenever I saw him. With each successive win, he made more money and Ryder's worth grew in his eyes.

Still, I had to wonder if that might be a double-edged sword. The more valuable he became to my father, the more reluctant he'd be to just lose him when Ryder and I could finally leave. We had no plans to tell him in advance, but if he wanted to find us, there'd be nothing in the world that would stop him. We could go to the ends of the earth, and if he decided he wouldn't let Ryder go, it wouldn't matter what we tried.

We'd be trapped here until my father decided neither of us were worth enough to care about.

His obsession with making me as miserable as possible seemed to ebb away as his fascination with Ryder fighting again grew. I wanted to believe none of it would matter when the time came and we could finally escape, but I knew with every day there existed a chance that all our plans would be for naught.

The private detective called me once a week to update me on his progress in finding my mother. My hope for seeing her again slowly dimmed as each time he said he hadn't located her, yet I wondered if I'd waited too long to look for her and she was long gone from the world. If that were the case, I knew who to blame.

Then one night Ryder returned home and I smelled a familiar, sickening scent. It wafted through the air as he walked toward me and leaned down to kiss me hello. I'd know that perfume anywhere. The sweet smell of it had never left me.

He smiled and patted my belly. "How are my two favorite people doing tonight?"

I inhaled deeply, taking the odor of that cheap perfume into my nose. "Where do you go when you go to train with Floyd?"

The surest look of guilt crossed his face before he answered, "The warehouse. When there aren't fights going on, we train there."

"Why don't you train here in the work out room? It's got all those machines, so I imagine you'd be able to lift or whatever you do, right?" I asked, my stomach turning from that smell.

Ryder chuckled and shook his head. "Training means more than just lifting. Most sessions, I spar with another fighter. I can't do that here."

"Is this training something you're keeping from my father? I can't figure out how you're making money for us to get away from here if you're just training every day."

His expression grew serious and he drew his eyebrows in. "Yeah, this needs to be kept a secret, Serena. Just trust me. I'm doing what I have to so we can get away from here."

I didn't want to not have faith in him, but I knew where that perfume had come from. He wasn't going to tell me the truth, though. I knew that too.

"Are we getting close to what we need?" I asked as sweetly as I could while inside every insecurity I had began to plague me just like when I first heard Ryder say he'd been with someone named Kitty.

He smiled and I wanted to believe him when he said, "Almost. I think before the baby comes, we can be out of here."

I watched for any sign of betrayal in his eyes, but I saw none. That smell hadn't come from nowhere, though.

"What do you say I get changed and we take a walk in the garden? It's not too cold out tonight," he said as he walked into the bedroom.

"It's April, Ryder. It's still chilly out at night," I yelled into him.

He poked his head out of the bedroom and smiled. "It's got to be fifty degrees out now. We'll only take a short walk if you get cold."

I couldn't say no to him when he looked so eager, so I got up and headed in to get my shoes. "I usually don't go out into the garden until it's warm enough that I don't have to wear anything on my feet. Fifty might be a little chilly for that."

Ryder stopped getting dressed and turned to face

me. "Instead of that, let's just stay here."

"Why? It sounded like you wanted to go, so let's go."

"No. I don't want to anymore."

He pulled me into his arms, and I knew what the sudden change was about. He'd remembered how much I hated wearing shoes. We hadn't talked about it in months, but he'd remembered.

"Are you sure?" I asked, wishing I hadn't just minutes before been thinking of him cheating on me with Kitty.

He nodded and kissed me on the forehead. "Yeah. Staying right here sounds much better."

I wanted to get lost in the feel of his arms enveloping me. I wanted to love how incredible his body felt against mine and revel in his touch.

But all I could smell was that overly sweet perfume of hers.

Her.

Pushing him away, I shook my head. "I can't. I can't do this."

Ryder grimaced, like my words hurt him. "Can't do what? Have me hold you? What's going on, Serena? What's this about?"

"Nothing," I said as I turned away, still shaking my head as I tried to get rid of the memory of that sickening smell that threatened to choke me if I stayed there next to him.

He followed me into the living room and grabbed my wrist to stop me. Spinning around, I looked into his eyes and saw anger like I'd never seen from him. Then I looked down at where his hand encircled my arm and felt how strong he was holding me there. He had the ability to crush grown men with his hands, but never before had I thought about how he could do the same to me.

Not until now.

"What's going on, Serena?"

I didn't want to do this with him, but my emotions began to spill out all over and the words tumbled out of my mouth before I could stop them.

"You fucking smell like her! Is that where you go at night instead of training? Do you go to see her? While I sit here pregnant and worried sick that you'll be hurt the next time you fight, are you with her?"

Ryder released his hold on my hand and shook his head. His mouth hung open in shock for a moment before he finally said, "I fight for you. For the baby. For us to get the fuck away from here."

"Then why do you smell like her? All I can smell is that disgustingly sweet perfume all over you," I choked out as my heart contracted at the thought that he actually might have been with her.

"Like who? There is no her, Serena. There's you and no one else. Just you," he explained, his eyes pleading for me to stop.

But I couldn't.

"That stripper you were with while I was in Italy. The one who was with my father at your fight that night. You smell like her, and it's making me sick!"

"Kitty?"

I hated the sound of her name coming from his mouth. "Don't say that name here. Don't!"

Taking a step toward me, he wrapped his arms around me, holding me tight. "Serena, I would never go with her. I made a mistake back then, but don't let what your father's trying to do tear us apart."

Even though I knew he was right, I couldn't stop myself from pushing him away. Not that it made much difference. He was so much bigger and stronger, so with every shove, he just held me tighter.

"I can't stand the thought that you were with her, Ryder," I sobbed into his chest as my emotions finally took over. "Tell me you didn't go with her now."

"Serena, I wouldn't do that," he whispered against the top of my head. "Don't do this. Don't let your father win."

I looked up and searched his face for the truth. Why would he smell like her if he hadn't been anywhere near her?

"Does she come around and watch you train, Ryder? Is that why her perfume is all over you?"

He shook his head. "I haven't seen her since that night, Serena. She's no one to me, so I don't even think about her. I don't know why I would smell like her."

Inhaling, I smelled his skin and now it seemed like that awful perfume was nowhere to be found. God, was I losing my mind? What was wrong with me?

Ryder tilted my head back and stared down into my eyes with a look that made me feel safe. "I love you, Serena. You're having my child. How could you think I'd ever be with anyone else?"

"I don't know. I hated seeing her that night, Ryder. She still cares about you, and there she was about to walk in where I'd just been like she was welcome too."

He pressed a soft kiss onto my forehead and smiled. "She wasn't welcome. I would have been happy to never see her again. Your father wanted to cause a fight between us, so he brought her around. I was actually surprised you didn't mention it that night."

I closed my eyes, embarrassed that I'd let myself think Ryder would ever be unfaithful to me. "I didn't want to talk about it. Ever."

His lips grazed mine before brushing my ear as he whispered, "Then we won't. I'd much rather talk about a million other things. Or not talk at all."

The smile in his voice made me open my eyes, and as he pulled back, I saw that look of desire all over his face that made him so sexy. I loved how much he wanted me, even now that my pregnancy had begun to make my body much softer and rounder than usual.

"I don't want to talk either."

He slid his hands up under my sweater to lift it over my head before unhooking my bra. Tossing it away from him, he cupped my breasts in his palms and smiled.

"You look so beautiful standing there looking up at me like that. It reminds me of that night in my room when you brought me the chocolate you made. I felt like the luckiest guy in the world, you know that?"

I ran my finger along the top of his pants and teased the head of his cock. "Because I made you chocolate?"

He winced as I took hold of him and began stroking. "No. Because you had that same look in your eyes. Like I was the only man in the world you wanted inside you."

Slowly, I dropped to my knees and flicked my tongue along the length of his cock, all the while staring up at him to see the effect I had on him. His eyes rolled back and his face grew relaxed before he let out a soft groan.

"You were the only man I wanted inside me. For weeks and weeks, I'd wanted to touch you, to feel your body against mine."

Ryder opened his mouth to say something, but I slid my mouth down the length of him and heard him fall silent, except for that sexy sigh he made whenever I sucked his cock down to the base. Just hearing that sound made me want him inside me.

And then he buried his hands in my hair and tightened them slowly until an erotic mixture of my pain and his pleasure filled me as he hoarsely groaned, "Oh, baby…God, I love the feel of your mouth on my cock."

Nothing was more masculine than when he told me how much he loved me sucking his cock. Not the way he fought and not even the way he protected me. I gazed up at him and watched the pleasure wash over him as inch by inch I slid him into my mouth and then slowly eased up to the tip of his cock, sucking the head between my lips in that way I knew he loved.

His hand pushed down on my head, forcing me to take all of him, and he fed me his cock as I closed my eyes and he set the pace. Above me, he grunted his desire and moaned with every swipe of my tongue across his skin, and I loved every second of it. I didn't care that with each tug of my hair, pain fanned out across the top of my head. All I wanted was to take him to that place that only I got to see.

That place where he wasn't my father's employee or a fighter in the ring. He was just a man in love with me who I could bring to his knees simply by sucking his cock.

"Fuck…don't stop…right there. Look up at me. I want to watch you take it all," he moaned as I felt the first twitch of his release against my tongue.

Grasping the base of his cock, he held it tightly as he came, flooding my mouth as he shuddered. I could have watched him like that forever, spellbound by how beautiful he looked because of what I'd done.

When he finished, he knelt down in front of me and kissed me softly on the lips. "I swear to God every time you do that, I think I'm going to black out. Now's your turn."

I shook my head and smiled. "Maybe in a little while. I just want to enjoy how incredible you look right now."

He grinned a guilty smile as he traced his finger across my lips. "I love you, Serena. You don't have to worry about me ever wanting another woman. You're all I want."

"Because of what my mouth can do?" I asked with a giggle.

"No," he answered, shaking his head. "Because of what every part of you does to me."

He looked at me like I was the only one in the

world that mattered to him, and I wondered how I could be so stupid as to think that he'd ever want someone like that Kitty.

✧　✧　✧

EVEN THOUGH I didn't want to let my jealousy get the best of me, I couldn't help it. No matter how I tried, I couldn't get the image of Kitty draped all over Ryder out of my mind. Every time he left to go to a fight or train, my mind filled with thoughts of them together.

"I'll be back late tonight," he said before kissing me goodbye.

"Okay," I said sweetly as I decided this would be the night I found out if my suspicions were correct or if I was just being stupid and irrational. "I'll try to wait up."

Ryder smiled. "I like when you do, but if you're too tired, don't push it." He cupped his palm over my belly and added, "You're sleeping for two, you know."

When he said cute things like that, I wanted to believe that nagging feeling in my gut was totally wrong. That he would never betray me like that.

"I don't think that's how it goes," I said as he lifted my t-shirt to press a soft kiss to my skin.

He looked up at me and grinned. "Well, however it goes, I understand if you can't wait up. I'm not fighting, so you don't have to worry."

"Okay. I'm going to try, though."

"I love you. See you in a few hours."

As he backed up toward the front door, I blew him a kiss. "Love you. Stay safe."

The door clicked closed, and I hurried to put my shoes on and grab my sweater. Ryder was driving my car, so I ran down to the garage and jumped into the one car I knew my father wouldn't even notice was missing. Never a fan of Janelle's choice of buying a Jeep, he never drove it and made sure it was parked in the part of the garage farthest from the door to the house.

At the front gate, I turned on the charm and lied through my teeth to the grey-haired guard named Jack, eliciting a promise from him to keep my leaving a secret since I was going to buy my father a surprise birthday gift. He'd worked at the gate since I was a little girl, and although I knew he might tell someone I'd left the estate, I gambled that he wouldn't since my father never even bothered to call him by name, instead referring to him as Joe or John or any other name that began with J when he bothered to speak to him at all.

Just as I suspected, Ryder drove to the warehouse. I parked far enough away to hide the Jeep but still be safe and snuck in through the side door into the dark hallway that led to the huge center room where the fights occurred. I stayed in the shadows to avoid being seen, and crept along the wall until I reached the room where the fighters' dressing room.

I saw no one in there, so I continued toward the second door and opened it a sliver to peek through. Unlike when I'd been there for fights, the place seemed empty now. Floyd, another man, and Ryder stood in the area where matches were held talking before the two of them backed away and began sparring while Floyd barked out commands for what he wanted them to do.

Was this what he'd been doing all these weeks? How was he making enough money so we could get away by hanging out with Floyd here? And was this where he saw Kitty and she left her disgusting perfume on him?

A noise startled me, and I turned around to see Dylan standing in the doorway to the dressing room. Quickly, I walked toward him, explaining, "I was just watching. Please don't tell Ryder I was here, okay? He doesn't like me to see him fight, and I'm sure he'd feel the same way about his training."

Dylan smiled and motioned toward the dressing room. "Come in here. They'll be going at it for a while since I'm not due out there for another half hour."

I followed him, and we sat down across from one another on two metal folding chairs. Hoping he could put my fears to rest, I asked, "Is it usually only you guys here at night like this?"

He didn't seem to understand what I really meant and simply nodded. "Yeah. There are a bunch of us who spar together."

"Nobody else comes here?" I asked, hoping to lead him to where I wanted him to go.

"You mean like your father? Nah. He doesn't show up except for fights. Nope, nobody other than us."

"I guess it's strange to see a female here then," I said, sure that would help him talk about any other women, if any ever came around.

Dylan chuckled. "Pretty much. This isn't like MMA. There aren't females who fight like we do."

His answer made me feel foolish for doubting Ryder even as it made me happy. I'd been so stupid. He probably hadn't even smelled like her that night. My mind was probably just playing tricks on me.

I stood to leave, pleased with the answer I'd gotten. "Well, I guess I better go. Don't tell Ryder I was here, okay?"

"No problem," he said with a smile. "I don't think he'd mind. With all the training and fighting he's been doing, you guys probably don't see much of each other anymore."

"You're right. He's here training every night, it seems."

"That's in addition to the two or three fights he's in each week. He's got himself on a grueling schedule, but he says he has to. Strike while the iron's hot, I guess," Dylan said, shrugging.

Two or three fights a week? My father only had him fighting a couple times a month, so who was he fighting for?

Was that how he was making the extra money?

A chill ran up my spine as I thought about what my father would do if he found out Ryder was fighting for someone other than him. If Dylan knew, then others did too. How long would it be before someone let it slip and my father learned the truth?

"I better go. Nice to see you again, and take care of yourself."

He smiled at my concern like Ryder did whenever I told him to be careful. "That's next to impossible in this business, but I'll do what I can."

Hurrying out into the hallway, I took one last look at Ryder sparring with that other fighter and then ran to my car. My fears that he was cheating on me were nothing but jealous nonsense, but now I had bigger fears about what my father would do to Ryder when he found out about what he was doing behind his back.

Chapter Twenty-One

Ryder

AFTER EVERYONE LEFT and the warehouse wasn't The Pit anymore but just a vacant building again, I sat in the room that at one time was my home and waited for the pain to subside. If it was just the normal aches and pains from a fight, I could have handled them, but as I sat there on that old metal folding chair wishing I was home submerged to my neck in a hot bath, I knew nothing about how I felt was normal.

I'd had two matches this week, and they'd followed two fights the week before. I'd won all of them, but those wins hadn't come without a price. The guy in the second match last week had been a fucking monster with fists the size of my head. Even though I was faster and ended up running circles around him just to stay on my feet, when he caught me on the right shoulder with his last few jabs, he got me good. Barely able to lift my arm a few inches, I'd been in searing pain nearly every minute since then.

If I didn't have a damn good reason to be fighting, I would have hung it up after that match. But I did, and every night when I returned to the apartment and saw Serena sleeping peacefully in our bed, I didn't have to remind myself of why I said yes to every fight Floyd could get me.

Closing my eyes, I tried to push away the pain in my ribs from that night's fight. The guy I'd defeated had used my sides like a punching bag for the first half of the match, and even though he'd definitely gotten the worse of it after I got back up on my feet, those blows hurt just as bad.

Between my shoulder injury from last week's fight and my ribs from tonight, merely moving hurt enough that all I wanted to do was curl up into a ball and sleep for three days. Hell, I'd take a straight eight hours.

"If I didn't know better, I'd say you're exactly what those people say you are. A beast. I can't figure out how you're doing it, but whatever it is, don't stop," Floyd said as he pulled up a chair next to me.

I opened my eyes and turned to look at him, groaning with each inch I had to move my head. "Right now, I feel like what the beast shit out."

He studied me for a moment and shook his head. "I'm wondering how long you can keep this pace up, Ryder. Four fights in two weeks looks like it took a toll on you."

Moving my head slowly, I looked up toward the ceiling, unsure how long I could keep fighting like this too. I didn't have a choice, though.

I'd barely made enough to get us away from the estate, but with a baby, we wouldn't be able to just stay anywhere. Over the years, I'd saved nearly thirty grand, but by my last estimate, I had to make at least five grand more to be sure we could afford a decent place safe enough for a newborn and everything a baby needed, and that was just for the first few months. I'd get a job doing whatever I had to in order for us to live, but I didn't want Serena or the baby to go without because I hadn't done enough now.

"I just have to make it a little while longer, Floyd. I can do this."

"Well, how much are we talking about here?"

I knew when I told him his eyes would probably bug out of his head. Five grand in our business was like a million dollars.

Without looking at him, I answered, "About five thousand dollars."

The sound of surprise I expected from him didn't come, so I slowly turned my head and looked over at him. "I figured I'd get some reaction from you on that."

He nodded and said, "Normally, I'd say that's a number you're not going to see for a while, but I heard from a friend of mine who got into the fight game a while ago and is doing pretty well for himself. He's a big deal in this town called Keyser in West Virginia. Not anywhere I'd want to spend my time, but different strokes for different folks, you know?"

As Floyd rambled on, my spirits soared at the mere thought that this guy he knew in this place I'd never heard of could get me closer to what I needed to get Serena and me away at last. When he stopped badmouthing this Keyser place, I jumped at the chance to get him to the point of his rambling.

"That's nice, but can your friend help me out?"

Floyd's eyes narrowed to slits. "Didn't I just say that?"

"No. You said anything but that. So what's the story with this friend of yours? What's he up to and how much is the take?"

"Nate's arranging a pretty big event in that town of his. Seems the cops are as crooked as a witch's nose, so he doesn't have any worries in that department. The place is pretty much a dead end in every way, so he's got no shortage of guys willing to risk themselves for even a small payday. It's a typical Appalachian town, you know?"

I thought about what I knew about typical Appalachian towns. The answer was not much. I'd seen something on TV one night when I couldn't sleep about how those places were fucked up from meth and things didn't look like they were going to get better any time soon. Other than that, I never cared to know anything about them until that moment.

But how much money could I possibly make in a place even Floyd had called a dead end? It didn't sound so great now.

"I'm not fighting some meth head, man. I'm desperate for money, but I'm not that desperate. You ever see those fuckers? They look like their faces are peeling off from that shit. And I know from experience guys high on something have the strength of like five guys."

Waving my concern away, he tried to reassure me. "No, no. It's nothing like that. The place is poor as fuck, but it's out of the way enough that big spenders like to bet on his fights. He's good at flying under the radar, if you know what I mean."

Well, that sounded a little better. Still interested, I pressed him to talk money. "Okay, what kind of prize are we talking about, Floyd?"

He grinned and leveled his gaze on me. "You'd end up with just over three grand after I got my cut."

Three grand! That was equal to a couple weeks' worth of fights. I wanted to jump at the chance to make that kind of money, but nothing this good came without having to give something.

"So what's the catch?" I asked, sure he was holding back some important detail.

Shaking his head, he frowned. "No catch. He wants a great fighter to go up against his best guy, and I thought of you."

"So what's the glum face about?"

I still wasn't convinced he wasn't holding out on me.

"I can't believe you would think I wouldn't tell you everything about this. You go down, I go down, so you can trust me."

"Yeah. You know how it is. If something sounds too good to be true, you better believe it is. No probably about it."

Floyd nodded. "Usually, I'd say I agree with you, but not this time. Nate's a decent guy, as far as promoters go, and he wants a good fight more than anything else. I think you can give him that. That's why I told him I'd talk to you about it."

I didn't have to hear any more. The money was good enough for me to travel to some two-bit town in West Virginia, and if Floyd's friend Nate wanted a good fighter, I was his man.

"I'm in. When's the match?"

Tilting his head left and right, Floyd grimaced. "That's the tough part. It's at the end of next week. You've got a fight for Robert just a few days after. Do you think you can do it?"

Whether I could do it or not had nothing to do with the answer I had to give. I needed money and fast, and this fight could give me it.

I stood from my folding chair and felt a whole new group of aches settle into my back and legs. Even Floyd would start to think I couldn't do it if I looked like a beaten up eighty-year-old guy, so I pushed down the urge to groan about how much like hammered shit I felt and flashed him a shit-eating grin.

"I've done it so far. You giving up on me?" I joked, hoping he didn't see how much fucking pain I was in just standing there.

With a smile, he shook his head. "No way. You've got a date with destiny, son. I'm convinced fate loves you, even as she's a fickle bitch with everyone else in the world."

"Good. I'll see you tomorrow then."

He said something about me taking it easy until then, but I wasn't listening anymore. The only thought in my mind at that moment was getting home and making it to that tub.

❖　❖　❖

ROBERT STOOD POURING himself a drink at the bar on the far side of his office as I walked in for a meeting he'd called for with me just an hour before. Thankfully, he hadn't ordered me in for one of his talks the night before because I probably wouldn't have been able to pretend I wasn't in agony. As it was, soaking in the tub for over an hour hadn't helped as much as I had hoped it would, but at least if I had to sit in front of him now, I could act like I wasn't feeling like shit.

He turned around and headed back toward his desk to sit down before he began talking. "So how is training going, Ryder?" he asked in a voice that made me wonder if he knew what I was up to on the side.

"Good, as always. Floyd's got me in great condition, and sparring more often than before has made me even sharper."

All of that was true. The lie was that I was training just for his fights.

Raising his eyebrows, he opened his eyes wide. "I hope he's not working you too hard. I need you in top condition for this next fight, and a tired fighter isn't going to get me what I want."

My blood ran cold for a moment as I studied his expression. I expected he knew how often I trained with Floyd, but did he know the real reason?

"No, I'm good. I'll do what I'm supposed to that night. You don't have to worry."

Robert's mouth turned up in one of his terrifying crocodile smiles. "Oh, I'm not worried. If you don't, Floyd better worry, though, because I'll be looking at what he's been doing with you in the past few weeks."

I hated the idea of Floyd paying the price if I didn't win. He was sticking his neck out as much as I was sneaking around behind Robert's back.

"Floyd's good. He knows the ins and outs of this business better than anyone else I've ever met. He won't do anything to hurt my chances."

"You two go way back. I forgot about that. He was the one who let you live in my warehouse before I found you. I'm just wondering if he's being too hard on you."

A nervous chuckle escaped from my throat. "I'm a big boy. Whatever he's doing in training is nothing compared to what other fighters can do to me. It seems to be working, so why fix what's not broken?"

Robert appeared to think about what I said and nodded. "As long as you don't get broken. I can't make money off a fighter who can't fight."

"I haven't found too many who can do it so far," I joked, hoping our conversation would end so I didn't have to sit there and dissect every word he said in an attempt to figure out if he knew what I was up to or not.

He let out a hearty laugh and threw his head back. "You're still one cocky son of a bitch, aren't you, son? Still that same kid I met that day who'd never been beaten, even though you've had your fair share of losses since then. I can appreciate someone who believes in himself. You remind me a lot of me at your age."

Sure I had no idea what he meant by that, I smiled and nodded while I wished he'd get bored talking to me and turn to that laptop of his. He didn't, though, and changed the subject abruptly.

"How is Serena? I haven't seen her around the house in weeks. Where has she been hiding?"

His sly expression told me he knew exactly where she was, so why ask?

"She's been worried about me, mostly. You saw her that night. My fighting makes her miserable because she's convinced I'm going to get hurt."

"I guess she doesn't share your cockiness?" he asked, raising one eyebrow to punctuate his question.

"Not really. She's not a fan of the fighting or anything that she thinks puts me in danger."

I didn't have to say it, but that included virtually everything I'd ever had to do for him. Working for Robert had put my life in danger from the day I met him in one way or another. The only difference now was I controlled what happened to me in fights.

"So all she's been doing is staying in that apartment of yours and worrying? That doesn't sound like my daughter."

Suddenly, I began to worry this meeting had

nothing to do with what I was doing behind his back but what Serena was doing to find her mother. If he even suspected she'd hired someone to locate her, he'd go to whatever lengths necessary to stop her.

Even if that meant harming her mother.

I couldn't let that happen. Finally seeing her mother again meant too much to Serena.

"Well, she did mention something about finishing her degree," I lied, hoping to force his focus to a topic I knew he'd have something to say about.

True to form, he frowned and shook his head. "That again? I swear that girl doesn't understand how life works. You need to convince her to forget that nonsense. I'm sure you can do that, can't you?"

I struggled to keep the look of disgust from my face. I didn't share Robert's dislike for Serena educating herself. All I wanted was for her to be happy. If that meant getting her degree, then I wanted that too for her.

Not that any of this was true since in just a few months we'd have a baby and school would probably have to take a backseat, at least for a little while. We couldn't let Robert know about the pregnancy, though.

"I'll see what I can do," I answered with all the enthusiasm I could muster for promising to dis-courage the woman I loved from doing what she'd always wanted to do.

Clearly happy with my answer or finally bored with our discussion, Robert opened up his laptop and began reading something as he said, "Good. I look forward to seeing that cockiness in your next fight. And tell Floyd I'll be watching to see if all he's been doing with you is too much."

I stood up and got the hell out of there before he decided he wanted to talk about anything else. As usual, our meeting had been like walking on eggshells, but that's how Robert liked dealing with people. He liked to think he was keeping us on our toes.

The truth was that's how tyrants acted, and he was nothing if not a tyrant.

SERENA MET ME at the door, practically jumping for joy as she wrapped her arms around my neck to hug me. "I can't believe it! It's finally going to happen!"

I held her to me and asked, "What? What's happening?"

She let go of me and kissed me like she hadn't seen me in weeks. "He found her! He found her, Ryder, and I'm finally going to get to see her again."

Tears welled in her eyes as she told me about the private detective finally locating her mother, and for the first time, she called her by name. Alita.

"I just got off the phone with him. He said he finally found her just a few miles away in a house she's been living in for years. After all this time, I'm going to get to meet my mother again. I tried calling Janelle to tell her, but she and Charles are off on another vacation. I'll just tell her when she gets back."

Serena kissed me again and twirled around, ecstatic about the news the detective had just given her. My distrust of her sister kept my happiness at bay, though.

As she whirled around, I stopped her. Holding her by the shoulders, I looked into her eyes and said, "Maybe it wouldn't be such a good idea to tell Janelle. That's pretty much a surefire way of letting your father know."

The smile slid from her face, and she nodded, accepting the reality of what would happen if her sister found out where her mother lived. "I guess you're right. She's never been really eager to see her anyway."

"It's still great news," I said, hating that I'd had to bring her back down to earth with that warning.

With a hopefulness in her eyes that never failed to make my heart swell with happiness, she said, "It is, isn't it? I can't wait to see her again. I just hope she's as happy to see me as I am to see her."

I cupped her cheek and kissed her softly. "Of course she will be. I'm sure she's wanted to see you every day since she went away."

Leaning into my palm, Serena smiled. "And in just a little while, she's going to have a grandchild, so this is perfect timing. I knew if I believed it would happen someday."

Nothing made me happier than seeing her excited about finally getting to know her mother. With the fight coming up that would give us enough money to leave and now this, it felt like everything was finally coming together for us. We'd had to wait longer than either of us had wanted, but at long last, I saw the light at the end of the tunnel that signaled a life after this place.

A life away from Robert Erickson and all the ugliness of his world.

Chapter Twenty-Two

Serena

E VEN THOUGH RYDER wanted to go with me to see my mother just in case something happened, I chose to see her for the first time alone. I knew he worried about me, especially now since I was pregnant, but this was my mother. She wasn't going to do any harm to me.

As I drove toward the address in New Windsor the detective gave me, I couldn't believe she'd been just thirty miles away all this time. Had my father known this?

I knew the truth was he probably had been the one to send her there, but I didn't want to believe that he'd known she was less than an hour away for all these years as I begged him to find her. My father had never wanted me to see her, but was he really that much a monster to do this?

Whatever he'd done or not done, I'd found her at last, and nothing would stop me from getting to know the woman who'd given birth to me. I wanted to share all those things I'd experienced with her, to see her face when I told her about growing up and then meeting Ryder. I wanted her to be in our child's life from the very beginning.

My GPS alerted me that I needed to turn left onto a long winding road leading to an enormous grey stone home in the distance. As grand as the one I grew up in, the very sight of it made me happy. I'd worried she had been forced to live in squalor because of my father's spitefulness, but the house I saw now said otherwise.

Pulling up in front of the home, I marveled at how beautiful her home was. My hands began to shake at the reality that in mere seconds, I'd finally be face-to-face with the one person I'd wanted to see for so long. What would I say first? Would she even recognize me after all these years?

I squeezed the steering wheel tightly and took a deep breath. This is what I'd wanted since I was six years old. I could do this.

But what if Janelle was right? What if she chose to leave us and didn't want to know her daughters? What if my finding her would be something she hated instead of a surprise she'd love?

Suddenly, I lost my will. I couldn't bear to finally meet my mother only to have her show me she never missed me at all.

My mouth grew dry, and my emotions began to spin out of control. If she shunned me like my father had always said she did when she left us, I wouldn't be able to handle it. The single dream I'd kept alive all these years would be dead, and everything my father had said about her would be proven right.

I couldn't face that.

Putting the car into gear, I looked in the rearview mirror to turn around and leave, but a knock on my car window stopped me. A man with light hair and a big smile who looked to be around my age motioned for me to put down the window. I didn't want to talk to him, no matter how happy he looked. This had all been a big mistake, and all I wanted to do was go home.

But he knocked again and I didn't want to just leave him standing there grinning at me without even telling him a lie that I'd gotten lost, so I rolled down the window and returned his smile.

"I'm sorry. I took a wrong turn and before I knew it, I was here. Sorry about that."

"Oh, it's no problem, miss. What were you looking for?"

My mind raced to remember a single road name I'd seen along the way, but not one came to mind.

Stammering, I tried to bluff my way out of what had already become an awkward conversation. "Oh…I…I mean…it's no big deal. I was just looking for a different place."

The man chuckled. "I got that. But what I'm

asking is what house were you looking for? This house sits on twenty-five acres, so wherever you were headed, you missed it by a mile."

"Or two," I mumbled, embarrassed by my lame attempt at lying.

We stared at each other in silence for a few moments until he introduced himself. He took his work gloves off and thrust his hand in through the window. "I'm Michael. I work the estate as the chief gardener."

I shook his calloused hand. "I'm Serena. I was looking for someone who lives here."

Michael looked puzzled by my statement. "Then you really must have the wrong house. Nobody lives here. At least not in the main house. It's been empty for years. The man who owns it comes to visit every few months, but other than that, it's more like a museum than a home."

Had the private detective gotten the address wrong?

"Oh, well, I guess I should go then and find the right house."

He stared at me for a moment and shook his head. "You wouldn't be looking for Alita, would you? I just noticed you look like her."

"Alita?"

"She lives here, but not in the big house. She lives in the carriage house at the back of the property. I think she's at home right now."

The carriage house? Why would my mother not live in the main house?

I wanted to ask Michael, but having a stranger explain her circumstances seemed wrong. But I needed to know who the owner of this house was, even though in my gut I had a sneaking suspicion of the name that would come out of his mouth.

"Who owns this property?" I asked and held my breath as I waited for his answer.

"The owner is Robert Erickson. I can get you his information if you'd like to talk to him, but I don't think he's looking for potential tenants for the house."

My heart sank as I heard my father's name. He had known where my mother was all this time, and he'd lied over and over every time I asked about her. Even worse, he'd hidden her out here and made my mother live in a carriage house while he left the main house empty, like she wasn't worthy of living in a home as nice as ours.

I hung my head as these thoughts got tangled up in my emotions and tears welled in my eyes. Maybe she had wanted to see me like I'd wanted to see her all these years.

"Are you okay? Is something wrong?" Michael asked.

Willing the tears away, I looked at him and

smiled as I turned off the car. "Maybe I'll take a look around, if that's okay."

He opened my door for me and spread his arms. "The place is yours to explore. If you have any questions about the gardens, please ask because I'm your man on that front. Anything else, I might have to bluff the answer, but I'll do my best."

"Thank you. Can I assume the gardens are Italian with sharp angles and the shrubbery formed into geometric shapes?" I asked as I began to walk around the main house.

"How did you know?" he said, calling after me.

Disappointed I'd been able to so correctly describe my father's taste, I forced a smile. "I had a feeling."

Left alone, I walked what felt like the entire twenty-five acres until I reached a tiny light grey cottage. My heart contracted as I judged the entire house to be little bigger than a garden shed. Why was she exiled here and to such a tiny home after living in our house? Her home now would practically fit in our entryway.

A mix of anger and apprehension swirled inside me as I walked toward the front door of the cottage. Flanked by pink rose bushes just beginning to bloom, its pale yellow color welcomed me. I wanted to believe that it opened to a warm home comfortable for her.

I knocked as my heart slammed against my chest and a lump filled my throat. My hands shook from fear that everything my father had ever said about my mother was true. Even if only some of it was, she might not have ever wanted to see me again.

The door opened and there she stood looking out at me like she was seeing a ghost. Her dark eyes so similar to mine grew wide, and her mouth opened like she wanted to say something to me, but no words came out.

She was as beautiful as I remembered her being. Dark brown hair fell in loose waves barely grazing her shoulders. Her tan skin looked warm and touchable, and I had to control my urge to reach out and brush my fingertips over her high cheekbones.

"Serena?" she asked quietly, her tone full of disbelief.

"It's me, Mom. It's Serena."

She buried her face in her hands, and I heard her sob, "I've dreamed of what this would be like for so long, but now that you're here, it's even better than I imagined."

I instinctively wrapped my arms around her and hugged her to me. "It's really you. I can't believe it. After all this time, I found you."

Lifting her head, she wiped the tears from under her eyes and smiled. "How? How did you find out where I was? Your father told me he'd never let you know."

"I hired a private detective to find you because he wouldn't tell me where you were. He said you disappeared."

She nodded her head sadly. "Yes, I assumed that's what he told you girls." Looking around me, she asked, "What about Janelle? Is she here with you too?"

"No, it's just me. Janelle doesn't know I found you. Nobody does. Well, except Ryder."

My mother closed the front door and smiled. "I can tell by the way your eyes lit up when you said his name that he's someone you care about. Your eyes always told the whole story, even when you were a little girl."

My hands cupped my baby bump. "He means the world to me."

Her gaze focused on where my hands sat, and her eyes grew wide again. "Oh, my God! Are you pregnant?"

"Yes, but nobody knows. I haven't told Daddy or Janelle. You see, Ryder and I aren't married and he works for Daddy, so…"

The myriad of reasons why Ryder and I hadn't been able to marry yet filled my head, but they were too difficult to explain. He loved me and I loved him, and that's all that mattered.

My mother gently placed her hand over mine

and closed her eyes. "You don't have to explain your father to me. I know all about him and what he can do to someone if he decides they went against his wishes. Just tell me he's not like the other men who work for your father and that's all I'll need to know."

I shook my head and sighed. "He's nothing like them. He's smart and brave, and he protects me, even from Daddy."

"Good. I worried you and your sister would get caught up in your father's world and never have the chance to be with someone you truly love. Ryder sounds like he deserves you, and that's all I've ever prayed for."

She led me into her kitchen, a quaint room painted in pale yellow like her front door and even more welcoming, and we sat down at a tiny table covered in a white tablecloth. As I watched her, I couldn't shake the thought that she belonged somewhere grander.

"Why did you go?" I blurted out, needing to know the answer to that question more than any other.

Frowning, she said, "I didn't have a choice. He sent me away, Serena."

"Why?"

She tilted her chin up and with a look of defiance explained, "I wouldn't accept his affairs and told him I was leaving and taking you girls with me. That night, two of his men grabbed hold of me as I walked from your room and drove me here. Your father was waiting for me and told me if I wanted to stay alive, I'd accept it. I didn't want to live for a long time when he sent me away from you girls, but I kept a tiny hope alive that one day I'd be able to see you again."

"Did you ever try?" I asked, knowing how unfair that question was but still needing to know.

"I asked about you every time I saw him, Serena. Every time, I begged him to let me see you, but by the time you were a teenager, he said you didn't want to see me ever again because I'd abandoned you. But I didn't. I swear to you I would have been there every day if he hadn't exiled me here."

"He told us you just disappeared one night. I couldn't understand why you would go," I said as the emotions from that time long ago came rushing back.

She reached across the table and touched my hand. "I never wanted to go. I missed you and your sister more than you can ever know. I pleaded with your father to let me come back. I promised I wouldn't take you anywhere. I even told him I'd look the other way concerning the other women, but it didn't matter. He always said no."

Choking back tears, I said, "A man kidnapped me when I was seven. When it happened, I actually convinced myself that you were behind it and had finally found a way to get me. I waited the whole time I was at that house for that man to say he was taking me to you."

Through blurry eyes, I saw my mother begin to cry. "Oh, honey, I'm so sorry. I should have been there for you. I'm so sorry, Serena."

"I had no one after that. Daddy took me out of school because I couldn't stop talking about it. I didn't know how to deal with everything. I just wanted someone to talk to, but nobody wanted to be friends with me because I just couldn't stop myself from…"

Pressing my lips together, I refused to let the words that had been in my head for so long come out. I didn't want to be that person anymore. Friendless. Alone. Poor little Serena.

I wasn't that person anymore. I wasn't alone now. I had Ryder.

My mother lightly squeezed my hand, and I saw the sadness in her eyes. I'd seen that same sadness every time I looked in the mirror growing up.

"If only I hadn't been gone from your life. You deserved so much better, honey. I would have given you that if I could have. I would have, Serena."

"I know. I know it wasn't your fault, Mom. I know that now. I do. I guess I'm just crying because I can't believe that after all these years you're finally right here in front of me. I'd forgotten what you looked like it's been so long. I look so much like you."

She smiled and wiped her tear-stained cheeks. "You're more beautiful than I've ever been."

"Maybe that's why Daddy always liked Janelle more. She looks like him."

"How is your sister? Is she happy? I'm sure your father was more than pleased with himself when he married her off to that Charles person I read about. His millions didn't hurt either, of course."

I didn't know how to answer her questions. I didn't want to lie, but to say Janelle was happy seemed at the very least not entirely truthful. Then again, her idea of happiness and mine had never been the same.

With a sigh, I said, "She's happy to be married to someone like Daddy. I don't think she's in love with Charles, but that didn't seem important to anyone at the time."

My mother furrowed her brow. "I'm happy you escaped that kind of arrangement, Serena. I just worry it's coming. I know your father."

"It already came, and he's gone, so you don't have to worry. I won't be letting my father or anyone else push me into another marriage."

Her eyes opened wide in surprise at my admission that I'd already been married off. "I had no idea. When? I've seen your father since Janelle's wedding, and he never said a thing."

Looking down at my wrist, I gently rubbed my scar through my sweater as the horrible memory of being forced to marry Oliver replayed in my mind. "It didn't go exactly how Daddy planned, so he probably didn't feel it warranted any mention."

"You said he was gone? What happened to him, or shouldn't I bother asking, knowing your father?"

I lifted my head and answered her question truthfully. "He died. I wish I could say I was unhappy about that, but I'm not. I never loved him and I begged Daddy to not make me marry him. I guess you can say we both know what good it does to beg him not to do something."

"I'm sorry, Serena."

"I'm okay. It taught me a lesson I'll never forget. I can't afford to be weak ever again."

My words made a look of sadness fill her eyes. "I wish you never had to learn that lesson, but in your father's world, it's one everyone learns at one time or another."

We sat silently across from one another, each of us knowing all too well what happened when you allowed yourself to feel even the slightest weakness around my father. We'd both learned the hard way.

"I hope you can find it in your heart to forgive me for not being there all these years. I wonder if I had been if things would have been easier for you."

I shook my head, unwilling to live in the past for another minute now that I had my mother back in my life again. "I don't blame you for anything. I blame him. He took you away from us and made sure you stayed away. I can't forgive him for that. I won't."

She squeezed my hand and frowned. "Don't let what he is infect you. You somehow came through all those years with the ability to love. Don't let it be ruined by your hatred of him."

"I can't forgive him for keeping you here all these years. He sticks you in this carriage house, intentionally leaving the bigger house empty. He's heartless, and one of these days, he's going to pay for what he did to you and us."

She looked around the tiny kitchen and smiled. "For a long time, I hated this house. It was a gilded cage, but a cage nonetheless. I was trapped here. He had people watch me twenty-four hours a day for years. I felt like a prisoner, put away for a crime I never committed. But then I guess I just accepted things, and it became my goal to wait him out. I would outlive him, and all I could hope for would be that you and Janelle would be willing to see me when the time came."

Suddenly, my conversation with the gardener outside made me worry for her safety. "I told that

Michael guy my name. What if he calls him? Are there still men who watch the house here?"

My mother smiled sweetly. "Not for years. I don't even think your father cares if you see me now. I imagine he thinks the damage is done and you won't be able to forgive me for all he's convinced you I did. And as for Michael, don't worry. Your father has never treated him with any bit of kindness, like he does with most of the people who work for him. Michael won't be interested in helping him anytime soon."

"But what if he mentions someone named Serena came to see you? I'd hate for you to suffer because of me."

"Don't worry. He won't. Your father doesn't frighten me anymore. Let him rant and rave. I have my daughter back and just in time for me to become a grandmother."

The sound of those words made me happy. My mother had her daughter back, and I had my mother back.

And nothing my father could do would change that.

Chapter Twenty-Three

Ryder

KEYSER LIVED UP to everything I'd imagined it would be, as far as Appalachian towns went. Empty streets that looked like they belonged in a ghost town welcomed us as Floyd drove past one after another abandoned building, and I half expected to see some tumbleweeds roll toward us when we got out at the building where the fight would be held.

"Booming metropolis," I mumbled as I followed him toward a vacant building.

"This place looks like the kind of place where at any minute zombies would appear coming down the road," he said with a nervous chuckle.

I turned around to take one last look at the street before walking into a dimly lit hallway. Cinder block walls on each side were covered in graffiti, and beneath our feet entire sections of concrete were missing, leaving gaping holes in the floor.

"Jesus, Floyd, this place is even worse than The Pit, and that's saying something," I joked as he led the way to a large metal door at the end of the hallway.

"It's no Taj Mahal, that's for sure."

He pulled hard on the doorknob and heaved the metal door open to reveal a huge, brightly lit space that looked nicer than I'd expected. It was no great place, to be sure, but at least it didn't look like meth heads had been squatting there as recently as a few hours ago, like I'd worried it would.

A large guy with long hair and glasses saw us and immediately walked up to shake our hands. "Floyd, you son of a bitch! It's good to see you, man," he said in a gravelly voice.

"Nate, long time no see. This place doesn't look like the shithole I thought it would by the way you described it." Turning toward me, he said, "This is the kid I was talking about. Nate, meet Ryder Rhodes."

The man gave my hand a firm shake and grinned at me, showing off a nice set of teeth that didn't seem to fit with the rest of his look. I threw Floyd a nasty look for the kid remark, even though compared to both of them, I would be a kid.

"I hear good things about you, Ryder. Floyd says you're unbeatable. Is that him just talking shit to get me excited, or is he right?"

Shrugging like I always did when someone asked me if I was as incredible as they'd heard, I said,

"Little bit of both, I guess. I haven't been beaten lately, so he's right about that."

"Lately?" Nate asked, obviously sensing that his friend had lied to him.

Floyd quickly answered, "He stepped away from fighting for the past two years, so I wasn't counting that last fight before he left."

Nate whistled and looked me up and down. "Two years? Damn! That's a long time to be away and come back to winning form. You must be good. I guess we'll see tonight."

"I guess," I said with a smile as I scanned the area behind him to see where I'd be fighting.

He noticed where my attention had gone to and looked back at the big empty space. "It's not much, but then again, there isn't much overhead so it's a win-win for everyone involved."

"Just point me in the direction of where I can get changed and I'll leave you guys to talk shop."

Nate turned back to face us and pointed to the corner of the room. "Just head back there. You're the first one here, so you get to take advantage of being the early bird."

"How many fights are you running tonight?" Floyd asked as that exact question ran through my mind.

"Just Ryder's and another one. He's got the main event, so he should be ready by seven since the first one is scheduled for then but it could be over quickly. You never know, do you?"

Floyd laughed. "No, you never do. I swear I'm the most surprised of them all sometimes, and I've been in the fight business for decades."

Nate and Floyd began to reminisce about their biggest shocks in the business, so I walked back to the changing room, happy for some peace and quiet before the fight. Floyd had talked my damn ear off the whole ride there, going on about some show he'd watched on TV the night before that had been just the best fucking thing since sliced white bread. By the time we got there, I was happy to be anywhere but in that passenger seat.

Even an ugly, down-on-its-luck Appalachian town that looked like all but misery had deserted it.

For about thirty minutes, I sat alone on an old wooden bench and thought about how great it was going to be when I surprised Serena with being able to leave after this fight. She'd come home so happy from seeing her mother for the first time since she was a little girl, and I wanted to add to that happiness with the news that we finally could escape Robert and everything that came with him.

I didn't mention it to Serena, but the thought had crossed my mind that once he found out we were gone, he might retaliate against Alita like he always threatened to. I didn't want to see her hurt any more than I wanted to see us hurt, but I needed to believe Robert's threat was just that, a threat meant to manipulate Serena and nothing more.

Maybe we could find a way to help her escape from his control too. I didn't know if that could happen, but I felt hopeful because of this fight. When I won, that money would be our ticket out.

All I had to do was win.

But like when I was undefeated two years ago, I had a reason to fight that no one else did. I was literally fighting for my future, not just money or bragging rights here in small town USA.

THE THREE OTHER fighters showed up around six-thirty, and I quickly figured out they all knew one another by how they joked around about whose turn it was to buy drinks that night after the matches. Each one checked me out for a second and then looked away like nothing about me concerned them in the least.

Smaller than most of the guys I'd fought, all three had a wiry look about them I knew could make them as dangerous as someone bulkier. I'd seen enough fighters get beat based on thinking they could handle someone because of how they looked to know better.

I sat silently as the crowd filled up the big room outside where we sat and the three local guys talked about what they were going to do with the money they won that night. Nate's fights paid out well, so it wasn't surprising they had money on the mind. If I didn't have Serena and the baby to think of, I'd be doing the same thing as they were.

Nate's voice boomed throughout the building announcing the fighters for the first fight, and two of the three guys headed out to their match. The third guy sat quietly on the other side of the room and looked like he might be uncomfortable without his friends around, so instead of making small talk I took the chance to really get a feel for him. Definitely wiry, his pale skin looked very white under the large tattoos of black dream catchers on his right arm and a steer head on the other bicep. He kept running his hands over his shaved head, and after a while, he closed his eyes and hummed some tune I'd never heard over and over.

Floyd came in as I studied my opponent for the night and pulled up a chair in front of me, blocking my view of the guy. "Hey, you ready?" he asked eagerly.

"Yeah. He's smaller than I've fought before, but I'm not letting that trick me. I'm not exactly the biggest guy in the ring most nights, and I do pretty well for myself."

Floyd turned around to look at the guy and then turned back to face me. "You'll be fine. I put down the money you asked me to, so that'll make the prize even better. I'm going to get back out there. Nate says those two are cousins or something like that and their fights are always brawls until there's blood all over. I'll see you after. We'll go for a drink at that bar I saw about twenty miles down the road."

"Okay. Your treat, right?" I joked as the sound of the crowd screaming filtered into the room.

He thought about it for a moment and finally nodded. "Okay," he grudgingly agreed. "Now I'm glad I bet some good money on you tonight too."

Cheap bastard.

I watched him walk out as the crowd exploded again, and the pale guy stood and walked across the room, stopping a few feet away. Looking up at him, I saw him glaring down at me.

"You sound pretty fucking sure of yourself. You shouldn't be. I don't care if you're unbeaten or not. I'm winning that money tonight."

The rage in his eyes made me wonder if he planned to begin fighting right there instead of saving it for the match. "Yeah, whatever. May the best man win."

"That's going to be me, motherfucker."

He turned on his heels and stalked back to his chair without giving me a chance to answer him, but I didn't have anything to say anyway. Not that I was against talking smack before a match, but I didn't feel like getting into a pissing contest with this guy before the fight. Better to save my anger for when it counted.

The sound of the crowd screaming died down, telling me the fight between the cousins had ended, and right after they stumbled into the changing room covered in one another's blood. I couldn't tell which fighter had won until the one opened his mouth to show his two front teeth knocked out and laughed.

"I lost some teeth, but I won the money, fucker."

The other guy waved him off and collapsed into a chair near the guy I'd be fighting in a few minutes. "Yeah, well, I got your teeth and I'm not giving them back."

Sure I didn't want to be around when they started fighting over the teeth, I walked out of the room and stood against the wall to wait for Nate to call us out. Pale guy followed me, and positioned himself nearby to glare at me before he started growling.

I turned to look at him and shook my head. "The last guy who thought this staring me down shit worked got pretty fucked up by me. Why don't you save the act for the fight, dude?"

If he thought the whole glaring and growling routine was scaring me, he was sorely mistaken. I didn't frighten that easily.

"I'm going to be the one doing the fucking up, dude," he answered, mocking me.

Shit talking like this was nothing new before a fight, but this guy seemed a little too jacked about it. I considered giving him a shove just to be an asshole but decided against it. I'd take my own advice and save my anger for the match.

Nate announced our names, and I found out the pale guy's was Justin Forte. Even his name sounded like it belonged on a jackass.

He trotted out to the crowd, and it erupted into cheers for him, with some people even chanting "Get it done!" like it was his catch phrase or something. Like his name, it fit him.

I walked out to a smattering of cheers at first but after the crowd got a good look at me, they began to scream and holler like I was one of their local boys they were used to watching. A few of the more rabid fans barked out, "Let's get started!" like they were about to do something more than drink and cheer for us to beat the fuck out of each other.

Nate drew us together and wrapped his arms around us before he leaned in and said, "You two know how this goes. First one to surrender loses. There are no rules other than two fingers and you're done."

I expected Justin to talk more shit, but he just nodded and I did the same.

Lifting his head, Nate said loudly so the crowd could hear, "Let's see a good fight, you two!" and I slammed my fists down on Justin's before we stepped back and the fight began.

As I expected, he came at me like a fucking wild animal, aiming for my nose and hoping for a quick show of blood for the crowd. I twisted out of his way and caught the back of his head with my elbow as he flew past me, and he grunted in pain as I spun around to face him when he came at me again.

"Wanna play games, little bitch?" he said, sneering at me. "Fight me like a fucking man!"

I laughed in his face. I didn't know what kind of fighting he'd ever done, but standing in one place while someone whales on you wasn't fighting. It was losing.

"You're gonna laugh at me?"

From the crowd, some guy yelled, "Stop fucking talking and fight! You're like fucking hens out there!"

Justin turned to throw a look toward where the sound came from, and I jumped at the chance to show him how fighting was supposed to be done. My arm came around in a right hook, and my fist connected hard with his face. I felt my knuckles slam against his cheekbone before they skated along his head, clipping his ear. He turned in shock to come at me, but he was too slow. By the time he raised his hand, my forearm was meeting his face. It slammed into his nose, breaking it and sending blood pouring out of his nostrils.

He staggered back while his hands filled with blood, but I didn't let up. I saw my chance to win, and I took it.

The next hit sent him to the ground, and as the crowd screamed its desire for me to kick his ass, I pounced on him, taking advantage of his weakness. Like a man on a mission, I beat him like I had to. My fists pounded his face and body over and over. The whole time he tried to defend himself, but it was no use.

I knew what I had to do, and I did it.

The sound of the crowd yelling all around me slowly faded away until all I heard was the noise my fists made every time they met his body. A deafening sound of pain that repeated again and again.

Every thought disappeared from my brain, except for one. I had to defeat him. I had to win to get the money to take Serena away from the world we were trapped in. To protect her. I couldn't lose and let her down.

I had to win. No matter what it took.

He struggled to guess where I'd attack next, so his hands never fully protected him. When he thought I'd go for his shoulder, I zeroed in on his face, by now bloody and busted so he was almost unrecognizable. When he believed I'd go for his face again, I focused on his chest, pounding my fists into his body over and over.

I was like a savage animal fighting for its life, and I didn't care. I didn't care that at one point I would have eased up at least a little so the guy I was fighting would have at least a tiny chance. I didn't care when he began begging me to stop.

I didn't care because I couldn't. I cared about two souls in this world, Serena and our child, and I couldn't afford to care about Justin.

The familiar two finger signal finally came after God only knew how long I beat on him, but I didn't stop. I couldn't.

My fists kept slamming into his face, his shoulder, his chest. Even though I saw those two fingers, my brain didn't get the message, so like the machine I was, I kept fighting.

"He gives up!" a voice behind me shouted as hands pulled at my shoulders to get me off him.

The words came out frantically, like the person saying them saw something that terrified them. I fought against their hold on me, but then another person joined in and finally pulled me off Justin. They threw me backwards, and I fell onto the ground in a confused heap of rage that suddenly had no place to go.

"Let me at him!" I screamed as I scrambled to

my feet.

Floyd jumped in front of me and held my shoulders so I couldn't move. He wore an expression of pure terror, but he didn't have to worry. I'd won. I'd gotten us the win.

"Ryder, stop! Stop! It's over!"

I looked around him to see Nate hovering over Justin, who lay in crumpled heap of his own blood and broken bones. My mind raced as it tried to find its way back to normal, even as my body craved more fighting.

Nate yelled something and a few men began pushing the crowd toward the doors. No announcement that I'd won or anything. Just a fight and then nothing.

"Floyd, get over here!" Nate said in a panic, and Floyd rushed over to where he sat crouched over Justin.

I watched as the two of them shook him by the shoulders and then stared at one another like they didn't know what to do. One of Nate's guys made a noise that sounded like he was in pain and then looked over at me in horror.

Was Justin knocked out? Had the people in Keyser never seen anyone knocked out before?

Slowly, I staggered over to where Floyd stood and said, "I guess these guys aren't used to real fights. He's out cold."

Nate turned his head and looked up at me with a sickening expression but said nothing. Floyd shook his head wildly and tried to speak but nothing came out.

Finally, I grabbed him by the shoulders. "What the fuck is wrong with you? We won. We won, Floyd."

His face twisted into a painful grimace and then he looked down at Justin and mumbled, "You beat him unconscious. Look at him. We have to get him to a hospital now!"

I shook my head in disbelief and stared down at Justin as he lay there completely motionless. He'd be fine. This was just a fight like all my fights were. Bare knuckle fighting with some blood and a whole lot of pain, but nothing more. He'd be damn sore for a few days, maybe weeks, but then he'd be okay. They always were.

"No. No way," I stammered out as the realization that Justin's chest had barely moved in the entire time I'd stood there.

"What the fuck are we going to do?" Nate mumbled.

Floyd began rambling on about the police and it wouldn't just be me that got charged because they were all involved with the fight, but all I could do was stare down at Justin's broken body with its bloody and busted face.

"No fucking way am I going to jail because this animal beat someone into a fucking coma," one of Nate's guys said.

"Nobody's going to jail or anywhere else," Floyd said as coolly as if he'd just told us to lock up on our way out. "We need to be smart about this, and I know someone who can help."

Nate slowly nodded. "Do what you have to. We'll take care of Justin."

"Ryder, come with me," Floyd said as he motioned for me to follow him back to the changing room.

Unsure my feet could even move, I nodded and did as he ordered. When I sat down on that same wooden bench from earlier, I looked up and saw he was on the phone talking to someone.

There was only one person in our world who could help now.

Chapter Twenty-Four

Ryder

SLOWLY, THE TERRIBLE events of that night filtered through my brain until the truth finally sunk in. For the first time in all the years I'd spent in underground fights, I'd become the beast all those people cheered for.

A fucking animal who beat someone mercilessly.

Not someone I'd been ordered to take care of. Not in defense of my life. Not to protect the woman I loved.

Not for any honorable reason at all. I'd done it for a few thousand dollars, and I didn't even have to. He'd given the sign, but I'd ignored it.

I hung my head and tried to imagine how I could have done such a horrible thing. I'd just wanted to win that money to get Serena away so we could live our happily ever after with our baby in that little house she dreamed of.

How could things have gone so wrong when all my intentions were good?

The sound of voices filtered in from where it

happened, and I braced for the police to come in and take me away. Away from Serena and away from our child. Away to jail where I'd spend the next few decades wishing things had been different.

And what would Serena do? I pictured her standing in front of her father as he introduced her to the next man he'd give her to. She'd beg him to reconsider, or maybe she wouldn't. Maybe this mistake would finally break her spirit, and she'd give in to what he wanted for her life. She'd become the wife of whoever he chose and my child would become their child.

All the while I'd rot away in a six by eight cell and know I'd ruined the one chance for all of us to be happy and free.

I heard footsteps and squeezed my eyes closed in one last desperate attempt to push the reality of the night away. The hollow sound stopped just inside the room, but the person said nothing. I felt their stare on me. I imagined it to look as full of judgment and condemnation as it should.

"If I'm not mistaken, the first time we met we were both in basically the same positions as we are now. You sitting in some shithole and me able to give you a life you'd only dreamed of. Does that sound about right, Ryder?"

Robert's anger resonated off every word so by the time he said my name, it came out from between gritted teeth. In my misery, I hadn't imagined what I'd say to him when I finally saw him that night. Now that I knew just how furious he was, I still didn't know what to say.

I looked up at him and nodded. "Yeah, that sounds right."

"And did I give you everything I promised I would?" he asked, his tone still laced with rage.

Hanging my head, I answered him. "Yeah, you did."

"When you broke my rules, I showed you what the punishment for that had to be, didn't I?"

The memory of that night he sent Serena away flashed through my mind, followed by the memory of getting beaten in my match two days later and ending up in the hospital. Robert never made a secret of his unhappiness.

And he wouldn't this time. Of that, I was sure. Just what he'd do to me before they took me away, I had no idea, but knowing him, it would be cruel and stay with me forever.

"Didn't I, Ryder?" he repeated, even more sternly than the first time.

I looked up into those dark eyes of his that showed nothing of the emotion I knew existed in him and nodded again. "You did."

"And when you betrayed me and followed Serena's wishes over mine, I once again showed you the consequences of your actions."

"Yes."

"Does it seem to you that our entire time together has been one long lesson you don't seem to want to learn, son?" Robert asked as he moved to stand in front of me.

I tilted my head back to look up at him and blew the air out of my lungs slowly. I'd never thought about it like that, but he wasn't wrong. Whatever he had tried to teach me after all this time, I still hadn't learned it.

"I guess it does."

"So now I find out from our mutual friend Floyd, who will suffer his own consequences to be sure, that you've been fighting behind my back and got yourself into a situation out here in wherever the hell this place is."

I hated the thought of Floyd suffering because of my mistake. Practically pleading with Robert, I said, "This isn't his fault. Don't make him pay for what I did. I came to him and asked him to help me. I basically didn't give him a choice."

Robert's eyebrows shot up into his forehead. "I'm intrigued. Have you taken to threatening poor Floyd to get what you want, Ryder?"

Shaking my head, I answered him truthfully. "No, I didn't threaten him. If anything, I begged him for his help. He just seems to have a soft spot in his heart for me and couldn't say no."

"Everyone seems to have a soft spot for you, son. Floyd, my daughter, even me. For example, I know I should have just told Floyd to let the police take you and solve a multitude of problems for me. But instead, here I am talking to you and considering what I might do to get you out of this mess you've created."

"Get me out?" I asked, confused about what he meant. "There's no getting me out, Robert. I beat that guy into a coma in the fight tonight. I'm going to get charged with at least assault, and they're going to put me away. There's no out from that."

My explanation of the situation seemed to amuse him, if the smile that slowly formed on his lips was any indication. Waving my ideas away like they were nothing to him, he rolled his eyes and said, "All this time you've known me and you say something like that. Of course, there's a way out. There's always a way out. The question is do I want to help you this time?"

I tried to speak, but nothing came out I was so shocked. It had never occurred to me that he'd want to help me. I'd betrayed him, and I knew what happened when someone betrayed Robert Erickson.

They paid, often with their life. So why would he help me when he could just let the justice system take me away so I'd pay for that betrayal?

"I have to admit, though, I'd be more inclined to help you if you hadn't lied to me."

I knew what we wanted. He wanted to know why I'd fight behind his back. He knew I didn't love fighting enough to do it for kicks. I'd have to tell him if I ever wanted a chance to see Serena again, assuming he didn't make never being with her from that point on one of the conditions of his help.

It didn't matter. I had to take the chance, even if it meant he sent me away from her. I couldn't spend my child's first years in prison. I couldn't do that to Serena.

"I asked Floyd to help me find fights for extra money. Serena's pregnant, and I wanted it to be right this time."

Robert's eyes opened wide in surprise. "Pregnant? I had no idea. And when you say this time, am I to understand the last time was your child also?"

I nodded. "Yeah, and that fuck Oliver found out and tried to kill Serena and the baby. He succeeded with the baby."

With a heavy sigh, he sat down on the bench next to me. "Well, that explains why you wouldn't have a problem with killing him when she asked you to."

I knew the moment had come to finally tell him the truth about how I felt about Serena. Turning to face him, I said, "I love her. I've tried to protect her from everything your world forces on her because she's not made for that. She's sweet and gentle, and you married her off to a man who thought nothing of pushing a pregnant woman down a flight of stairs to kill her and her baby."

Robert said nothing and the look on his face said he wasn't so much surprised by my admission that I loved her as much as resigned to the fact. But I knew if I wanted his help I had to say what he wanted to hear or there'd never be a chance for Serena and me to escape this life after tonight.

"I'll do whatever you want. You name it. I'll do it. Just let her be, Robert. Don't make her marry another man. We love each other, and that's not going to change. We've been through too much already to let anything come between us."

"Other than you being in prison," he said casually, like he was taunting me.

"Please don't do that to us. I'm begging you, Robert. I'll do whatever you want. I just want to be allowed to be with her and our child. Make me your errand boy or the gardener who shapes the hedges into those funny bird shapes. It won't matter as long as I'm with her. Make me work off the cost of helping that guy once he wakes up. Assuming he wakes up."

He stared at me for a long moment without saying a word, and then abruptly stood up from the bench. "Fine. You and Serena can be together, and I won't marry her off to anyone else. You'll come back and work for me, not as a fighter since there's no way anyone's going to want to fight you now. Even if I can clean this mess up, and that's going to take some money, I'm sure, the rumors will get out and there won't be a goddamned man around who will fight you anymore."

I wanted to jump for joy at hearing his words. Whatever he made me do, it couldn't be worse than being away from Serena and the baby. As long as I had them, I'd be okay.

He stuck his hand out and I shook it as I asked, "What will you have me do?"

That crocodile smile of his slowly lifted the corners of his mouth. "Nothing you can't handle, Ryder."

Chapter Twenty-Five

Serena

A KNOCK AT the front door startled me from a nap, and I answered it to see Jesse, one of my father's men standing there. Large and dopey-faced, he looked uncomfortable, like he didn't want to do whatever he'd been sent to do.

"Yes?"

"Uh, your father…I mean, Mr. Erickson called and said he wanted you in his office when he came back."

As he spoke, he fiddled with the zipper on his windbreaker like a child forced to give a speech would. His hands shook too, and I wondered if he was always this fidgety or just tonight.

"Did he say for what?" I asked, knowing as soon as the words left my mouth that I'd wasted my time in even saying them. Jesse didn't look like someone my father would keep as a confidant. His job was simple.

He was merely muscle, or as he was forced to be now, messenger boy.

Jesse looked away and shook his head. "He just said he wanted you there, miss…I mean ma'am."

"Do you know when he'll be back?"

He had to know that answer.

Directing his attention to the top of the doorframe, he said, "Uh, he said he'd be here in the next ten minutes."

"Okay. Thanks."

I closed the door to put both of us out of our misery and threw on a big white sweater that covered me to the middle of my thighs. As I headed out the door, I wondered what my father could possibly want to see me about. Even more, why did he want to see me alone? He didn't ask to see Ryder, which was good since he was training with Floyd tonight.

My stomach twisted into knots at the mere thought of dealing with my father. I'd successfully avoided him for the past few weeks, thankful to not have to hide my rapidly growing belly since the last thing I wanted was him knowing about my pregnancy.

Tugging at the bottom of my sweater, I slowly walked down the stairs toward the door to the main house, all the while thinking of the reason why he would have sent one of his lackeys to get me. Had something happened to Janelle?

Then it dawned on me. I stopped as I turned

into the main hallway, and my heart sank. He'd found out I'd gone to see my mother. Only that reason made sense. There was no other reason that explained why he'd want to see me alone.

My palms instantly grew sweaty as fear raced through me. Would he hurt her now because I'd dared to disobey him and find her on my own? A painful feeling of sadness wound its way into my chest, and I had to stop myself from crying. I'd been so sure that no one else had known what I was up to, but somehow he'd figured it out. I felt sick at the thought of her paying for my arrogance.

He'd probably found out from the private detective. I'd asked that man if he knew my father, and he'd claimed he didn't. Did he lie? Was he actually someone my father hired himself, so he'd known all the while what I was planning? Was that why the private detective took so long to find her when there she was living less than an hour away from here?

As these thoughts raced through my mind, I made my way to my father's office and stopped outside the door to steady myself. Taking a deep breath, I tried to calm my fears. If I called my mother immediately after talking to him, maybe it would give her enough time to get away to somewhere safe before he could send his thugs to do something horrible to her.

Silently, I prayed to God that he hadn't already set his men on her and this meeting wasn't to merely announce what he'd done.

"Serena, I'd know those footsteps anywhere. Come in here."

The stern sound of his voice rattled me, but I closed my eyes and took another deep breath. "I'm coming."

I stepped into the room and stopped dead at the sight of Ryder sitting in one of the red leather chairs in front of my father's desk. Why had that oaf Jesse made it seem like only I had been summoned?

Stress and fear ebbed out of my body as the thought that this meeting was about my mother faded from my mind, and I smiled. "What's going on? Why the formal request to see me, Dad?"

Extending his left arm, he offered me a seat next to Ryder. "Come. Sit down."

I did as he said, and Ryder took my hand in his, bringing it to his lips in a kiss before lowering it onto the armrest of his chair. Surprised he'd do that in front of my father, I looked down at where our hands joined and then up at Ryder to see something strange in his eyes.

What was it? Fear? Dread? Why? What happened?

I wanted to ask him, but instead I smiled and waited for him to smile in return, but when he didn't, I turned to face my father. "What's going on?"

"Ryder won't be fighting anymore for me. He's coming back to work as security," my father said matter-of-factly, his face expressionless.

"Okay. Did something happen? Did he lose?" I asked before turning to look at Ryder. He didn't look like he'd been beaten.

"No. He'll tell you later, I'm sure. I just wanted you to know that his time as a fighter has ended. He won't be returning to that again."

His words sounded so final, but I couldn't see any evidence on Ryder why he wouldn't fight again. No bruises, no broken bones. Nothing that would mean he couldn't fight anymore.

I turned my attention back to my father. "What's going on here? You were the one who wanted him to fight again, and I see nothing to explain why suddenly he can't now. What happened?"

My father merely arched one eyebrow and shot Ryder a nasty glance, so I swiveled in my chair and asked him the same question. "What's going on? Did you get hurt?"

Ryder just shook his head but didn't say a thing. Back and forth, I looked at him and then my father for some answer as to what was going on, but neither of them said a word.

Finally, I stopped and stared at Ryder. "Say

something! What's happened?"

He hung his head and quietly mumbled, "I…there was a fight and I…"

Whatever it was, he couldn't get the words out, no matter how hard he tried. His face twisted into a look of agony, as if even trying to say what happened hurt him. He squeezed my hand tightly but couldn't even face me. What had he done?

"Ryder, what happened? Are you hurt?"

He shook his head sadly but still refused to look up at me. "No. I'm fine."

The way he said those words told me he wasn't fine at all, but sitting there in front of my father wasn't where we needed to have this discussion. For now, I held his hand as he clung to mine and hoped he knew whatever had happened, I was there for him.

"I hear congratulations are in order, Serena," my father said, tearing me out of my sadness for Ryder.

Unsure what he referred to, I turned my head to look at him. "For what?"

His gaze drifted down my body and stopped just above my waist. "We're going to have a baby in the house, I hear."

Shock washed over me. He knew I was pregnant. But how? Who told him?

My father smiled and looked over at Ryder to answer the question that must have been written all over my face. Why would Ryder ever tell him about the baby? We agreed to keep the pregnancy a secret, especially from my father, so why would he tell him? What had suddenly changed so much that he was back to working for him as one of his men and he felt he should share our secret with the one person I wanted not to know?

Did he know about our plan to leave too?

Then suddenly, fear tore through me. Had Ryder told him about me finding my mother? Had he betrayed everything we were for some unknown reason to work for my father again?

"Well, I think we've had enough excitement for one day, so you two go. I'm sure you have a lot to talk about."

My mouth hung open in shock, and I watched Ryder stand to leave, still holding my hand. I stood and followed him out, unsure what to say. I had no idea what had gone on between them, but now everything felt different.

He didn't say a word all the way back to the apartment. All he did was walk and hold my hand tightly, like he feared if he let go I'd run away and he'd never find me again.

But I didn't want leave him. I wanted answers to why all we'd planned suddenly seemed to have changed in a matter of hours. He'd left to train with Floyd, and he'd come back a different person, and I wanted to know why.

I closed the door behind us, and as he walked toward the kitchen, I asked, "Now that we're alone, would you mind explaining to me why my father knows the one thing we didn't want him to know, Ryder?"

He didn't answer me, so I followed him and found him finishing off a glass of whisky and pouring himself a second one. Whatever happened, he looked shaken by it, and my heart went out to him.

Touching him on the sleeve, I said, "Tell me what's wrong. Please. Don't keep it all inside, whatever it is."

Ryder tilted the glass back and swallowed the last of the whisky in it before he poured another glass of it. Placing the bottle on the counter, he sighed and turned his head to look at me, his eyes full of that same sadness they'd had back in my father's office.

He reached for the glass and his hand shook so violently he had to put it back down. I slid my fingers through his and squeezed them, but he continued to shake uncontrollably.

"Ryder, what's going on? What happened? Why does my father know about the baby?"

Opening his mouth, he tried to say something, but nothing came out. He hung his head and pulled me into him, wrapping his arms around me tightly.

"I fucked everything up, Serena. I didn't have a choice. If I didn't do it, you and the baby would have been left alone, and I couldn't let that happen. I'm sorry. I didn't mean to."

The anguish in his voice tore at my heart. Ryder was the one person I turned to for strength, and there he stood broken and devastated leaning on me.

Holding him to me, I whispered, "Whatever you did, we'll get through this. Just tell me what happened."

He leaned back away from me and frowned. "I've been fighting behind your father's back. Floyd would get me fights, and I'd go to earn more money so we could leave. Tonight's win would have gotten me enough to finally get you away from here."

The words got caught in his throat, and he stopped for a moment before he said, "But something went wrong. I don't know what happened, Serena. One minute it was like any other fight, and the next minute…"

Ryder backed up across the kitchen until he hit the wall. Shaking his head, he lifted his hands up in front of him and stared at them like he was sickened by them being a part of him.

I tried to take him into my arms, but he pushed me away like my touch hurt him. I reached out and gently put my hand on his shoulder. He looked at me like he didn't even know who I was.

"Honey, it's me. It's Serena. You don't have to hide anything from me. It's okay."

He shook his head and winced in pain. "It's not okay. It's not okay."

"Whatever happened, we'll be okay. We will," I said as his face twisted in agony.

"Like when I killed Oliver or his brother or any of the other people your father had me take care of?"

"What are you talking about? Tell me."

He pushed past me, mumbling, "I can't do this with you right now. I can't."

I'd never seen Ryder like this. His rage frightened me, but I couldn't stand by and let him torture himself over whatever had happened. I followed him into the bedroom and watched him sit down on the edge of the bed and hold his head in his hands. He looked broken.

Standing beside him, I quietly said, "Please don't shut me out. I know you're a good person. You've protected me from the moment we met. Whatever you did, I still love you. We'll be okay. I promise, Ryder."

He didn't look up at me, so I took his hand and placed it on my belly. "You were fighting for us. If my father found out and that's why he won't fight you anymore, that's okay. He didn't look that angry, to be honest. I think we'll be okay."

For a long moment, he stayed hunched over

holding his head in his hands, but then he looked up and wrapped his arms around my waist, pressing his cheek to my belly. "I'm sorry, Serena. I just wanted to be able to take you away from here before our baby was born, and now I've ruined everything."

I gently stroked his soft hair as I closed my eyes and came to terms with the reality that whatever he'd done meant we wouldn't get to leave this place before the baby came. Tears of disappointment welled in my eyes at how cruel fate could be. We'd been so close, and now that chance had been taken away from us again.

He looked up at me with such sadness. "I'm sorry. I didn't have a choice. I fucked up. I fucked everything up. I just couldn't bear the thought of losing you."

"I don't know what happened, but you'll never lose me, Ryder. Just tell me, what did he make you promise to do?" I asked, dreading what his answer would be.

I knew my father. He'd get his pound of flesh for whatever he'd caught Ryder at tonight.

"I have to work for him. That's it."

Neither of us believed that, but it didn't matter. Fate had given my father what he wanted, and he took it.

"We're not getting out of here, are we?" I asked, looking away because I couldn't face him when he said the words that would mean everything we'd dreamed of was gone.

"Not now," he said quietly, his voice sadder than I could bear.

I couldn't stop the tears from coming, and they rolled down my cheeks as everything began to overwhelm me. All our plans over.

"Can you forgive me?" he asked in that same tortured voice that made me feel like he had his hand around my heart and was squeezing it.

I sat down on the bed next to him and kissed him, my lips wet from tears. He slid his thumbs over my cheeks to dry them and again asked, "Can you forgive me, Serena?"

The answer to that question was the simplest thing in the world. Ryder had shown me love I'd never known before. Forgiving him came as naturally as breathing.

"There's no need. I don't need to know what you did that you think you should ask for forgiveness. Whatever it was, I know you wanted to protect me and the baby. How could I blame you for that?"

He pressed his forehead to mine and whispered, "I'm not giving up, Serena. I'm going to find a way so we can escape this world of your father's. I promise."

"I love you, Ryder. It doesn't matter where we are. That won't change. I just need to know one thing. Does he know about me finding my mother?"

Shaking his head, he said the words that made me hope not all was lost. "No. He didn't say anything that made me think he knew."

"Then we can get through this like we've gotten through everything else. In a few months, we'll have a baby and no matter what he tries to do, I promise I won't marry another man, no matter what he does."

Ryder took a deep breath and let it out slowly. "He swore he wouldn't do that. I won't let him if he tries. I swear to God, Serena, I'll find a way to stop him if he does."

"He won't. He has what he wants. I don't know if it's you under his control or me, but he's got both of us, so he's happy."

With a look of hopefulness I loved seeing in his eyes, Ryder shook his head. "He won't always control us. Someday, we're going to leave here and we'll be the ones in control."

I didn't know if he believed that or just said it to make me happy, but I hadn't given up on finding some way to have everything we'd dreamed of. So it would have to wait a little while. I'd waited my entire life for it. I could wait a little longer.

Chapter Twenty-Six

Serena

MY MOTHER AND I met three days a week at a tiny, out-of-the-way inn a few miles away from her house so no one would know I'd found her. I reserved the room for four weeks, hoping she'd stay there and finally leave that house my father had consigned her to, but every time she insisted on returning in the belief that if she didn't, he'd take it out on me.

I didn't know if he would or not. I just wanted her to be free of him.

The Two Cross Inn sat off the road a ways and never seemed to have many guests staying there, so it had an abandoned feel to it. The peeling dark green paint around all the windows only accentuated that. We made sure to hide our cars behind the building every time we met. The room we met in, Room 9, was dark and old, with heavy forest green draperies covering the windows and ensuring our privacy.

My mother settled in to a brown upholstered chair next to the old TV on a metal stand as I crossed my legs and got comfortable on the bed. "This place has cheating spouse written all over it, don't you think?" she asked with a chuckle.

I looked around at the deep beige walls and strange geometric brown and green patterned bedspread beneath me and cringed. "Maybe in a horror movie. I'd hate to be the woman whose guy can only spring for this place for our rendezvous. Talk about killing the mood."

She laughed louder at my comment, and I watched as she became more beautiful with each time she smiled. Warm and inviting, it lit up her face.

"I'm so sorry I didn't get to see you all those years. I think about how many times I would have felt so much better just seeing your smile."

A blush made her cheeks pink, and she sighed. "I wish we had gotten to have all those times together, Serena. I try not to think about it, though, because it makes me sad."

"Well, don't be sad. That's in the past, and now, we can make up for lost time," I said in my cheeriest voice to cheer her up.

She smiled, but it didn't go all the way up to her eyes this time.

"Is something wrong, Mom?"

Shaking her head, she said, "I'm just worried he's going to find out what you've been up to. I don't want to see you get hurt, honey."

"He has what he wants now, so I hope he wouldn't even care."

Her eyebrows drew in with concern, and she leaned forward toward me. "What do you mean has what he wants now?"

I took a deep breath and searched for the words to explain what had happened with Ryder a few nights earlier. Unable to find the right way to say it, I simply said, "He has Ryder back working for him, so I think he'll be happy for at least a little while."

"Why is he so obsessed with him, Serena?" she asked, her expression even more worried now.

Shaking my head, I answered truthfully, "I don't know. He found Ryder when he was fighting in his underground fights and brought him home one night. He used to even refer to him as his adopted son, showing him off at parties like he used to with me and Janelle. When he caught us together a few months after he brought him to the house, he sent me away and made sure Ryder was beaten in his next fight so badly that he ended up in the hospital. Then he offered him a job as one of his men when he got out, and Ryder took it, but just recently, he decided he wanted him to fight for him again. Now, as of a few days ago, he says he can't fight ever again and he has to work for him as security again. I don't know why, and I've never understood his obsession with

Ryder."

"I want you to be careful, honey. Your father's obsessions never end well for anyone but him."

"Has he ever done this before with anyone else?" I asked, curious to know my father through her eyes.

Frowning, she nodded. "I remember a man named Anderson Jarrett. This was before you were born and when Janelle was only just walking, so she wouldn't have been even a year old. Your father became fixated on him. It was almost as if he fell in love with him. He was barely into his twenties and had come into a company that worked with your father's mining business when his own father died. I don't remember what the company did, but I don't think it was that important. But your father talked day and night about this Anderson person and his company. Serena, if it had been a woman, I would have been sure he was cheating with her."

I'd never heard the name Anderson Jarrett before, not from my father or from anyone associated with him.

"What happened with this person?"

"Nothing good for him," she said with a sigh. "Your father practically courted him like a mistress for over a year, and then one day Jarrett disappeared from our lives. He used to have him at the house a few times a week for dinner and drinks, and then never again. I even asked your father what happened to him, and he waved the mere mention of him away like it meant nothing to him. But he was obsessed with him. I found out later that Anderson Jarrett lost his company to your father and swore until the day he died a few years later that your father stole it from him."

"Died?" I asked, sitting up straighter at the mention of his death. "I thought you said he was only in his twenties."

"He was. One night he was found floating in the pond behind his house. It was ruled an accidental drowning, but in the weeks leading up to his death, he began making a lot of noise about how he believed your father had no right to his company because he stole it from him."

As much as I hated to believe it, this story sounded very much like what I'd heard about my father's business from Ryder. I didn't want my mother to know that the man I loved and the father of my child and her grandchild could be involved in something like that, though. Ryder was more than just one of my father's men.

"So you see, that's why I don't like to hear your father is so preoccupied with your boyfriend, Serena."

I slid my palm over my pregnant belly, wishing more than she could ever know that Ryder and I could escape my father's obsession. "He knows we're together and doesn't seem to have a problem with it. I was hoping that meant his interest in him had started to wane."

"Unfortunately, that would probably leave you as his main obsession again, wouldn't it?" my mother asked in a sad voice. "He always did have an unhealthy need to control everything you did, Serena."

"Why is that?" I wondered aloud.

Shaking her head, she shrugged. "I don't know. It's who he is, I guess. He became obsessed with me the minute he met me, and he pursued me like a demon. Then when Janelle was born, he seemed to lose interest in me and become fixated on her. But when you were born, it actually scared me a little to see how obsessed he was with everything about you. I had hoped it would diminish over time, but it never seemed to. What about when Ryder came to the house? Did he become less interested in you and your sister then?"

I thought back to those days when he was so hell-bent on marrying the two of us off. Part of that had been to benefit him, but I knew another part was his bid to control our lives through who we married.

"No. It just changed a little to forcing us to marry men we didn't love but who could help him. Janelle seems to have found some way to live with it, but I couldn't."

My mother stood from her chair and leaned across the bed to hug me. "I'm sorry he did that. He had no right. I'm happy to hear your sister has been able to make her peace with it, though. I just wish she could do the same with me."

I did too, but I didn't trust Janelle to keep my secret. "I'm sorry I can't let her know I've found you, Mom, but she'll tell Daddy. I know she will. She believes all the lies he told us about you."

The disappointment showed in her expression, and she looked away, frowning. "Maybe someday, right?"

Taking her hand in mine, I squeezed it gently. "I hope so. I hope someday the three of us can all get together and we don't have to hide it from anyone."

She turned back and smiled sweetly at me. "Promise me you'll be careful, Serena. From what you've told me, nothing about your father has changed, and his need to control you and Ryder frightens me. I know you may not see it because it's all you've ever known, but I can tell you it's not normal, honey. Not at all."

"I know. We want to get away. We had even planned on doing it sometime soon, but…"

I let my sentence trail off, not knowing how to explain what had happened with Ryder. But I didn't want her to think I liked living the life my father had forced upon me.

Cradling my face in her hands, she nodded, even if she didn't understand what I struggled to say. Her dark eyes filled with sympathy I knew came from living the life I had to endure now.

"I just want you to remember that you don't need your father's blessing to live the life you want. You or Ryder. You're still young, so go out and make your own way in the world, okay?"

"We will. It won't always be like this. I promise. Someday soon we'll be free of him. All of us."

"I hope so. I've gotten used to my life, but I don't want you to be like me, a bird stuck in a gilded cage. I wanted more for you and your sister than that."

Covering her hands with mine, I kissed her. "I promise you I won't let that happen."

She had no idea how long I'd told myself those exact words. I meant them from the first moment they came into my head long before Ryder came into my life, and until the day I escaped my father's world with him, they'd be my mantra.

✧　✧　✧

BY THE TIME I got back to the house, Ryder was waiting for me. He sat on the couch with a bottle of whisky on the coffee table in front of him, his near constant companion since returning to work for my father.

"You're home early. I thought I'd get here before

you," I said as I sat down next to him.

"He had me doing my stand guard thing in his office all day, which amounted to doing nothing for nearly eight hours, and then he said he had somewhere to be and let me go," Ryder said in a low voice.

I put my head on his shoulder and closed my eyes. "You were tossing and turning all night last night. You must be exhausted. Why don't you go lie down for a while?"

Picking the bottle up from the table, he lifted it to his lips and drank a mouthful. "I can't sleep, even when I'm tired."

I wished I knew what was troubling him. Ever since that night, he'd seemed lost in his own thoughts. Nothing I said helped, and more and more, I felt like he was sliding into something I recognized all too well.

I'd seen depression firsthand, and everything about Ryder now said whatever my father had done was killing him inside. I wanted to help, but I didn't know what to do, and every minute he was back around my father only made things worse.

If only we could find a way to leave this place and everything that came with it.

Gently, I turned his face so he had to look at me. I searched his eyes for any sign of that wonderful intensity I'd seen in them so many times, but all I found was sadness.

"I'm worried about you. It feels like you're slipping away ever since you went back to work for my father, and I don't know what to do. Tell me what to do, Ryder. Tell me, and I'll do it."

All he did was shake his head.

Taking his hand, I stood up and pulled him to his feet. He looked down at me with a look of complete confusion, but I had to try something. "Dance with me."

"Serena, I..."

I placed his hand on the small of my back and held the other in my hand out to the side of us. "I remember the first time you held me like this. It felt like you hated even touching me," I said with a smile.

He smiled for the first time that day and kissed me softly on the forehead as we began to sway back and forth. "I've never hated a moment I got to spend with you. Being with you is like a dream come true."

Standing on my toes, I kissed his lips and felt the unbearable sadness in him. I wanted to make him see no matter what, we had each other and that was enough.

"I love you, Ryder. Tell me what you need and I will do whatever it takes to get it. I can't stand seeing you like this."

His eyes slowly closed, and he whispered, "I

don't know what to do. I fucked everything up, and now it's just a matter of time."

He stopped talking, but what he said made no sense. "What do you mean it's just a matter of time? For what? Does he have you doing something, Ryder? What is it?"

Opening his eyes, he leaned down and kissed me tenderly, lingering against my lips as he said, "I love you, Serena. You have no idea how much it hurts to even think about living without you."

We stopped dancing, and I stared up at him in horror, holding his face in my hands as panic shot through me. "What does that mean? Why would you have to live without me? Tell me! Did he say something like he was sending you away?"

Ryder shook his head and frowned. "No, but it feels like at any minute he's going to order me to do something that will make you not love me anymore. You'll see what I've become…and you'll leave, like you should."

Pressing my lips to his, I kissed him, desperate to make him understand how impossible it could be for me to not love him. I looked up into those green eyes so full of despair and hated that he couldn't see how loved he was because of what my father had done to him.

"You are a good man, Ryder. You protect, and that's never a bad thing."

"The things I've done for him. I try to tell myself I had to so I could protect you, but…"

I couldn't let him do this to himself. "Look at me. None of that was your fault. Oliver would have hurt me again if you didn't do something to stop him. The others my father made you do. Don't do this to yourself, Ryder."

Hanging his head, he said quietly, "Do what? Accept who I am?"

His phone vibrated in his pocket, and he reluctantly pulled it out to see who'd messaged. "He wants me down in his office."

Grabbing his hand, I held it tightly. "Don't go. Tell him you were asleep. Tell him you were drunk. Or I'll tell him. Just don't go. Stay here with me."

He stood and shook his head. "I don't have a choice."

I held onto his hand, reaching so my fingertips still touched him, but he walked away toward the front door. "Hopefully, I won't be long."

As I sat there hating what my father was doing to Ryder and me, my mother called. I quickly answered and heard her voice full of fear.

"He was here, Serena. He knows. He warned me if I spoke to you again, he'd make me pay. Be careful, honey. He was furious."

"Are you okay?" I asked, my heart racing in

terror that he'd hurt her.

"I'll be fine. I'm worried about you, though. You know how he is with anyone he thinks has deceived him."

Suddenly, his message to Ryder seemed ominous. If my father wanted to punish me, the surest way would be to hurt Ryder.

"I have to go, Mom. I'll call you tomorrow to check up on you," I said as I hurried to get down to my father's office.

"Be careful, Serena. He's dangerous when he thinks he's been betrayed, and right now, that's what he feels we've done."

"I will. I promise. I love you, Mom. Be careful too."

Tearing down the steps, I broke into a run down the main hallway to my father's office and found him sitting behind his desk like nothing was wrong. I looked around, but Ryder was nowhere to be found.

"Where is he? Why did you tell him you needed him if he's not here?"

My father looked up at me and said nothing for a long moment. "I sent him on an errand I needed him to do for me."

"What does that mean? Did you need milk? Want a pack of cigarettes? Does your car need the oil changed? What errand did he have to do for you?"

Chuckling, he shook his head. "You sound

frantic, Serena. Don't you trust our Ryder?"

My blood boiled at the way he referred to him. "He's not our Ryder. Why are you so obsessed with him? If you care that much about him, why can't you let him be happy? Why do you have to make him miserable?"

"He gets from me what he's given me. He understands there are consequences to his actions. Why haven't you ever been able to understand that?"

"So that's why you're like this with him? You feel he's done something to deserve you making him miserable? What? What did he ever do except fall in love with Robert Erickson's daughter and treat her like a queen, like you always said I should be treated?"

I waited for him to answer me, but then a terrible thought entered my mind. "What did you make him do, Daddy?"

"Ryder understands sometimes choices have to be made."

"Please, tell me you didn't make him do what I think you did!" I screamed as tears streamed down my cheeks.

He simply smiled that crocodile smile I knew meant he'd done exactly as I'd feared. I didn't give him a chance to answer me before I ran to the garage and grabbed the Jeep keys from the box.

My hands shook and my tears made seeing the road nearly impossible, but I pressed the gas pedal to the floor and drove as fast as I could to get to my mother's before Ryder did something I knew neither one of us would be able to forgive.

The miles raced by as I convinced myself he wouldn't do that to her. He couldn't. He loved me too much to hurt her, even if my father ordered him to. He'd find a way to make sure I wasn't hurt, and he'd protect my mother just like he protected me.

Chapter Twenty-Seven

Ryder

THE HOUSE FELT eerily quiet, and as I walked through the front door, all I wanted was for this night to be over. If I could just lose myself in enough whisky to dull my senses and the feel of Serena next to me, I could make it to tomorrow.

That's all I tried to do each night. Sometimes the demons that haunted me hid, chased away by alcohol and Serena's arms around me so I fell asleep and didn't have nightmares of Justin's face as he lay there on the ground, beaten senseless by my hands.

Other times, the ugliness of that night refused to let me be, and I sat awake staring at the TV watching B movies and infomercials as I prayed to God to keep my hands off the gun never far from my side. All that kept me from blowing my head off lay in the bed next to me, that gentle creature who knew nothing of who the man beside her really was.

Sometimes I'd look over at her and think about all those dreams we had. Then I'd cup my hand over her pregnant belly and the regret I felt nearly overwhelmed me. All I'd wanted was to get Serena and the baby away from Robert and his world, but now all that was just what it had always been.

Dreams.

I'd thought fighting would get us to that place we dreamed of, but now that was gone too.

I stopped at the Robert's office door and looked in to see him standing in front of me. His eyes stared out at me with a hollow look I knew meant nothing good.

"Did you take care of everything?" he asked in a tone that said he didn't think I'd done exactly what he ordered me to.

"Yeah. Where is everyone? I saw Jesse leaving as I drove in," I said as I looked around the office and found no one.

Robert grinned and turned to walk back to his chair behind his desk. "I sent him on an errand. I would have sent you to do it, but I didn't think you were up to it. Come in and sit down. I want to talk to you."

"Can this wait, Robert? I'm tired. I just want to go home and see Serena," I said as I moved to leave.

"I want you to know I was happy to pay for that fighter's hospital bills. He'll be taken care of for the rest of his life. Not that he needs it. I mean, he's back to fighting, for God's sake. But that's neither here nor there, I guess."

As much as I didn't want to talk about that horrible night, I knew my role at the moment. "Thanks. I appreciate it. I have to go see Serena."

"She's not here, Ryder. She left a little while ago."

Serena would only leave for one person other than me. But if she left, that meant Alita called and…

"Why would she go out so late at night?" I asked as I walked toward him, stopping at the corner of his desk.

"She's almost due, isn't she? Just another few weeks and we'll have a baby on the estate again," he said almost wistfully, like he looked forward to his first grandchild's arrival. "I was thinking that you and Serena will move back into the main house here when he or she comes. You can have Serena's old room, and we'll change Janelle's room to a nursery."

"Where is she, Robert? Did she say where she was going?"

He leaned back in his chair and folded his arms across his chest. Leveling his gaze on me, he turned to a different subject. "You know, as much as I am loathe to admit it, you passed every test."

"What?" I asked, confused as his quick change from talking about the baby to whatever he referred to now. "I need to find Serena. She shouldn't be out late at night."

"I think when she says she loves you she actually means it. I never put much stock in love, but I think she loves you. I have no doubt you love her. I think a part of me knew the minute I brought you into this house that you'd fall in love with her."

"And still you've done everything you could to try to make her not want to be with me. You don't care that I make her happy. I don't even think you want her to be happy. You sure as fuck don't want me to be happy. I need to go find Serena."

On my way out of his office, I heard him say something about the cost of love, but I didn't stop to ask what he meant. I had a sick feeling I knew.

SERENA'S CELL PHONE went directly to voicemail for the third time in a row, and I tossed my phone onto the passenger seat in frustration before jamming the gas pedal to the floor. I needed to get to Alita's before she did and ran into Jesse. I didn't know what orders Robert had given him, but I couldn't know making sure Serena remained unharmed was part of them.

Or if he hadn't decided to kill two birds with one stone.

Mile after mile, I thought about the horrific possibility that Robert had told Jesse to take care of not only Alita but Serena herself. Would he follow through on that order? I wanted to believe the guy I knew would never knowingly hurt the woman I loved or her mother, but Jesse was entirely beholden to Robert.

And if tonight was the night he decided to punish Serena for finding her mother, Jesse's job might just be to get rid of both women.

I couldn't let him do that. I wouldn't. He'd have to kill me first.

But that could only happen if I reached Alita's house before he did. He had a good ten minute jump on me, but looking down at the speedometer, I saw my speed top one hundred miles an hour, and that wasn't the only advantage I had.

I knew exactly where Alita's house was after driving out there to make sure Robert didn't have it under surveillance before Serena went to meet her that first time. Jesse didn't, and he had no idea that taking the route the GPS gave wasn't the fastest way there.

Turning off the main road, I wound through a back road so dark I knew at any moment something might jump out and I wouldn't have time to swerve out of the way. I reached over and grabbed my phone again to call Serena, but it went directly to voicemail.

Never before in my life had I felt so helpless to stop what I knew was about to happen. Serena could be on a collision course with Jesse and his orders, and even if she wasn't a target, she might still get hurt.

Or worse.

I pushed that possibility out of my mind and focused on the road ahead of me. Just a few more miles until I reached the back of the estate and Alita's carriage house. I had to get there before he did.

JUMPING HARD ON the brakes, I skidded to a stop and ran up the path to the back door of the house as adrenaline once again pumped through me. A light in the kitchen gave off a warm feel that made me want to believe I'd beat Jesse there. I listened for any sound coming from the house, but I heard nothing.

My heart sank at the possibility that he'd been there already and done his job. I looked through the back door window and saw no one inside.

"Who are you?" a male voice asked behind me.

I turned around to see a man around my age with a shovel in his hand ready to bash my head in. Holding my hands up, I quickly tried to explain what I was doing there.

"I'm looking for Alita. Are you Michael?"

He lowered the shovel to the middle of his chest and nodded. "I am. How do you know my name?"

"Serena told me she met someone named Michael who worked as the gardener here. She said you were a friend of Alita's."

"I wouldn't exactly call myself her friend, but I

care about her. Is something wrong?"

I turned to look into the house again and then faced him. "I think someone's coming for her right now. If you care about her, you need to get her away from this place before he gets here."

Michael dropped the shovel and ran past me through the back door. I followed him to the front of the house where Alita sat in a chair in the living room.

She looked at him and then me and opened her mouth to speak, but nothing came out. Michael pointed at me and said, "He knows Serena. He says someone's coming for you tonight."

"Now," I corrected him as I stepped toward where Alita sat. "I'm Ryder, and as much as I wish we could take the time to get to know one another, at the moment we don't have the time. He'll be here any minute, so if you don't leave now, you won't have a chance. Have you seen Serena tonight?"

"No. I called her to tell her Robert had been here to see me and was furious. He knows she and I have been meeting. She told me she'd call me later, but I never heard back from her."

Standing, she looked out the front window as headlights from a car driving toward the house began to draw closer. Unable to tell if they were from Serena's car or Jesse's, I pushed Alita and Michael toward the back door.

"You need to get her out of here now. Do you have a place to go or at least some money to hide out for a while? Do you have a car to use?"

He nodded and smiled. "I've been planning for this what seems like my whole life."

"Go now. Go as far as you can, and then wait for me to call you. Only answer if you see Serena's number, understand? He will find you if you don't lay low. I'm going to do everything I can to make sure that doesn't happen, but you have to go right now."

Alita reached out to touch my arm and smiled. "Thank you, Ryder. Thank you for taking care of Serena and us."

I pushed them through the kitchen and opened the back door. "Thank me later. Now just go. Get as far away as you can."

They ran down the dirt path to an old garage, and in seconds Michael raced away with Alita. Now I just had to worry about Serena.

A knock at the front door made my heart skip a beat, and I slowly walked to the front of the house to answer it. Pulling out my gun, I slowly opened the door as I held my breath, hoping it would be Serena I'd see instead of Jesse.

Outside in the dark a figure stood off to the side, and I only needed one look to know it was her.

"Ryder, what did you do? What did he order you

to do?" she asked as she marched into the house and began looking for her mother.

"She's not here, Serena. She and Michael left already."

Her shoulders sagged. "Why? Is that what he ordered you to do? Send them away so I wouldn't be able to see her ever again? Why would you do that to me, Ryder?"

I pulled her close and hugged her as she began to sob. "No, that's not what happened. I think your father sent Jesse to kill her, so I drove up here as fast as I could to stop him. I got here in time and told her and Michael. She's going to be okay, Serena."

She tilted her head up to look at me, clearly confused. "So she's okay? You didn't…"

It broke my heart to know she thought I had come here to hurt her mother. I deserved it, though. After all I'd done, why wouldn't she think that?

"I'd never do that to you, Serena. I've done a lot of bad things, but I've never hurt a woman. Not even for Robert."

Cradling my face in her hands, she kissed me sweetly on the lips and shook her head. "I'm sorry. I should have known you wouldn't hurt my mother. I just worried my father was threatening you with something, and you didn't have a choice. I should have known better. Please forgive me."

Before I could tell her I loved her and she never

had to ask for my forgiveness for anything, I saw headlights coming down the road toward the house. Jesse. My stomach tensed as I knew what would happen next. I couldn't risk Serena being there for that.

As she stared up at me, fear reflecting in her eyes, I kissed her and hoped I hadn't made the biggest mistake of my life.

"I want you to go. Run down the path to the road and get into the car. Drive away as fast as you can back to the house and wait for me."

She shook her head. "I don't want to go, Ryder. I don't want to leave you here with him."

"It's not me he's here for. He's here for your mother. I need you to leave now."

"Then why do I have to go?" she asked in horror. "Why can't I stay here with you? He won't hurt me."

Taking her hand, I directed her toward the back door. I couldn't tell her the truth—that I worried her father had told Jesse to take care of her along with her mother. Even I didn't want to believe Robert could be that kind of monster.

"I just want you to go now, Serena. I don't want you around this. Go, and I'll follow in a few minutes."

I opened the door and guided her out onto the porch, but we'd run out of time. Jesse stood there on the path looking almost surprised to see us there.

Pushing Serena behind me, I whispered to her, "Run to your car. I'll keep him busy."

"Don't bother running. I'm here for her mother, not her."

"She already got away, so you failed. Go back and tell my father he won't get her tonight," Serena snapped.

"You need to go, Jesse. She's not here. Go tell him she was gone when you got here."

His eyes opened wide in terror at what we both knew Robert would do when he found out Jesse failed. He walked through the kitchen door and shut it hard behind him.

"I can't do that, man."

Serena and I took a few steps backward toward the living room. I felt her squeeze my hand in fear and wished to hell I had gotten her away from this.

"Yes, you can. You can do it and you have to because she's not here."

Wincing, he took a step toward me and shook his head. "You know what he'll do to me if go back and tell him I failed. Just tell me where she is and you won't have to be involved in this anymore."

"You know I can't do that, Jess. I can't let you hurt Serena's mother. I don't care what Robert ordered you to do. Just turn around and go back. I'll do whatever I can to help you with him, but I can't let you hurt her."

He reached behind him and pulled out his gun.

Waving it around, he sighed like this was all too much for him. "Why, man? Why did you have to get involved with his daughter? Jesus, didn't he warn you like he warned everyone else? Why couldn't you just keep your hands off her?"

The way he talked about Serena pissed me off. I gripped my gun until my palm hurt. "Don't say another word about her. Not another fucking word. Now turn around and leave here before you get hurt."

"You told me yourself about how he called you a stray that first night he brought you to the estate. He can claim you're his adopted son all he wants, but when it comes right down it, Ryder, you know you aren't one of them. You and I aren't like them."

Serena leaned around me and pointed her finger at Jesse. "You don't know anything. You're just like my father."

I pushed her back behind me and hoped I could somehow get through to him. "Jess, I know how you're feeling. I've been there. But you don't have to do this. Go back and tell him she was gone when you got here."

Frowning, he shook his head. "I can't do that, Ryder. I'm sorry. I'm going to find her and when I do, I have no choice. You know that as well as anyone else. Just accept this is how it has to go."

Nothing Jesse said was wrong. I knew he had no choice. None of us did in Robert's world. That didn't change the fact that I'd sooner die than let him hurt Alita.

"I'm sorry, Jess. I can't let you do that."

"You don't have a choice, man. Don't fight this. You have the girl. Let the mother go and he'll be happy."

I pointed my gun at him and hated that I knew what he said wasn't true. "No, he won't. He'll never be happy, and there's nothing you and I can do to change that."

There was nothing more to say. I never wanted to hurt Jesse or anyone else. I didn't have a choice.

None of us did.

I squeezed the trigger and felt the shot explode out of my gun, and then a second later I heard a second shot. Had I pulled the trigger a second time? Serena let out a terrified scream behind me. I wanted to turn around to see if she was safe, but I couldn't. All I could do was watch as Jesse collapsed onto the floor in what looked like slow motion before my legs gave out and I fell.

"Ryder! Talk to me! Please, say something!" Serena begged over and over, each time her voice sounding farther and farther away.

Until all I heard was silence.

RYDER AND SERENA'S STORY CONCLUDES IN

IF WE FALL (CORRUPTED LOVE #3)

GET YOUR COPY TODAY!

About the Author

K.M. Scott writes contemporary romance stories of sexy, intense, and unforgettable love. A New York Times and USA Today bestselling author, she's been in love with romance since reading her first romance novel in junior high (she was a very curious girl!). Under her Gabrielle Bisset name, she writes erotic paranormal and historical romance. She lives in Pennsylvania with a herd of animals and when she's not writing can be found reading or feeding her TV addiction.

Be sure to visit K.M.'s Facebook page at **facebook. com/kmscottauthor** for all the latest on her books, along with giveaways and other goodies! And to hear all the news on K.M. Scott books first, sign up for her newsletter today and be sure to visit her website at **www.kmscottbooks.com**.

Books by K.M. Scott:

If I Dream (Corrupted Love #1)
If You Fight (Corrupted Love #2)
If We Fall (Corrupted Love #3)

Crash Into Me (Heart of Stone #1)
Fall Into Me (Heart of Stone #2)
Give In To Me (Heart of Stone #3)
Heart of Stone Volume One Box Set
Ever After (Heart of Stone #4)
A Heart of Stone Christmas (Heart of Stone #5)
Unforgettable (Heart of Stone #6)
Unbreakable (Heart of Stone #7)
Heart of Stone Volume Two Box Set

Temptation (Club X #1)
Surrender (Club X #2)
Possession (Club X #3)
Satisfaction (Club X #4)
Acceptance (Club X #5)
The Complete Club X Series Box Set

SILK (Volume One)
SILK (Volume Two)
SILK (Volume Three)
SILK (Volume Four)
SILK Box Set

K.M.'S BOOKS ARE IN AUDIOBOOK TOO!

Books by Gabrielle Bisset:

Vampire Dreams Revamped (A Sons of Navarus Prequel)
Blood Avenged (Sons of Navarus #1)
Blood Betrayed (Sons of Navarus #2)
Longing (A Sons of Navarus Short Story)
Blood Spirit (Sons of Navarus #3)
The Deepest Cut (A Sons of Navarus Short Story)
Blood Prophecy (Sons of Navarus #4)
Blood Craving (Sons of Navarus #5)
Blood Eclipse (Sons of Navarus #6)
The Sons of Navarus Box Set #1
The Sons of Navarus Box Set #2

Stolen Destiny (Destined Ones Duology #1)
Destiny Redeemed (Destined Ones Duology #2)

Love's Master
Masquerade
The Victorian Erotic Romance Trilogy

9 781941 594544